What the critics are saying...

"...yet another delightful read from the talented pen of Ms. Kelly. One can safely say that she is un-paralleled in writing romances that make you hot and bothered at the same time as rolling on the floor laughing...This is a perfect blend of humor, romance and great mystery..." ~ *Sam, All About Murder (awarded five dagger rating)*

"...This novel has everything, action and adventure, love and hate, jealous ex-lovers and murder all tied into one plot...This story is very enjoyable all around and an excellent read." ~ *Angel Brewer, The Romance Studio/Blue*

"...*Peta and the Wolfe* is Sahara Kelly's debut into the contemporary suspense category, and she certainly did a good job. Amidst a suspenseful subplot the reader finds herself tangled in a web of mixed emotions and passion created by the two main characters and the "supporting" cast of characters...the sort of story that will make you smile but will get you teary eyed as well. Do not miss this one." ~ *Mireya Orsini, Just Erotic Romance Reviews*

"...One of the best things about a Sahara Kelly novel is that the reader is guaranteed incredibly hot sex scenes, but not at the sake of the plot or characterization. She writes a fully developed story, with incredible eroticism, and completely satisfies the reader...For a story guaranteed to heat up the nights as well as please the romantic inside, I highly recommend *Peta and the Wolfe!*" ~ *Terrie Figueroa, Romance Reviews Today*

"...I was ensnared right from the opening paragraph. Kelly has created wonderfully complex characters that constantly change and develop as the story progresses...The mystery sewn throughout the book is interesting and well plotted with a number of likely candidates for the killer...." ~ *Tara James, Romance Junkies (awarded five blue ribbons).*

PETA AND THE WOLFE
Guardians of Time

Sahara Kelly

Guardians of Time: Peta and the Wolfe
An Ellora's Cave Publication, March 2005

Ellora's Cave Publishing, Inc.
1337 Commerce Drive Suite #13
Stow, Ohio 44224

ISBN #1419951718

Edited by: *Briana St. James*
Cover art by: *Scott Carpenter*

Warning:

The following material contains graphic sexual content meant for mature readers. *Guardians of Time: Peta and the Wolfe* has been rated *E-rotic* by a minimum of three independent reviewers.

Ellora's Cave Publishing offers three levels of Romantica™ reading entertainment: S (S-ensuous), E (E-rotic), and X (X-treme).

S-ensuous love scenes are explicit and leave nothing to the imagination.

E-rotic love scenes are explicit, leave nothing to the imagination, and are high in volume per the overall word count. In addition, some E-rated titles might contain fantasy material that some readers find objectionable, such as bondage, submission, same sex encounters, forced seductions, etc. E-rated titles are the most graphic titles we carry; it is common, for instance, for an author to use words such as "fucking", "cock", "pussy", etc., within their work of literature.

X-treme titles differ from E-rated titles only in plot premise and storyline execution. Unlike E-rated titles, stories designated with the letter X tend to contain controversial subject matter not for the faint of heart.

Also by Sahara Kelly:

A Kink In Her Tails
Beating Level Nine
For Research Purposes Only: All Night Video
Guardians Of Time 1: Alana's Magic Lamp
Guardians of Time 2: Finding The Zero-G Spot
Hansell and Gretty
Joshua 4.0 (*Ellora's Cavemen: Tales from the Temple I*)
Knights Elemental
Madam Charlie
Magnus Ravynne and Mistress Swann
Partners In Passion 1: Justin and Eleanor
Partners In Passion 2: No Limits
Persephone's Wings
Sir Phillip Ashton's Eyes (*Mesmerized*)
Sizzle
Tales Of Beau Monde 2: Miss Beatrice's Bottom
Tales Of Beau Monde 3: Lying With Louisa
Tales Of Beau Monde 4: Pleasuring Miss Poppy
Tales Of The Beau Monde 1: Lying With Louisa
The Glass Stripper
The Gypsy Lovers
The Sun God's Woman
Visions (*Mystic Visions*)
Wingin' It
Irish Enchantment

PETA AND THE WOLFE
Guardians of Time

Prologue

Bloody hell.

Peta Matthews fought with the wheel of her small two-seater, struggling to keep it in the ruts carved through the snow by the tires of other cars. Other larger cars.

Most people in Mayfield had either minivans or SUVs, but not her. One look at the green low-slung convertible and she'd drooled. It was the car of her dreams, but in these damned New England winters it became more of a nightmare.

And this late snowstorm was one of the worst. Heavy flakes piled up around her windshield wipers, and even with the defrost control on full she had a hard time seeing more than a couple of car lengths ahead.

She slowed even more as the road curved toward the bridge leading to Acorn Street and her house.

The fact that she was in a blazing temper didn't help matters much either.

Damn Max Wolfe.

She'd gone to the bar to find him and try and explain to him, in the politest of terms, that he was a week late finishing up an edit she needed two days ago, and if he didn't get his arse in gear she'd take great pleasure in firing him.

She gritted her teeth as the road tried to wrench the steering wheel out of her grip.

Her life seemed as out of control as her driving at this moment. She'd found Max, all right, but he'd been plastered all over some little tart with breasts the size of cantaloupes, and she had turned away disgusted, without delivering the pithy diatribe she'd rehearsed so carefully on the way there. She gripped the wheel tightly as she negotiated the tricky road surface.

To top it all off, Cary Stiles had come in just as she was leaving, and made yet another pass at her. Life, she thought, as yet another patch of ice made her rear end skid, really did suck at times.

It would have sucked a lot less if she could rid her mind of the image of Max Wolfe. Even as she peered through the sludge on her wiper blades in an attempt to keep her car on the road, she could still see him. His tall muscular body and his darkish blond hair haunted her dreams, a vision that drove her to toss and turn and wake up in a sweat, sometimes milliseconds away from climaxing. His hazel eyes had captivated her, his sexy voice echoed in her ears, and sometimes she wondered if she was becoming obsessive about him, and should seek professional help.

She sighed and tried to banish all thoughts of Max from her mind as she squinted through the snow and tried to see the turning for the bridge.

There — there it was. She flicked on her turn signal and moved the wheel to the left.

Obediently, the car turned left. But not quite far enough. There was little traction beneath the small rear wheels, and not enough weight to keep them where they were supposed to be.

With a gasp, Peta realized she wasn't going to make the turn. She stamped her foot on the brake in an automatic response to the sight of the wooden railings looming in front of her headlights.

It was too late.

With a crash and a shriek, Peta Matthews and her little convertible sailed off the icy bridge into the swirling blindness of the snowstorm and the River May beneath.

Oh BOLLOCKS!

Chapter 1

Someone was playing the drums. Loudly and energetically, and behind her right eye.

Lovely. She was dead and had arrived in heaven with a migraine.

Peta groaned and shifted a little, waiting for the pain to shoot through her body. She remembered the odd sensation of her car flying, but not much else.

"Easy, dear. Just rest a moment."

The voice was quiet and soothing, and Peta obeyed it without question, since it was telling her to do what she wanted to do anyway. Rest. For perhaps a few thousand years.

"Mama, she's got pitty hair."

Heaven had child angels? What were they...oh yes, cherubs.

"Yes she does, Lalla. Now why don't you go and play with Hannah for a little while so that Mama can take care of this nice lady and make her feel better?"

"Don't wanna."

Oh good. Cherubs were annoyingly obstinate too, just like their earthly counterparts.

"Lalla?" The voice held all the maternal authority common to a mother whose eyebrows were raised and whose hands were planted firmly on her hips.

"It's not faaaaiiiir." That was definitely a whine.

"You may come back later and say hello if there's time."

There was silence for a moment, and Peta imagined the cherub's wings fluttering as she thought about this statement.

"Hooookay."

"Good girl. Now run along."

Footsteps fading away indicated that the cherub had left. Walking. Perhaps she hadn't graduated from flying class yet.

Cautiously, Peta raised one eyelid, and then the other.

A lovely woman was bending over her, stroking her hands over Peta's body, and looking worried.

Peta risked a look around her. The room was large, and sunlight shone through the wide openings that passed for windows. Birds sang loudly, a little too loudly for Peta's comfort, and a couple of other women were fussing with something in the far corner of the room.

They were all gorgeous, and clad in something soft and silky.

Oh fuck. Heaven really was a Victoria's Secret catalogue. No wonder they'd put those fluffy wings on their models.

So why was she here? Were they going to introduce a new line of lingerie for the volume-enhanced? Girdles that could shape her body into something resembling an hourglass rather than a grandfather clock? Victoria must truly be an angel with incredible powers if they were going to try *that*.

"How do you feel?" The woman spoke quietly, still touching Peta, running her hands across her naked skin.

Shit. She was *naked*.

Peta winced. "Headache," she muttered. "And I'm naked."

The woman grinned. "I can help with both. Close your eyes."

Peta was too confused to do anything else, and as she lowered her eyelids, she felt the woman's hands on her forehead. They moved slowly and felt both cool and strangely warm at the same time. Within seconds the pain behind Peta's eyes was gone.

"You may open your eyes now."

Cautiously, Peta did. The woman was drawing a soft silk sheet up over Peta's body, and with a sigh of relief, Peta found she could move and tug it all the way up to her chin.

She said the first thing that came into her mind. "Where am I? This is heaven, right?"

A low laugh greeted her words, and the woman pulled up a chair next to the bed. "Some people think so," she smiled. "Actually, it isn't. This place is called Anyela, and it exists outside of your time. Outside of most people's time, as a matter of fact."

Peta blinked. "Who *are* you?"

"My name is Neala. My husband is the Guardian here."

"I'll bet he is," answered Peta wryly. She glanced at the other women. "What is this, some kind of harem or something? I never learned about *this* in church. Must give St. Peter a few gray hairs."

Neala chuckled. "There is much to tell you and little time in which to do it. But I should let my husband explain it all to you." She looked carefully at Peta, her black eyes focusing intently on her. "Headache gone?"

Peta blinked. "Now you come to mention it, yes. And the rest of me seems to be intact, which is odd..." Questions and images flooded her mind. "I drove off the bridge...my car...I —"

"Relax, my dear. All will be explained to you. Ah, here is my husband now."

Peta moved on her pillow and saw a tall man entering the room. His long hair was tied back and his eyes were the most unusual turquoise blue. In his arms he carried a very innocent-looking little girl, who was snuggled comfortably against his chest.

Neala stood up. "Lalla. *What* did I tell you?" There was no anger in the words, just a typical motherly reprimand.

"But *Mama*..." Big blue eyes widened. "You said to go play with Hannah and I was going to go play with Hannah. But I found Papa on the way and you said it was good to spend time with Papa, and Papa said..."

"Enough, Lalla." The man's voice was deep, and accompanied by a light kiss on the top of his daughter's curly blonde head.

He looked at his wife and they shared an identical eye-rolling moment of parental communication. They grinned.

Peta watched the byplay with interest. Two gorgeous people — beings — angels, whatever they were, and they still let themselves be manipulated by a tiny elfin child. Some things never changed.

"I'm glad you're awake. We have to talk."

Neala lifted her daughter from the man's arms. "We'll leave you to it." She headed off, letting Lalla wave a little hand to Peta.

Peta, to her surprise, found herself waving back. Those big eyes were irresistible.

"Now, Ms. Matthews. I expect you have lots of questions." He seated himself in the chair next to the bed, and crossed his long legs. "Do you know where you are?"

"Um...Mrs...Neala said something about a place out of time? Which is a polite euphemism for being dead?"

He laughed. "No, Ms. Matthews. You're not dead. You're in Anyela. This is a place where the Guardians of Time keep an eye on the Universe and its progress. Occasionally, things go wrong and it's up to us and our representatives to correct any problems."

"Ah." Peta's head swam as she tried to follow his words.

"I am the Guardian, one of the people who supervise the entire process."

He settled back in the chair, and Peta found herself staring at his unusual eyes. He was a corker, all right.

"You are Peta Matthews, born and raised in...um..." He frowned a little in thought. "...England, yes?"

"Correct. How did you know—"

"Never mind how I know. I just do, that's all. You're here for a special reason. It was not time for you to die."

Peta gulped. "I suppose that's a good thing?"

"Well, yes and no. It meant that we had to bring you here before sending you back. There are things you must do, Peta. Important things."

"Oh?" She couldn't imagine what. Publish a best seller? Clean her kitchen floor? Her life wasn't exactly what she'd call "important" to the overall scheme of things. Not as far as she could see, anyway.

"Your life is now entangled with a certain person's, and that person must continue to live out his allotted time span. I can't tell you why, but it's imperative."

"Really? Who?"

"Max Wolfe."

"Oh shit." Peta closed her eyes. "Excuse my language."

The Guardian laughed. "Don't apologize. I've heard worse. And from my own genies too."

"Genies?" Peta opened her eyes at that. "You mean like magic lamps and stuff?"

The Guardian cleared his throat. "Upon occasion, yes. But not this time. We do train suitable candidates for our genie program. They're men of great—er—prowess, shall we say? But you, you're a special case."

"Oh. That's nice." Peta's mind was still struggling with a variety of concepts, none of which made any sense. And it figured that Max would have to be in there somewhere.

The Guardian grinned. "Let me see if I can simplify this for you. We need you to return to your world, almost to the moment you went off the bridge. From that point on, events will unfold that will place you in a position to be of the utmost assistance to Max Wolfe."

"Do I get my own lamp?" Visions of belly-dancing costumes and veils flashed through Peta's mind.

"No. Sorry. We can't use that technique on this occasion. In fact, you won't even remember you were here. It is essential that time progress in a quite ordinary fashion, and that you both follow the course which has been set out for you."

"I don't get any inside information? Any useful tips? What am I supposed to do?"

"Sorry again," said the Guardian. "Our job is simply to make sure that the timeline continues uninterrupted on its course. Your death at that moment would have messed it up. Badly."

"But Max Wolfe? I can't help *him*. He's too busy chasing every randy little skirt that blinks at him."

The Guardian snorted. "You overestimate Max's interests, and underestimate your own potential, my dear."

Peta snorted at that. "Oh, right. I have mirrors, you know."

"But do you see clearly when you look into them?"

The Guardian's question took Peta by surprise. She thought for a moment. "Look, Mr. Guardian or whoever you are. I have no illusions. I know what I am. There are no lavish breasts here. No slender waist. It's all dropped to my hips. Which wobble on occasion. Yes, I see quite clearly what I am when I look in the mirror."

The Guardian's lips curved in a warm smile. "Not all attraction is based on the physical, Peta. And Max is already interested."

"He *is*?" Damn. She'd squeaked.

"He is. And that attraction must be allowed to grow, to develop into something special between the two of you. It is imperative that Max learn to trust you."

"Why?"

The Guardian's face turned sober. "Because you, Peta Matthews, must save Max Wolfe's life."

Chapter 2

"Oh Max...oh Max...oh *MAX!*"

The woman screamed his name long and loud, and Max Wolfe winced at her ear-splitting enthusiasm. The fact that he was buried to his balls inside her pulsating body and doing his best to keep her going until he reached his own orgasm was not very helpful against such a vocal assault. The steady squeaking of the bedsprings didn't help either.

He closed his eyes and imagined riotous chestnut hair and a pair of stern gray eyes that would have softened when he slid into her. She would be panting now, not screaming loud enough to shake the plaster off the peeling walls. She wouldn't *have* peeling walls.

She'd have him. Max Wolfe. Deep inside her. He grinned to himself and came, spurting hotly into the still-whimpering woman beneath him.

"Oh Max." She sighed and deflated into a smiling and boneless heap of satisfied hormones. The old bed gasped out a last creak and stopped its infernal racket.

Enormous breasts pillowed his chest as he tried desperately to remember her name.

"Well, my gosh, um, honey..." he improvised. What the hell *was* her name? Something calendar-ish, May? June? No, wait, it was April.

"That was some fuck, April." He smiled winningly at her.

Surprisingly, she scowled and pulled away from him sharply, ripping her sweaty flesh from his like an old band-aid and almost taking the condom along with her.

"The name is Tuesday."

"Oh. Sorry. I knew it was something from the calendar. Tuesday, that's an unusual name..." He removed his protection with a deft twist and deposited it neatly in the trashcan beside him.

Max stretched out on the bed and put his arms beneath his head as his erstwhile playmate struggled into her too short and too tight dress.

"That's what you said in the bar. God, get yourself some new lines, will you? You're a good fuck, but not much of a conversationalist." Tuesday pulled her thigh high boots up with a snap and grabbed for her coat and purse.

"Thanks for the thrill, Max. Let's not do it again." The door slammed behind her.

Max sighed.

Mr. Peebles ventured out from his hiding place.

"You know, Mr. Peebles, it occurs to me that my sex life is not what it once was."

Mr. Peebles did not respond to this comment, just sat watching Max inscrutably from large amber eyes as his whiskers twitched.

"I used to be able to bring a woman to orgasm within minutes. I would have any number of ladies falling over themselves to give me their phone numbers, their room keys, their panties...where has that gift gone?"

Once again, there was no response from his silent audience.

"Sometimes I envy you. Perhaps I should have been castrated at an early age as well. It would have made life a lot simpler, wouldn't it?"

Mr. Peebles' eyes revealed nothing of his innermost feelings. He yawned delicately, showing a lot of rather sharp teeth. Correctly deducing that little in the way of further activity was going to take place on Max's bed that evening, he carefully stepped onto the rumpled covers and circled a time or two before settling himself into a comfortable lump. He was purring himself off to sleep within minutes.

"And a fat lot of help you are," scoffed Max. He watched the antics of this unusual cat with affection. "This is what it comes down to, does it? A quick fuck and then the brush off by someone whose name should have been removed from the list of possible things parents are allowed to call their offspring. Followed by a nice night's snuggle with a cat who ignores my every attempt at communication."

Max sighed again. "It's all her fault, you know. If it wasn't for her, I'd have been long gone, and you'd have some other sucker running themselves ragged for kitty treats."

Max got up from the bed, used the bathroom and slipped into a pair of silky shorts. He carefully got back under the covers without disturbing Mr. Peebles' tranquil repose.

"Yes, Mr. Peebles, 'tis a sad man you see before you — or you would if you'd open those feline eyes of yours for two seconds, you lazy lump..."

A polite snore greeted this request.

Max wished he could sleep as thoroughly as Mr. Peebles, but he knew that once he closed his eyes she'd be there, and that would be it—he'd be fighting a wet dream for the rest of the night. He was getting damn tired of waking up with a painful hard-on and making do in the shower each and every fucking morning.

All because of his boss. The delectably munchable Peta Matthews.

He lowered his eyelids, and yep—there she was. Hands on those luscious hips of hers, staring at him with contempt radiating from her gray eyes. Her skin was like ripe peaches with a dash of cream, soft, velvety and very lickable. Max's mouth watered and his cock stirred.

She'd be speaking to him in that delightful almost-British accent, scolding him for something or other he'd done, or forgotten to do.

How the hell was he supposed to remember all that stupid editing shit when she stood there in front of him, her body sending out messages like some kind of sexual radar, and his satellite dish homing in on each and every one of them?

The snow began pelting against his windows, hard now, with the force of a good gale behind it. There was a nice, old-fashioned Nor'easter shaping up outside, and for a moment Max wished he could share it with Peta. Snuggling with her under the covers or in front of a blazing fire.

Of course, he had no fireplace in his dingy little apartment, but hell, it was his fantasy and he could have whatever he wanted in it. Including Ms. Matthews.

He'd just bet she was tight and hot, and he knew just how to get her ready for him. Her breasts were small, but would fill his mouth to perfection, and the rest of her would feel like satin against his skin.

He wondered if her pussy was bare or if she'd left her pubic hair intact. He didn't care. Either way would be just fine with him. All he needed was her, any way he could get her. One night. One fuck—or maybe two or three, depending on his mood, and she'd be out of his system. He could then pack up and head off to wherever the wind blew him.

Like he'd been doing for the last year or so.

He grinned into his pillow, as he imagined the delight of sliding past Ms. Peta Matthews's inhibitions and into her boiling cunt.

It would be explosive. Cataclysmic.

The wind howled, and the little apartment trembled. A night like this cried out for hot sex with an even hotter woman. They'd shake the world together.

And exactly at the moment he had that thought, Max Wolfe's world shook—and collapsed.

* * * * *

"You cooking something, were you? Or jumping around?"

Max's landlady, Mrs. Lee, stared angrily at him from beneath her straight black bangs.

"Absolutely not, Mrs. Lee. I was in bed, for chrissake."

Max shivered in the blanket that a fireman had thoughtfully bundled around him as the rescue crew picked their way through the rubble that had once been Max's little apartment. Before the ceiling had collapsed, that is.

"You do something. I know. You bad man."

Max sighed. At least the interior of the ambulance was warm, and the EMT had wiped away the blood from the cut on his head. A large lump of plaster had narrowly missed him, but left a nasty gash as a parting gift.

A plaintive yowl came from the cat-carrier next to him. Thank God country EMTs were supplied with a variety of odd equipment. With surprising presence of mind, Max had rescued Mr. Peebles and grabbed his cell phone and wallet as he'd fought free of the debris. He'd clean forgotten he was in his shorts and it was snowing. His feet were freezing.

Mrs. Lee was now gesturing and shouting at the fire chief in Chinese. He sighed again. Good luck to her. He was out a place to live and a wardrobe. She was going to have to deal with insurance companies, construction companies, and the resulting mess. If she'd ever taken the time to have the place inspected she'd have known it was barely fit for human habitation.

A buzz came from the phone resting on top of Mr. Peebles's carrier. Frowning, Max picked it up. What now?

"Max, I just heard. Poor darling. I'm on my way. Got some clothes here if you need 'em."

It was wonderful, precious Phoebe Dunford. His guardian angel and owner of Mayfield Masterpieces, the small publishing company where he attempted to perform the duties of editor. She had taken it upon herself to mother him. Occasionally it was annoying. This *wasn't* one of those occasions. "Bless you, Phoebe. Be careful, will you? It's still snowing a bit."

"This? This is nothing. Wait until we get a *real* snowstorm."

Max laughed. "Right. I'm sitting here in my skivvies, the temperature has to be about twenty below zero, and you're telling me this isn't a *real* snowstorm?"

"Look, I don't have time for idle chit chat. Peta's been in an accident."

Phoebe's words sent Max's senses reeling onto high alert. "What? How bad? Where is she?"

"I'll tell you in a sec..."

Headlights pulled up next to the remaining fire truck, and Phoebe herself slid out of the huge SUV, closing her cell phone as she did so.

"Evening, Miss Phoebe." The greetings came from the fire department and the EMTs, most of whom knew Phoebe. Hell, thought Max. She knows everyone in Mayfield. She could probably tell them about their grandparents too.

"Can I take him off your hands, John?" She looked up at the EMT who grinned affectionately at her.

"He's all yours, Miss Phoebe. Just a nasty abrasion on the head. No sign of concussion or anything else. Damned lucky if you ask me."

The little woman reached Max and smiled at him. "Come along, dear. Let's get you out of the cold."

She was a tiny gray-haired whirlwind, and within moments, Max found himself comfortably settled in her car, toasting his toes beneath her heating vent. Mr. Peebles sneezed on the back seat.

"What about Peta?" Max spoke the first words that came into his mind.

"Drove that silly car of hers off the bridge. It's why you've only got one ambulance here. T'other had to take her over to County General. She's unconscious right now. I'm going to drop you off and then head over."

"I'll come too."

"No you won't." Phoebe's mouth snapped shut. "You're chilled through, mostly naked, and have just had a ceiling drop on you. If Peta comes around I want her to recover gently, not die of shock at the sight of you."

Max grimaced.

Phoebe was right. He was still dusted in plaster, a large band-aid covered a good portion of his forehead, and although he was warming up, silk shorts were not the best attire for visiting a sick friend in the middle of a snowstorm.

Shit and fuck. "But..."

"But nothing, young man. I'm taking you over to the office. You can clean up in that little bathroom, get a bit of rest on the old couch in the staff room, and I'll be there right after I've seen Peta. Then we'll figure out what to do."

"We will?" Max was surprised at himself. He was agreeing to everything this senior dynamo was suggesting. Must be shock or something.

"We will. Now be a good boy and do as you're told."

Max blinked and found himself deposited at the offices of Mayfield Masterpieces with a bag of clothing in one hand, the keys in the other and Mr. Peebles at his feet.

"I'll be back soon..." With a spray of icy slush, Phoebe spun her tires and expertly steered the SUV back onto the road.

Max shook his head and looked down at Mr. Peebles. The cat was expressing his opinion of the entire episode.

He'd turned his ass to the front of the carrier and was ignoring the world.

Max wished he could do the same.

* * * * *

There seemed to be a lot of voices muttering in her bedroom.

Peta wished they'd shut up and leave her alone. Then the pain hit her. Like a freight train rolling across her ankle.

"Nothing worse than a bad sprain and some bruises. Girl's extraordinarily lucky, Phoebe."

"Thank God."

Phoebe. Peta recognized the woman's voice and attempted a little smile. It froze as someone stuck a pin in her.

"Ow."

"Sweetie, you're awake at last," said Phoebe, rushing to the bedside. "How do you feel?"

"People keep asking me that," mumbled Peta through her haze. "Where am I?" Damn. She'd said that before too. Talk about déja vu.

"You're in the hospital, darling. Your car went off the road. Fortunately, you're okay."

Peta, whose body was now telling her otherwise, grimaced. "Define *okay*."

"You're a lucky young lady, Ms. Matthews. Just a couple of bruises, some abrasions and a rather nasty sprain of your right ankle. Other than that, well...it's quite miraculous." The doctor joined Phoebe at Peta's bedside.

Peta wanted to snort. If he thought this kind of misery was miraculous, then heaven help her if her injuries had been any worse. She ached from head to toe, had a million questions trembling on her lips, and the world was starting to fade away before her increasingly blurry gaze.

"I just gave you a small shot to help you rest, dear," added the doctor.

"Good idea," endorsed Phoebe. "I'll be back to pick her up tomorrow. I've got it all arranged."

There was an odd note of satisfaction in Phoebe's voice, and Peta tried to scribble a mental note to herself to check it out.

Her mind dropped the pencil and couldn't find the paper.

She slipped into unconsciousness once more, and for the split second before the darkness swamped her, she could have sworn she heard birds singing.

Chapter 3

The drinks had dulled Sandra Dean's brain. Too many tequilas and not enough food. She didn't care.

The carpet felt rough against her bare skin as she lay, sprawled and naked, waiting for the next touch. Her mind tried to focus on his hands, but instead she could only feel the heat between her legs as something almost cold touched her pussy.

Her hands slid to her breasts, feeling her hard nipples budding from a combination of the cool temperature and the arousal she was experiencing.

It was fabulous.

The butterfly fingers were dancing all over her body, touching her in all the places she liked most. It had been so long since anyone had cared to find them. Too long.

She sighed and widened her thighs, waiting, anticipating, and needing to be penetrated. To be taken to those heights she remembered so well.

Blearily she remembered she had to be at work early the next morning. She was going to be alone, since Ms. Matthews was on some kind of sick leave and Miss Phoebe had phoned her, asking her to open the office and "handle things" until she herself could get in.

Again, she realized she didn't care. Mayfield Masterpieces was part of the real world. Not part of where she was now.

Her hands were pushed aside, and another set took over. Pulling hard on the nipples, tugging, teasing, flicking with just the right blend of savagery and tenderness.

Sandra moaned. This was wonderful.

She felt her hands raised above her head and something rough looped around her wrists, securing her in place. How did he know? How had he figured out that she enjoyed the feeling of helplessness? Of being under someone else's control? Of being able to surrender herself totally to another and let him do anything he wanted?

Her mind fogged again as her legs were forced roughly apart.

Now — perhaps now, she'd get the fucking she so desperately wanted.

But no, not yet.

He was raising her knees, playing with her, slipping something around her wet cunt and sliding it down to her ass.

Oh God. Yes. It was sliding into her ass, into that place that always turned her on like wildfire.

It was big, stretching her, and her muscles tried to relax as it filled her.

She felt her body lifted by hands that dug sharply into her buttocks. It was his cock that was inside her ass. And moving, too. Jesus Christ. He was big.

She could vaguely hear his grunts as he ass-fucked her. Desperately, she struggled, wanting to get her hands to her clit and bring herself off.

Coming like this was incredible, her muscles clamping around something thick up her ass and her fingers sliding in and out of her own cunt, catching her clit in that perfect spot to send her spinning into bliss.

Mike had known how to do it just right. But the law had taken him away from her, burying him in the State Prison and denying her these pleasures. Sure, she'd divorced him, but she'd never forgotten the heat of their fucking.

And never found it anywhere else, either. Until now.

He tugged his cock free of her and plunged deep into her cunt. She wanted to cry out from need, and the shock of his movements.

His hands gripped harder, hurting her now, clenching her buttocks and digging fingernails into her flesh as he pounded fiercely deep inside her.

She felt him lean forward and fasten his teeth to her nipple. He bit down, hard. It hurt, but only added to the fire consuming her flesh. He did it again, and she cried out from the pain/pleasure of it.

"Sandra," he breathed against her stinging breast. "Where is it?"

"Where's what?" She moaned and wriggled to get her clit against his body as his balls thumped her buttocks.

"The box. Where is it?"

"I dunno...so many boxes...oh God..."

A sudden slap surprised Sandra. He'd hit her. Hard. Across the face.

"You know the one. We were talking about it earlier."

Her face hurt and she tasted the bitter metallic tang of her own blood as her lip split. But this was how she liked it — rough and violent. It seemed he knew her darkest desires. Her desperate needs.

She spat the blood away as her body, so near to coming, cried out for more. "I don't know. It could be anywhere. Oh Jesus, fuck me. So close..."

He slapped her again. "Think, Sandra, think..." He stopped moving and let her tremble on the brink of her orgasm.

Think? How could she think? Her cunt was screaming for release.

"I don't know where it is. I told you. I DON'T KNOW. In the office maybe. Christ, finish me, will you? I'm dyin' here..."

She wriggled frantically, unable to move her arms as he began to thrust into her again, driving her down into the harsh carpet.

"Yes, I'm afraid you are," came the quiet sigh.

He pounded himself harder than ever against her, and she felt her backside drop onto the carpet.

Strong hands slid up her chest to her throat.

She was coming...she could feel it now. Her clit was on fire, and her cunt beginning to twitch and spasm around that fabulous cock of his.

She was soaking wet, the sounds of their fucking were adding to her excitement, and she began to whimper as her orgasm began. She couldn't catch her breath — it was mind blowing.

She tried to scream out her pleasure, but something was trapping the air in her windpipe.

His hands...

He was tightening them.

Vainly, she tried to open her eyes and tell him to stop, and her legs started to thrash, not from her orgasm but from terror. A red haze was seeping beneath her eyelids and her lungs felt like they were full of fire.

She struggled for air, adrenaline coursing through her, making her heart beat triple time and her body sweat in fear.

"N...n...no..." she rasped.

The hands never moved.

As her consciousness faded, Sandra tried to get her mind around the idea that he was REALLY going to kill her. What the fuck?

It was too late.

Chapter 4

Peta heaved a sigh of relief as Phoebe drew the car up into the driveway next to her house on Acorn Street. The small Victorian looked as lovely to her now as it had done four years ago when she'd bought it.

All she wanted to do was go inside, lock the door, have a nice cup of tea and then sleep off the lingering after-effects of the "wee shot" that dratted doctor had given her last night. She'd slept like a log and woken up feeling like one as well. Heavy, wooden-limbed, and stiff.

But to her surprise, the front door was opening.

To her even greater surprise, Max Wolfe was coming out. Of *her* house. And he was wearing a pair of the ugliest sweatpants she'd ever seen, not to mention a parka that was about three sizes too small. In puce.

Those drugs must have been a lot stronger than she supposed. She blinked. This couldn't be happening.

But it was. Within seconds he was at her door, all hazel eyes and tousled hair, and smiling at her, unfastening her seat belt like she was three instead of twenty-seven.

Ineffectually, she batted at his hands. "What are you...what...wha—"

"Quiet. You're still fuzzy from the medications. Come here." His voice soothed her and crept into her brain like another kind of drug. A horribly arousing one.

His arms slid beneath her and lifted her out of the car like she was a feather. God, the man was strong. She was no feather. More like an entire duck and *then* some.

"I...what are you doing? Mr. Wolfe. Put me...*ouch!*"

Her ankle bumped the car door as she was hoisted against his chest. His nice, manly chest. The one that had figured largely in several of her private fantasies. She sighed.

"Sorry. But you're in no condition to walk and you know it."

Carefully, Max carried her into the house, while Phoebe fluttered behind them.

Peta stared at him helplessly, trying to stop her arms from slipping up and around Max's neck. God forbid she should let him think she was enjoying being carried around. Well, she was, but damned if she was going to let on to *him* about it.

He carried her into her living room, and gently eased her into the recliner that was now arranged before the fireplace. A fireplace that was presently filled with a rather energetically crackling fire.

Dammit. She'd never been able to get one to do that. Her attempts had resulted in more of a smoky glow. This one snapped and popped very nicely.

She felt her temper rise. "Would someone tell me what the hell is going on?" She looked at Max and Phoebe who stared back at her. "Why are you two here? What's all this about?" She waved at the fire.

Something large and black landed on her lap and made her jump. It kneaded her thighs and resolved itself into the purring weight of a big black cat.

"And who the hell's *this*?"

Max calmly reached down and extended the footrest. Peta noticed that the cat glared at him in much the same fashion as she herself was doing right about now.

Phoebe settled in a matching chair, and Max perched on its arm.

"Max is your houseguest and caretaker, dear." Phoebe smiled serenely.

"What?" Peta's screech disturbed the cat who mumbled beneath Peta's hand. Odd how cats just seemed to be able to get people to stroke them. She rubbed his ears soothingly, and he purred.

"That's Mr. Peebles," grinned Max, nodding at her lap. "I'm afraid we're a pair. Love me, love my cat, as they say."

Love me? For a blissful second, Peta's eyes closed and she wished she could. Naked skin and all.

She blushed.

"There was another accident last night, Peta. While you were in the hospital, Max's apartment ceiling caved in. He was lucky to get out alive." Phoebe nodded at Max.

Peta stared and noticed the large band-aid that was partially hidden by that glorious hair. The silken strands that just shrieked for a woman to run her fingers through them. Her color deepened. "Oh. Uh...sorry to hear that, Mr. Wolfe."

"Please, Peta, call me Max. Seeing as we're going to be roomies, we can dispense with the formalities, don't you think?"

"Roomies?" Her eyes opened wide. "What do you mean, *roomies*?"

"Well, darling, it makes perfect sense." Phoebe gazed at Peta placidly. "You have a bad sprain there and can't get up and down stairs. In fact you have to stay off it for a day or so at least. Max has nowhere to live for the time being, but is pretty much all in one piece. Except for the clothes, of course. They were Claude's..." Phoebe's voice trailed off as she glanced at Max. "And you probably should think about shopping, dear boy. They don't really fit you very well..."

"They seemed like designer originals to me last night, Phoebe, and I can't thank you and Claude enough," smiled Max.

Peta's heart wobbled. Damn the man. When he smiled like that he could charm the bloody birds out of the trees.

"Well, I'll pass along your thanks when I go visit Claude's grave next time. I'm sure he'll appreciate it."

Given that Claude had passed on to his reward some twenty odd years ago, Peta now understood the oddness of Max's attire.

"I take it you lost everything, Mr. — er — Max?" Politeness forced her to inquire. Her mind broke out into a sweat as it considered the rather naughty idea that he might be naked under those dingy pants.

"Just about. Got my cell phone, my wallet, Mr. Peebles, and the fire department bravely rescued a couple of pairs of shorts. But that's about it, I'm afraid."

Well *shit*. There went that fantasy.

"I'm sorry to hear that. But you can't stay here — "

"Of course he can, dear. In fact, it's absolutely necessary. You can't be left alone, you know. Not for the next twenty-four hours, at any rate. Concussion and all that. Max has to wake you every couple of hours, just to make sure you're okay."

If Max was going to wake her every couple of hours, the one thing she wouldn't be was *okay*.

"Look, darling, I'm going to make us some tea, and Max is going shopping. You just take a nice nap for a while, and when you wake up we'll sort out the details. All right?" Phoebe stood up.

The heat from the fire and the warmth of Mr. Peebles purring contentedly on her lap soothed Peta, and she allowed exhaustion to creep in to her befuddled brain.

"Okay." It was a weak response, but the comfort of being in her own home, warm and safe, was overwhelming. Funny thing, that. Having Max around was making her feel *safe*.

She closed her eyes with a sigh, and let her mind drift.

* * * * *

Max watched her sleep and as he did so he wondered if his new jeans were a size too small.

He'd shopped for clothes and stocked up Peta's fridge in record time while Phoebe stayed with the invalid, then arrived home, handed Phoebe her keys and shooed her out the door. He'd worry about his own car later.

Right now, he just wanted to be alone with Peta.

And watch her. Watch her chest rise and fall under the crocheted throw he'd tucked around her, and watch her eyelashes as they quivered on her cheeks. Her ankle was bandaged, and she'd taken off her shoes, but her toes were perfect.

Max snorted at himself. Since when had he been interested in a woman's feet unless he was nibbling on them prior to moving up her legs? Since when had the curve of a woman's cheek stirred his cock to life?

She looked all soft and tranquil, and the few bruises he could see were fading. Her knuckles were skinned.

He had the oddest urge to pick up her hand and kiss the scrapes better.

He shook his head. Where the hell had *that* come from?

His youth had been spent at the best schools, the best summer camps and the best college, and certainly hadn't included things like getting boo-boos kissed better. His parents didn't have the time. His father was on his way to a distinguished judicial career, his mother active in every charity known to mankind and then some, and neither had given more than a cursory hug to their son.

He hadn't cared, particularly. He'd insulated himself at an early age from *that* sort of thing, and considered himself lucky to have enjoyed the life of the privileged few. He could ride, play *chemin de fer*, knew good clothes — with the possible exception of these jeans — and had a pretty good grasp of life in general, not to mention a degree in business which he hadn't used since a certain nasty episode in Boston nearly a year ago.

He considered himself intelligent, well-read, and knew he was attractive. The scores of conquests that had paraded through his sex life had reinforced that idea.

So why did he want to heal Peta's knuckles?

It was a puzzle. But the clock was ticking the afternoon away, and he knew he had to wake her. Puzzles could wait for later.

He knelt down by her chair and for a second his senses swam as her fragrance hit him. Hard.

She was flowers and hospitals and woman, and he closed his eyes, breathing in that insubstantial *something* that was uniquely her.

Gently he raised his hand to her cheek and stroked it. "Peta?"

She stirred slightly.

"Peta, honey, wake up."

Her eyelids flickered and then rose. She stared at him sleepily, and for a moment or two he could swear he saw something hot behind her eyes. Her lips curved in a welcoming smile. "Hullo, Max," she said.

Her voice went straight to his crotch. Jesus Christ. Two words spoken in that charming British voice and he was hard as a brick.

Mr. Peebles jumped up onto Peta's lap and she suddenly snapped into awareness. "Oh heavens. What time is it? Is something wrong?"

"Nope, nothing's wrong. I just have to wake you every now and again. We have to check you out for concussion, remember?"

She sighed and stretched, wincing a little. "Oh yes, now I remember. Lord, I'm stiff. And you—" she glanced down at Mr. Peebles "—aren't helping."

"Come on, down from there," said Max. He reached out to pick up the boneless lump of black fur. The lump became a rather irate feline.

"No, he's all right, Max, really. I was just joking. Leave him. I like the warmth. It's...it's comforting. We always had cats when I grew up..." Her voice trailed off as

41

Max leaned over her chair and stared into her eyes. "What...what are you doing?"

"Checking your pupils. If they're dilated we have to call the doctor."

She stared back at him, their faces only inches apart. "So," she breathed. "Are they dilated?"

Max was busy swimming in gray pools, and for a moment didn't even hear the question. "Uh, what?"

"My pupils. Are they dilated?"

He wondered how he was supposed to tell. It didn't help that her gaze had dropped to his mouth, and she was licking her lips. He wasn't sure if it was conscious or not, but if he was reading her right her mind wasn't on the state of her pupils.

Come to think of it, neither was his.

The fire was warming them, the room was quiet, Mr. Peebles was purring happily on Peta's lap, and Max wanted nothing more than to lower his head and taste her.

"I think..." he said quietly. "I think they're good."

"That's nice," she answered, never lifting her eyes off his lips.

Max couldn't have stopped himself to save his life. He lowered his head and closed the distance between them, almost brushing her mouth with his.

She sighed.

And the doorbell rang.

* * * * *

Peta jerked back from Max's mouth and disturbed Mr. Peebles, who leaped from her lap with a yowl.

Peta wanted to yowl too. She'd been so close to having Max Wolfe's lips touch hers.

"Er...I'll get that," said Max.

"Yes. Perhaps you'd better." *Before I say to hell with this ankle and rip your clothes off.*

Dear heavens. What was she thinking? Just because the man had no place to live and was taking care of her for a couple of days didn't mean that she was going to let him seduce her.

Besides, she had no illusions about Max. For him, she was probably the most available port in the storm at the moment. After all, he couldn't possibly bring one of his little bimbos over to Peta's house. That, she would never allow. If there was going to be any bimbo-boinking, then *she* was going to be the bimbo who got boinked.

She sighed. No one could be further from a bimbo than she was.

Peta gave up worrying about it, listening instead to the sound of voices from the hallway.

There seemed to be a long and enthusiastic conversation going on. Peta could hear a woman's voice and another man's, as well as Max's. Funny thing, that. She could distinguish Max's deep rumble quite clearly, but the others just blurred for her.

They sounded as if they were arguing, or at least having an energetic discussion about something.

Then there was quiet, and Max re-entered the room, followed by two people.

"Um, Peta? You have visitors. You feel up to it, hon?"

She tried to ignore the little thrill that traveled through her at his casual usage of the term "hon". It was probably natural to him. Doubtless he called all his girlfriends "hon". Did he look upon her as his girlfriend? Oooh. Now *there* was a thought.

She wrenched her mind away from the attractions of Max Wolfe and focused on her visitors.

Oh Gawd, *NO*.

Standing with polite smiles on their faces were the two people she could have happily spent the rest of her life *not* seeing.

Cary Stiles and his sister Diana.

Chapter 5

"Oh you *poor* darling."

Diana Stiles' elegant tones gushed into the quiet room, and Max gritted his teeth. "Does it hurt much? I'm so sorry. We came as soon as we heard."

The word "why" trembled on the tip of Max's tongue.

"Poor sweetheart," soothed Cary. He moved over to Peta's chair and knelt down next to it. In exactly the same spot that Max had occupied only moments earlier. Max wondered if a swift boot up the rear of Cary's designer pants might be appropriate.

"Er, well. This *is* a surprise." Peta's words held a slight edge. Max could hear it clearly, but apparently Cary couldn't, since he was busy trying to take one of her hands in his own.

"You must have known we'd come by and see if there was anything we could do," said Diana. The fact that she hadn't moved from his side didn't escape Max.

"How nice," said Peta noncommittally.

"Yes, how thoughtful," added Max.

"And here you are with your very own private nursemaid, too," cooed Diana. "Aren't you the lucky girl?"

Max removed his arm from Diana's grip. It was akin to wrenching a limb from a vise.

"I'll fix us something to drink," he said.

"Ooh, lovely, darling. I'll help you." Diana-the-vise was back.

"Make mine a scotch and water, will you?" called Cary. He remained glued to Peta's side.

"Sorry, Cary. No alcohol. Peta's on medication. You'll have to make do with coffee." Max tried not to let the satisfaction creep through into his voice. He wasn't a damn waiter.

"Um, Max?" Peta craned around Cary to catch his eye. "It'll have to be tea. I don't have any coffee, I don't think."

Max grinned at her. "Yes you do. I went shopping."

"Oh, darling. What a good person you are," said Diana, giving him her worshipful blue-eyed look. The one that had lured him into her bed several months ago.

"Yes, aren't I?" He bit the words out and turned to the kitchen. Diana followed close behind. Very close. If he'd stopped short, she'd have broken her nose.

He hated leaving Peta alone with Cary, but he really had no choice in the matter. And hard though it was to see Cary all over Peta, it would have been even worse if Diana had chosen this moment to be indiscreet.

Fortunately, she waited until they reached Peta's kitchen. *Then* she was indiscreet.

She slid her hands around Max from behind, stroking up and down. Quite a long way down. Over his crotch, in fact.

"Ooooh, Max. I've missed you so, darling," she breathed.

"Diana, I —"

"No, no, don't say anything. Just let me feel you." She felt him. Enthusiastically.

For some reason, Max found his cock unresponsive. He had a moment's blinding fear that he'd died and nobody had told him. Then the truth dawned on him. He had no sexual interest in Diana. Not anymore.

She left him colder than the stone birdbath that sat full of snow outside Peta's kitchen window.

Her fingers found the button on his jeans, but before she could unfasten it he pulled her hands away and stepped to the counter, putting some distance between them.

Diana pouted. It was one of her favorite expressions. She probably only had about four of them. Worship, pout, lust, and another, rather irritated narrowing of the eyes that he was getting right now.

"What's the matter, Max? Afraid that little pumpkin next door will hear us?"

Max frowned. "Peta is not a 'little pumpkin'. And we are presently in her house. I think a small measure of respect is in order, don't you?"

Diana's eyes narrowed even further. "That didn't seem to worry you at Edward Sharp's Christmas party, now, did it? I seem to remember you found a good use for that linen closet..."

She backed him up against the counter and rubbed her ample breasts against him. "It was fun, Max. Let's do it again."

Max's mind flooded with distaste. He'd never liked being pursued. In his traditional mind, it was the man who should do the chasing. Old-fashioned, yes, but he still harbored a dislike of overly aggressive women. Especially ones who seemed to feel that they had a right to glue their bodies to his. In someone else's kitchen.

"Diana, that night was fun. No arguments there. But we've both moved on. And you know why."

Diana went back to expression number one. Pouting.

"But darling—"

"No buts, Diana. I prefer my sex to involve *two* people. Any more, and I'm gone. I made that plain." He turned away from her, pulling free and reaching for the new coffee pot he'd added to his shopping cart earlier.

If Peta thought he could exist on tea while he stayed with her, she was in for a big, and nicely fragrant surprise.

"Well, it could be just the two of us again, Max. You know we were good together. Let's give it a try, hmmm?"

This woman never gave up. Max heaved a sigh. It was time to bring out the big guns. He filled the pot with water, put the coffee in the filter and plugged the thing in, while he considered his next words.

"Diana, I—"

He was interrupted by a sound from the next room. It sounded like a cry for help.

Fortunately, Diana moved out of the way, or he'd have run her down in his haste to get to Peta.

She was still sitting in her chair, but now there was the light of battle in her eyes, and she was glaring at Cary with lips clenched.

"I'm so *so* sorry, sweetheart..." Cary was sputtering.

"The reason I'm in this chair, Cary, is that my ankle is sprained. And you might remember that fact the next time you lean on it."

Max felt his temper flare up. "Are you all right?" His words were calm, cold, and he caught Peta's gaze on him as he crossed the room to her side, rather unsubtly forcing Cary to move away from her.

"I am now, thanks, Max. Cary—Cary bumped my ankle, that's all." Her lips were white, and Max couldn't even begin to guess how much it must have hurt.

"You clumsy idiot." Max aimed his words at Cary, watching as he shrank back.

Wisely, Cary backed away. "I...I...didn't mean to. It was an accident, honestly..."

Diana chuckled as she leaned against the doorway. "That's my brother. Always having accidents."

"Shut up, Diana," hissed Cary.

"Max, could *you* reassure Cary that I'm just fine here? That I certainly don't want to come and stay in his house while I recuperate, nor do I need him to interrupt his busy schedule with visits here *every* day?"

Max certainly could. In fact it would have given him great pleasure to make each one of those very points with his fist. How *dare* this jerk try and lure Peta away from her own home? And him?

Max found his fingers clenching, and did his best to relax them. Getting into a fight, satisfactory though it might have been, wouldn't solve things and would probably upset Peta. Her mouth was tight, and he could see the color flushing her cheeks.

He had to get rid of these two. Now.

"Look, I'm sure accidents happen. But Peta just got out of the hospital, and right now she needs rest more than anything else. Thank you both for coming by...let me get your coats for you."

It wasn't subtle, or tasteful. But it was effective.

Cary was not to be outmaneuvered, however. Crossing to Peta's chair, he reached for her hand, ignoring the fact that she'd buried it beneath Mr. Peebles's ample tummy.

Mr. Peebles, however, objected. He hissed, and obviously made his point clear. Cary halted, and settled for a warm smile.

"You just let me know if there's anything, *anything* at all, I can do, Peta dear. You understand?"

"And Max..." Not to be outdone, Diana was sliding all over him as she shrugged into her fur coat. "Remember our little—*conversation*—in the kitchen. We'll talk more when you're..." she glanced at Peta with a smug smile, "...free."

Max closed the door behind them both with a huge sigh of relief.

The coffee was perked, and he grabbed a couple of mugs for them both before returning to Peta.

As soon as he walked in, he knew he was in trouble.

* * * * *

Peta was burning. Her ankle throbbed where that idiot Cary had leaned on it, her temper was boiling at some of his suggestions, and to top it all off, it looked like Diana was still having an ongoing "*thing*" with Max.

Unwisely, she spoke the first words that came to her mind. "So. Are you sleeping with Diana, or what?"

Max's eyebrows shot up, and Peta realized that she'd sounded like a fishwife. "God, I'm sorry. It's none of my business what you do. Or with whom."

He passed her a mug, and she sniffed. It was coffee, and not bad either. Cautiously she took a sip. "Hey, this is quite nice."

Max grinned and settled in the chair on the other side of the fireplace. Mr. Peebles deserted Peta and came to check out the lap situation from this new perspective. Apparently he found it satisfactory, and as Peta watched, he lowered his large rump into Max's crotch and proceeded to knead Max's knees with great thoroughness. Max winced.

"Ouch, fella. Watch the claws." Carefully, Max eased the flexing paws out of his jeans and the legs beneath. His touch was gentle and Mr. Peebles took the hint, merely rearranging his limbs and closing his eyes in bliss as Max rubbed one ear.

"Peta, it seems that perhaps we should get a few matters settled between us, seeing as I'm going to be staying here for a bit," began Max.

Peta chewed her lip. She wasn't sure if she was ready to hear whatever Max was about to say.

"First off, you can ask me anything you want." He paused. "Provided, of course, I get to ask you anything I want in return. Fair enough?"

Peta thought about that for a moment. "Well, yes. I suppose so. It's better to ask about things and get it all straight up front, isn't it?"

"Yep. Total honesty. You want to know something? Just ask. I'll tell you the truth."

Peta swallowed. Total honesty from *Max Wolfe*? Good Lord, she wouldn't know where to begin. Thousands of questions trembled on the tip of her tongue, none of which she could spit out. All of which were extremely inappropriate, and many revolving around the issue of genital size. *Is it as big as I've heard?*

"Now, seeing as Diana made some implications a moment ago, let's talk about it and get it out of the way."

How could he sit there, so cool and collected, sipping his coffee and staring at her from those gorgeous hazel eyes, while discussing another woman? She held her breath.

"First off, I didn't fuck her in your kitchen. No matter how she made it sound."

Peta lowered her eyes. "I really didn't think you did. You didn't have time—"

She caught herself, and felt the color flood her cheeks as Max grinned.

"Clever girl. You're right. I do like to take my time."

His words did nothing to cool her blushes. She badly wanted to ask him how much time he did take, but her natural caution held *that* question back too. Thank God.

"As far as sleeping with her goes, well, yes I did. And no, I'm not anymore."

"Oh." What more was there to say? How was she in bed? Why did you two split up? Would you consider sleeping with me?

"You're wondering why, right?"

Good grief. He was a mind reader, too. She looked down at her mug. "I wouldn't presume." It was polite, noncommittal, and hopefully didn't show the screaming curiosity that was coursing through her.

Max snickered. "Can't hide from me, Peta." He rubbed Mr. Peebles absently. "Diana and I had a brief— *thing*—a few months ago. Yes, she's very attractive, and yes, she's very sexual. Both of which I found appealing at the time."

Peta suppressed a snort. Max and everyone else in Mayfield, she suspected.

"However," he continued, "her tastes and mine— differed. A lot. I won't go into it, but after a couple of nights together, I realized that we weren't on the same wavelength. I haven't dated her or slept with her since."

Okay. Good to know. Peta sighed a little internal sigh of relief.

"Now supposing you tell me about Cary Stiles." The question was firm, quiet, and demanded an answer.

Peta thought for a moment. "Well, there's not much to tell. He's been making passes at me for a while now. I turned him down. Every time. Now I think it's a matter of principle for him. I'm probably the only woman in Mayfield who's said no to him. I'm sure he means nothing by it, it's just that I've become this sort of...challenge to him, if you know what I mean?"

"So he hits on you every chance he gets?"

Peta wrinkled her brow. Sometimes Americanisms took a little translating. "Um, yes, I suppose you could say so. He was quite insistent just now that I come and stay with him. He's got this huge place on the other side of town." She pursed her mouth. "With all those 'Cary's Cafés' he manages, he can well afford it."

"Nice places."

"Yes they are. And successful too. I hear the chain is opening restaurants in several new venues soon." She leaned back and gazed into the fire. Somehow, Max was easy to talk to, like this. Casual, friendly, not intimidating at all. She wondered why she'd never seen it before, this gentle side of Max Wolfe.

Then she glanced at him and caught something in his eyes that wasn't gentle at all. It was downright hot.

She shivered.

"Damn, you're running a fever, aren't you?" Max was at her side in an instant, touching his palm to her forehead. If she hadn't had a fever before, she was well on her way to having one now.

"No, no, really, Max..."

"Don't 'no no' me. You should be in bed." He glanced at the clock. "And it's time for a couple more pain pills too, I think."

Peta groaned. "Do I have to?"

"Yes, young lady, you do." Max stopped. "God. I'm turning into your mother."

Peta couldn't help the laugh that escaped her. "No you're not. My mother is alive and well and growing ghastly amounts of vegetables in Florida."

She saw the answering smile lighten Max's eyes.

"Nevertheless, I think it's time to get you more comfortable. Do you want something to eat, or shall I take you straight to bed?"

Oh my. Now *there* was a question to give a girl pause. Peta swallowed. "I think perhaps bed, right now. I'm not hungry at all." *Except for a few things I shouldn't be thinking of at this moment.*

"Smart girl. Come on." He bent to the chair and picked her up in his arms, amazing her once again with his strength.

"Max, I—"

His face was close to hers. "What?"

"I just can't get over the way you do that. Pick me up. Carry me around. I'm not a lightweight, you know."

Max snorted as he carefully made his way up the stairs to the second floor and Peta's room. "You're just fine. Don't worry about it."

Oh *right*. The deliciously delectable Max Wolfe was about to carry her into her bedroom like some character from a romance novel, and he was telling her not to worry about it.

"Can I have a shower?" She wanted a shower. She wanted to get clean, and find herself again. She wanted him to scrub her back. She wanted him gone from her house and she wanted him to never put her down.

Her head ached as the conflicting thoughts dueled inside her mind.

"Nope. You have to stay off that foot, remember? If you're a good girl, you can have a bath in the morning."

She chuckled. "Oh goody. Something to look forward to."

Max lowered her gently onto the side of the bed. "Most certainly," he grinned, his hands brushing her breast as her weight settled on the comforter.

She wondered if it was accidental. The warmth between her thighs certainly wasn't. That was a direct result of his touch.

"Get undressed."

"I beg your pardon?" Her breath caught in her throat.

"I said get undressed."

"Not with you in the room. What *are* you thinking?" Peta felt her eyebrows hit her hairline.

Max turned back to her, and for one instant a bolt of heat shot from her ears to her toes. His eyes were gleaming with an expression she couldn't put a name to. Lust? Nope. Desire? Maybe. Impatience? Most likely.

"I'm thinking I don't want you falling and making that ankle worse. Where's your nightclothes or whatever?"

"My jammies?" Peta colored up as she realized what she'd said. He must have really caught her off guard. She seldom shared such intimate details with anyone, let alone the man of her dreams.

He grinned. "Yeah, those. Where are they?"

"Behind the bathroom door." She waved helplessly at the small bathroom that led off the master bedroom, and Max disappeared to fetch her jammies.

Her *jammies*. Well, that killed any sensual mood she'd been hoping for *stone* dead.

He returned, bearing her flannel pajamas. "Cows?"

Defensively, she raised her chin. "I *like* cows."

Max gave her a look that was so full of humor, she couldn't help but smile back. "Me too."

She looked around helplessly as Max laughed.

"I'm going to wait outside. You get undressed. Get into your jammies, and I'll carry you to the bathroom. Yell if you need help."

Peta watched the door pull to behind him, and obediently began to get undressed. *Carry her to the bathroom indeed.* Over her dead body. It was hard enough taking her clothes off knowing he was outside her bedroom door. If he imagined she could pee with him anywhere near her, he didn't know her bladder.

Which of course he didn't, and as she struggled into her pajamas, she realized he probably wouldn't, nor would he get to know any other parts of her body anytime soon, either.

It was a depressing thought.

She hopped quietly on one foot into the bathroom and freshened up, secure in the knowledge that she was, temporarily, alone. At least she could wash her face and brush her teeth while balancing one-legged on the sink.

She ran her hairbrush through her hair and straightened the worst of the tangles. It would have to do.

She opened the door and fell smack into a broad chest.

"*What* did I tell you?" Max's voice was stern.

Peta closed her eyes. This was awful. He'd been outside. While she'd peed. And brushed her teeth. Was nothing sacred any more?

Once again she was swept up into his arms and deposited on her bed. He'd turned the covers back, and she couldn't suppress her sigh of relief as she felt the smooth sheets and the soft warmth of her own linens.

"Now stay put." Max left the room, only to enter a few moments later with a glass of water and two pills. "Take these."

She glared at him. "Should I salute?"

His grin softened his stern expression. "You have to rest, and get that ankle better. I'm trying to follow doctor's orders here, kid. Don't make it hard."

I'd love to make *it* hard, she thought wistfully, taking the pills and washing them down with the water he was holding out to her.

"Good girl. Now lie back." He fussed around her with a good deal of efficiency, settling her comfortably.

She watched him, letting her muscles relax as the pain pills began to do their work. "Max?"

"Hmm?"

"Why are you doing this?" She was so comfortable now, her arms and legs were getting heavy, the pain had gone and her heart was singing. Max Wolfe was taking care of her. All was right with the world.

"Because I'm a nice guy?"

"Yes, you are. Funny thing, that..." She sighed, and with the memory of a pair of incredibly handsome eyes lingering in her brain, Peta fell asleep.

* * * * *

There were black and white cows in the field around her. They were making those soft sort of cow sounds—a munch and a swish combined with the occasional grunting kind of moo.

Peta felt the grass against her spine as she stretched in the sunlight, and realized she was naked. Some part of her registered this fact with detachment. The rest of her just relished the warmth on her skin and the blue sky that soared above her.

Then something else was soaring above her. It was Max Wolfe.

All hazel eyes and flying hair, he was swooping in for a very nice three-point landing, and—oh boy—his landing gear was down and locked.

He smiled as he touched the grass at her side, and within seconds he was lying on top of her.

She didn't feel crushed, just warmed from head to toe by his body and his expression. His cock was hard between her thighs, and she felt herself getting wet as he rubbed his skin across hers.

"Moo?" His voice was low and suggestive and she sighed with pleasure as it reverberated through her chest.

"Oh moo," she breathed.

His hands roved across her skin, bringing tingles of electricity in their wake and his lips found her breast. He suckled, teasing her with his tongue as he did so.

"Mmmmmoooo."

She couldn't have agreed more. Her legs parted as she struggled to get him where she needed him most.

His hip bones fit between hers like he'd been made for her, and when his cock slid over her clit, she gasped in pleasure.

"*Mmooo....*"

The palms of her hands ran over his back, tracing his muscles, learning his contours, and pulling him to her. She wanted him. She wanted to fuck him until...until the cows came home.

He raised himself on his hands, pulling back a little and dazzling her with the light shining from his eyes. All heat and passion, his gaze sought her very soul.

"Mmmooo?"

"Mmmoooo," she sighed, thrusting her hips up to leave no doubt as to the answer to his question. It definitely was "mmmooo" or never.

She was ready. Oh so ready.

It was going to happen. Finally, at long last, she'd get what she'd yearned for since he walked into her life.

She was going to fuck Max Wolfe.

He poised his cock at the entrance to her cunt and she gasped at the feel of it. So...*wonderful*.

A new sensation made her blink. Something was sitting on her foot.

Max turned slightly, and his cock slid away from her body. She nearly cried. They both looked down at a large cat who had draped himself over Peta's sore ankle.

"Oh MOOOOOOOOO."

Chapter 6

Max eased himself into Peta's room for the third time that night, and crossed to the bed. The first couple of times, he could have sworn she was mooing in her sleep. Well, hell, if she insisted on wearing cow pajamas, it wasn't a surprise.

He'd shooed Mr. Peebles away from her injured ankle, and wondered if he should wake her, but she was smiling a little. He'd crept from the room, leaving her to what was obviously a pleasant dream.

This time, he stayed.

He watched her sleep, noting the way her breasts rose and fell with each breath. He'd have to wake her soon, but was reluctant to do so. She seemed to be resting comfortably.

He shivered a little. Damn, she kept her house cool. Must be one of those leftover British things. She certainly had plenty of them.

He smiled as he looked around him. A couple of photos stood on her dresser, featuring an older couple holding vegetables. Her parents, he guessed. A small fuzzy toy sat next to the photos, and charmed Max. Who'd have thought the ever-so-proper Ms. Matthews would like cuddly toys?

Then again, he remembered how she'd felt, snuggled into his arms. Oh yeah. No matter what image she presented to the world, she was a cuddler, all right. He crossed to the window and briefly pulled the heavy drapes apart, gazing out on the winter wonderland that was Mayfield after a hefty snowstorm.

The moon had risen, and the temperatures had dropped significantly. The weather reports called for record low temperatures, given that it was early March. Everything was crisp and white and glistening, and Max allowed himself a rare moment to appreciate it.

He wondered at the paths his thoughts were taking. It was as if he'd stepped into Peta's house and left the "other" Max Wolfe on the doorstep. The one that wanted to fuck everything that moved, and then head out of town to new and challenging conquests.

Somehow, it had become less about fucking and more about—something else.

He glanced at the sleeping woman. Yeah. More about her.

A dark shape was curled up comfortably at the bottom of the bed. Mr. Peebles certainly knew how to find the perfect spot for his evening nap. Once Max had let the fire die down and closed the glass doors on it, Mr. Peebles had given him a look of disgust and disappeared.

Apparently, he'd found the soft comforter. And to add insult to injury he was snoring. The very least he could have done was come to Max's room and warm *his* feet. He'd saved the damned cat's life, for God's sake. That was feline gratitude for you.

Peta stirred, and moaned slightly.

Max was at her side in an instant. The nightlight reflected a glimmer from her eyes as she struggled to open them.

"What...wha..."

"Hush, Peta. It's time to check you out for a minute. Look at me, babe."

Max sat next to her and slid his arm around her shoulders, lifting her off the pillow and pulling her to his chest.

"Max?" Her tone was curious, not concerned.

"Yes, sweetheart. I'm here. Open your eyes, Peta."

"Oh yeah, the pupil thing..." She smothered a yawn and stretched, wincing a little as she moved her legs.

Max carefully peered into her eyes and heaved a sigh of relief. They looked just fine to him. All sleepy and gray and quite delightful. He wondered how they'd look when she orgasmed.

His cock stirred at the thought, and he wished for a second he had a good solid flannel robe instead of his shorts and a t-shirt. But he'd never worn a robe *or* pajamas and wasn't about to start now. No matter how cold this damn house was.

"Looks fine, honey," he said. "Time for more pills I think. You in much pain?"

Peta sighed and let him lower her back to her pillow. "Yeah, some. It's sort of throbbing, you know?"

He reached for the water and the pills he'd set next to the bed on an earlier visit. "Here we go...easy now." Once again, he lifted her as she swallowed the pills.

"Thanks Max," she said. "Sorry to be such a nuisance."

Max snorted. "You're not a nuisance. *He's* a nuisance." He glanced at Mr. Peebles who had decided to investigate the goings-on that had disrupted his nap.

Peta smiled sleepily. "No he's not. He keeps my feet warm. And he knows better than to sleep on my sore ankle. Don't you, sweetie?"

Mr. Peebles accepted the endearment and the caress as his due.

Max shivered. He couldn't help it. He wanted her hands stroking him like that.

"Max, you're cold. Silly thing. Wandering around half naked." Peta's voice was slurred, but tender. He rather liked it.

"I'll warm up. Don't worry about me."

"But I do. Don't know why. You're so annoying."

"I am?"

"Yes," sighed Peta. "Why don't you get under the puff and warm up? Can't have you getting sick. I need you."

Max froze. Did she realize what she was saying? Had she been reading his mind? Staring at his cock? What?

Hell. Why was he even hesitating?

Putting the glass carefully back on the bedside table, Max slid beneath the comforter. He assumed that was what she meant by getting under the "puff". Unless she had something else in mind.

"Oh that's nice," she breathed.

Without a trace of hesitation, she snuggled herself into his arms and yawned again. "What about work, Max?"

Too involved in processing the incredible feel of Ms. Peta Matthews as she snuggled her flannel-cow-covered body against his, it took Max a moment to realize that she'd asked him a question.

"It's all taken care of. Don't worry about a thing. Sandra is going to open the office tomorrow, your laptop is all set up, and we've brought the files we need over here. Just relax, honey. Go to sleep now, okay?"

"Yes. All right."

She nuzzled her head onto his shoulder, and apparently found the perfect spot. Her breasts pushed against him and she slid one thigh over his.

With a little sigh, she closed her eyes. "You're not cold anymore, are you?" she chuckled.

"Er, no. No, I'm not."

"Good. I'm glad. I heard you were a cold man, Max. But it was a lie. You're hot."

Now how was he supposed to answer that? *Yes, I'm hot enough to melt a good portion of the Arctic ice cap? I'll get even hotter if you let me take this damn flannel top of yours off and suck on those delightful breasts that are squished up against me?*

"The pain is going away."

Damn. He couldn't do any of the twenty-four things he wanted to do. The woman was recovering from an accident, for chrissake. He'd be a louse to try anything. He wasn't *that* much of a louse. Not at this moment, anyway.

Sadly, his cock wasn't listening. It knew what it wanted—it wanted to be buried in a hot, wet place that was tucked between Peta's thighs. It didn't matter that it was hidden beneath a field of black and white cows.

Max gritted his teeth and permitted himself the luxury of running his hand gently up and down her spine.

"Mmm, lovely," she murmured.

"Isn't it," sighed Max. His cock throbbed.

Sometimes, being a gentleman was a real killer.

* * * * *

Peta opened her eyes to the muted sunshine that struggled through the thick drapes on her windows. Something rather rough was licking her face.

A pair of slanted amber eyes, inches from hers, stared at her as Mr. Peebles continued his self-assigned task of washing her face.

She giggled. "Cut that out."

"Wasn't doin' anythin'."

The mumble from the pillow next to her shocked her rigid. She blinked and realized that a heavy arm was resting across her breasts and her legs were lying quite comfortably over a pair of hard thighs.

Dear God. She was in bed with Max Wolfe.

She shivered. It was her dream come to life. Impossible, utterly and completely improbable, but real.

She hurriedly checked her pajamas. They were buttoned up tight, and everything was where it was supposed to be.

Well, bugger it. What had she expected? To be seduced by a man known for his sexual conquests and whose dates resembled fashion models or playboy playmates?

Here she was, hips and all, covered in cows. The ideal outfit for a seduction - *NOT*.

Max moved next to her, stretching and brushing her breasts with his arm as he did so.

She tried to suppress a little shiver, but it was no good. The object of her fantasies was finally where she'd wanted him, in her bed, and he was draped all over her and around her like he belonged there.

She knew she had to move, or some of those damned cows were going to find themselves in a rather soggy field in a very few minutes.

Gingerly she eased away from his heat.

"Where do you think you're going?"

She turned her head and met the full blast of those incredibly hot hazel eyes. They were more green than gold this morning, and they were wide open, pinning her to the mattress.

"Um...I'm getting up?"

Max sighed. "How's the ankle?"

He didn't seem inclined to move, so she stayed where she was. Hell, she didn't want to move either, but pretty soon she was going to say bedamned to her ankle and jump his body. His very warm body. Which seemed to be wearing a light T-shirt. She wondered what lay beneath the covers. And oh dear God, did she want to find out.

"It's fine, thank you." Her polite answer drew a raised eyebrow in response. Max said nothing, just waited.

"Oh all right. My leg's stiff, the ankle still throbs although I think the swelling's gone down, and generally I feel like someone who drove her car off a bridge and into the river. Happy now?"

Peta knew she was snapping at him. But the combination of a sleepy and rumpled Max Wolfe along with her own thinly suppressed inclinations was driving her bonkers. "I have to get to work."

Both eyebrows rose at that statement, and Max yawned and stretched.

Peta looked away. Some things were too much, even for her.

"No going to work for you today, Peta. Don't you remember? I told you last night. It's all been taken care of, and your laptop's set up to handle the light editing stuff."

Peta frowned. "Last night?"

"Yeah," grinned Max. "Last night. When you so generously offered to share your warmth with me."

A blush rose to Peta's cheeks. "I did?"

"Well of course you did. I don't usually creep into an injured woman's bed uninvited, you know. What do you think I am?"

Peta wasn't about to answer that question. Nor was she going to pay any attention to the large lump that had appeared in her comforter, right around the area of Max's crotch.

She swallowed. "Well, that was — um — very gentlemanly of you, I'm sure. However, I'm quite ready to get up now."

"Yeah, me too."

Peta bit her lip and pulled away, swinging her legs over the side of the bed and turning her back on Max and his — his assets.

She heard his sigh and felt the bed move as he tossed the covers back and got out the other side. "You want to use the bathroom?"

She closed her eyes and prayed for strength. "Max." His name was supposed to come out like a firm exclamation, not a yearning plea.

She cleared her throat and tried again. "Max, thank you. Your attentions have been most...most thorough. But I think I can manage. I *know* I can manage. You may leave now."

He ignored her. "Here. I found this last night."

She turned her attention away from her toes and found he was holding out a cane.

"It was in a huge packing crate full of junk in your back hallway."

Peta chuckled. "Phoebe's been at it again. That woman loves flea markets like...like some people like designer shoe sales. She's always grabbing stuff, and then dumping it here. We go through it together and she picks what she thinks is fun and I get the privilege of disposing of the rest of it."

"Well, this time, she may have found something useful, although I doubt she realized it at the time. Let's see." Max put his arm around Peta, and she shivered a little, hoping he wouldn't notice that two cows in particular had developed bug eyes. The ones that covered her nipples.

Gently he raised her to her feet and she put her weight on the cane. It held, and she looked up with a quick grin.

Okay. That probably wasn't the smartest thing she could have done.

Max was looking at her with a mixture of amusement and heat, and he damn near took her breath away.

His muscles showed through the thin shirt he was wearing, and his boxer shorts did nothing to hide that fine piece of equipment that had doubled as a tent pole beneath her covers.

Dropping her eyes, Peta blushed. "Uh...good. That's good. I can manage from here." Bloody hell. If he didn't get out of her room she was going to embarrass herself even more than she had already.

"You sure?"

"Yes. Go away." It was more of a moan than an order, but Max seemed to take the hint.

"Okay. I'm going to grab a quick shower, and then fix us some breakfast. No doing anything but freshening up, lady. Be a good girl and you'll get a bath later. I have to check that ankle first. So dining will be informal this morning. Cows are welcome. I'll come get you when you're ready."

He flashed her a quick grin and left her, leaning on her cane.

Peta sighed. It *so* wasn't fair. She was ready now. She couldn't get more ready. Oh *bollocks*.

Chapter 7

"I don't care how long you stare at me, you're not getting bacon for breakfast. Yours is there." Max nodded at the dish containing perfectly acceptable cat food.

Mr. Peebles gazed at him in that particularly eloquent way that cats have developed over eons of dealing with humans. The way that said "You expect me to eat that shit when you're cooking something that smells so much better?"

Max had become accustomed to it and did the only thing possible under the circumstances. He ignored it.

Sliding bagel halves into the toaster oven, he stepped over Mr. Peebles and grabbed the cream cheese from the fridge. It would have surprised his many bed partners if they could have seen this efficiently domestic side of him.

Hell, he was surprising himself. But apparently, he was quite able to function around a kitchen—in fact he was rather enjoying it. The small table was laid with plates and mugs, the coffee was almost ready and the crisp bacon seconds away from perfection.

All he needed was Peta.

And that was the understatement of the year.

Waking up next to her and seeing her all soft and warm, wrapped in her *jammies*, had done quite awful things to his libido. And since when did his libido respond to flannel? He'd never gotten a hard-on from cows before.

He shook his head at himself, stepped over Mr. Peebles again, and retrieved the bagels.

Breakfast was ready. Time to get the lady downstairs.

"Stay away from the bacon, you hear?"

Mr. Peebles did the feline equivalent of "Yeah? Make me" by twitching his whiskers. Max narrowed his eyes and placed a plate upside down over the forbidden treat. It wasn't that he didn't trust Mr. Peebles, it was just that he...oh well, yeah, he didn't trust Mr. Peebles.

Satisfied that breakfast was safe for a few moments, Max hurried up the stairs and tapped on Peta's door. "Breakfast is served, Madam. Your ride's here."

A smothered chuckle followed his words. "Come on in."

She was sitting on the side of the bed, face scrubbed clean, hair pulled into a fairly neat bunch behind her head and wearing the most god-awful robe he'd ever seen.

She looked beautiful.

Max blinked. There must be something seriously wrong with him. No lace, no slinky lingerie, no makeup, not a hint of skin revealed, and she was still turning him on. He sighed.

"Let's go. I don't trust the cat to be in the same room with bacon for more than two seconds." He lifted Peta easily from the mattress as she grabbed the cane.

"You know I could probably do this myself," she protested.

"Sure. And I'd have to pick you up at the bottom of the stairs, call Phoebe for her car, and drive you back to the hospital. No thanks. We're doing this my way for a while."

Cautiously they made their way downstairs, and Max noted with satisfaction that Peta's eyes widened as he lowered her into the kitchen chair.

"Max. Really. This is too much..." She stared wide-eyed at the breakfast that awaited them. "Bagels? Cream cheese? And all this other stuff?" She sniffed at the bacon and closed her eyes. "Good Lord, I hope that's low fat cream cheese and pretend bacon."

Her stomach chose that moment to rumble loudly.

Max grinned. "Nope. It's the real McCoy. And don't even think about stupid things like calories. You didn't eat yesterday, you've got a belly full of medications, and the last thing you need to worry about is dieting."

Peta snorted, but reached for a bagel anyway. "Oh yes. Right. So speaks a man who probably has a metabolism faster than a freight train." She spread the cream cheese on the bagel and took a bite. "Mmmm. Oh God. Heaven."

Max helped himself to coffee and uncovered the bacon. Mr. Peebles moved over to sit next to his chair.

"Forget it, fella. I told you where your breakfast is," said Max.

Peta reached for a couple of pieces of bacon. "I can't remember the last time I had an honest-to-God, sit-down-at-the-table type breakfast. Not since I left home, anyway."

Mr. Peebles crossed to sit next to Peta's chair.

"When was that?" asked Max, around a mouthful of bagel.

"A while ago. Mum and Dad decided to head south, and I was busy here, so it seemed natural. Time to be my own person, as it were. Get out and stand on my own two feet."

"And did you?" The fragrance of the coffee swirled up Max's nose as he watched Peta busily making a large dent in her breakfast.

"Yes indeed. I found this place, got an excellent deal on it, and I've been here ever since."

Max ignored the hand containing a small sliver of bacon that slipped under the table. He could, however, see Mr. Peebles's tail twitching in appreciation. He sighed.

"It is a nice house." He also ignored the sound of Mr. Peebles's sharp teeth demolishing the forbidden snack.

"Thank you. I think so."

Max glanced around, realizing he'd spoken the truth. It *was* a nice house. Peta had clearly put her own stamp on the place, because there were whimsical little pieces here and there, the walls were bright and colorful, and the air was one of welcome, of—contentment.

The thought surprised him. He had never expected to feel *content* anywhere. Sated, yes. Horny, definitely. But up until now, some kind of sexual wanderlust had always driven him on. He had never really bothered to wonder what he was looking for— the search had been too much fun. But now he had a chance to experience something different. Something that didn't require satin sheets, a willing woman, and any sexual gymnastics at all.

It was strange.

"So, Max. You don't have any particular place you call home?" Peta was raising her eyebrows at him as she sipped her coffee. "My, this is very nice. I have to tell you I'm usually a tea person in the mornings, but I think you might just have converted me."

Max stifled the thought that he'd like to convert her to something else for breakfast as well. And bagels weren't involved. Cream cheese, maybe...

He cleared his throat. "Yeah, I guess you could call me footloose and fancy-free."

"So I've heard." The comment was dry, but Peta's eyes twinkled over the rim of her mug, taking the sting out of them.

"Now, Peta. You can't believe *everything* you hear."

She snorted.

"Well, all right. You can probably believe most of what you hear." Max found himself unable to come up with any diverting words. Something about Peta's gray eyes dug inside him.

"Better." She smiled at his honesty. "So are you some kind of sexual predator?"

Max nearly blew his coffee out his nose and across the table. "Fuck, no." He bit his lip. "Sorry. You caught me by surprise."

Peta chuckled. "Not a problem. I have heard the word before, you know. Even used it myself a couple of times."

Max felt relieved. "I'd wondered. It must be the British accent. You sound like the sort of person who wouldn't say 'shit' if she had a mouthful."

Peta laughed out loud. "Max, seeing as we pretty much invented the language you Americans take such delight in mauling, let me reassure you that most, if not all, the curses you use so colorfully originated hundreds of years ago in England."

"Well, if you say so." Damned if he was going to argue semantics at this hour of the morning. Of course, it had diverted her attention away from his sex life.

"So you never found one woman to settle down with, huh? Still looking for the right one?"

So much for diversion. "Uh, I guess. Though once..." He let his words trail off, not sure if he wanted to go any further in that direction.

"Once?" Peta, of course, couldn't let that one pass, could she?

Max swallowed. "Yeah, once. I met a woman. I thought I could play with her. She was gorgeous, hot, had a body that wouldn't quit..."

"But?" Peta's question prompted his memories, and images of a Cape Cod summer home flooded his mind.

"But...she was crazy for somebody else. Married him, too. She wasn't for me. Not that I minded, I had a second string to my bow, so to speak."

"But you cared for her?"

Max paused. Had he "cared" for Emma Hansell? He'd lusted after her, that's for sure. But she'd turned out to be so much more. She'd touched his arm and given him her apologies when he was the one who should have done the apologizing. It had been a defining moment for him, a moment when something had shifted slightly in his world. Of course, he'd gone right back in the house and fucked the shit out of Jasmine, but Emma's memory had lingered long after Jasmine had disappeared from his life. Onto the Internet.

"Max?" Peta recalled his attention. "Did you care for her?"

"I'm not sure." And that was about as honest as he could get. "She was special and I learned something from her. Let's leave it at that, shall we?"

Peta nodded. "All right. I'm sorry. I didn't mean to pry into your private affairs."

He grinned. "Yes you did."

She grinned back. "Well, yes, I suppose I did, really. But this is all most unexpected. To have the notorious Max Wolfe waiting on me hand and foot...well...you must admit?"

Max chuckled at her British phrasing. She wiped her mouth with her paper napkin and heaved a sigh of relief. "My word, that was excellent. I feel a thousand percent better now."

"Good. So, in all probability, does Mr. Peebles."

Peta had the grace to blush. "Never could resist those hungry-cat eyes. And I only gave him a little."

"Don't worry about it." Max stood and gathered the dishes, frowning at Peta when she attempted to rise from her chair.

"Stay."

Peta snorted. "Right. Do I get a dog biscuit?"

"Sorry. I just want you off that ankle as much as possible."

"Look, Max. I appreciate all your concern, but I have to move around soon. I need to get some work done, I need to take a shower..."

"Uh uh. No shower. Let me put these in the dishwasher, and then we'll discuss a bath."

"What's to discuss?" Peta's mouth tightened.

"We will discuss how hot you want the water. We will discuss if and how you're going to keep your ankle out of the water. We will discuss whether any of your other abrasions need some ointment or anything on them. We will discuss whether you need a pain pill or not."

Peta closed her eyes. "Okay. You've made your point."

Her eyes remained closed as he reached for her and carried her upstairs.

* * * * *

"Thank you, Max. That will be all."

"I'm not your damned butler."

Peta bit her lip. "I'm sorry. No offense meant. I just...I...what are you doing?"

She stared as he carried her through her bedroom and into the small bathroom. He deposited her on the closed lid of the toilet.

"Sit. Stay."

"I'm not your damned dog," she muttered.

He grinned. She found herself wishing he wouldn't do that. Flash that wonderfully warm and affectionate grin at her. It was almost as if he *liked* her or something.

Wistfully, she thought she'd rather have a hot and heavy lustful leer. But at this point, she'd take what she could get.

Max turned on the faucets and held his hand under the running water until the temperature satisfied him. He flipped up the drain lever and looked around.

"Want anything in it?"

"Pardon me?" She struggled with his question.

"The bath. Do you want anything in it? Bubbles? Some of that frou-frou stuff women like?"

Peta snorted. She'd never been frou-frou in her life. "There's a cube of bath salts on the top shelf over there."

Max rummaged in her bathroom cabinet, and Peta winced as she suddenly remembered that her birth control pills were in there, along with several other *very* personal items. The open mirrored door hid his face, but she could hear his chuckle.

"My, my. Interesting."

She felt the color flood her face. *Bollocks.* He'd found her vibrator. "Did you find the bath cube?" Translation — get the hell out of my private life. Or lack of one.

He closed the door and turned, and she waited for his next, probably embarrassing comment.

To her surprise, none was forthcoming. "Yep. Got it here. English lavender. That okay?"

"Um, yes, that'll be fine. Just crumble it under the tap."

"That would be the faucet, right?"

Peta rolled her eyes.

Max followed her instructions, and within minutes the tub was filling with creamy fragrant water. Peta couldn't wait to sink into it.

"Right. Thanks. I can manage from here," said Peta firmly. Enough was enough.

"You sure?" Max's expression was innocent, but his eyes weren't.

"Quite sure, thank you." *Unless you'd like to get naked and join me.*

Max sighed. "If you need anything, just shout, okay? I'm leaving the door open a little. And don't..." He glared at her. "...*Don't* put any weight on that ankle. Or pain pills will be added to the breakfast menu."

Peta did *not* want any more of those damn pills. They muddled her mind and made her much too susceptible to this dynamic man who was presently dominating the little bathroom.

"I hear you, Max. I'll be careful. Just...just go away now, please?"

Max nodded and left her, and she sighed, missing his presence. But the bathwater beckoned, she felt grubby as a worm, and within moments had sunk carefully into the steaming tub, with a huge feeling of sybaritic pleasure.

Breakfast with Max, a bath drawn by Max, carried around by Max. Peta closed her eyes and sank even deeper.

Sometimes a girl's fantasies did come true.

One good scrub, an awkward shampoo, and several dunkings later, Peta felt almost human again.

The water was cloudy with soap and bath salts, and as she gently moved her knees, she caught sight of her legs.

Holy fuzzies. She hadn't shaved in she couldn't remember how long. Quickly she grabbed her razor from the side of the tub and cleared the undergrowth from her armpits, thinking that her Mum may have been wrong after all.

Wearing clean underwear in case of an accident wasn't half as important as shaving beforehand. Of course, that pre-supposed that one knew an accident was about to happen, but so did the clean underwear thing.

She reached for her legs.

It was awkward, keeping her injured ankle away from the sides of the bath, and she put the razor down on the edge as she adjusted her position.

It fell with a clatter onto the tiled floor, along with her can of shaving cream.

Peta swore colorfully. Several ancient Anglo-Saxon words were involved.

"May I be of assistance?"

Peta squawked and grabbed the facecloth, holding it to her breasts.

Max was leaning casually against the doorjamb, watching in amusement.

* * * * *

Something had drawn him back to that partially open bathroom door time and time again. He'd noted when she'd finished washing and started shampooing. He'd listened as she'd slid beneath the water and come up sputtering, ready to leap in and help if she needed him. But she hadn't. Not then, anyway.

Now she did.

And what a sight she was. A small towel was wrapped around her hair, an even smaller facecloth was clutched to her breasts and she was glaring at him with a look that would have made even Mr. Peebles quail.

"No. I'm fine. Go away."

"Oh I don't think so," purred Max. "You've dropped your razor. And your shaving cream. Want them back?"

Peta seemed caught. "I...er...well..."

"A clever man such as myself would deduce from this that you are intent on shaving something." He let the deliberate innuendo hang between them. He ignored the little tingle that ran up his spine.

"Very bright of you, Sherlock Holmes. But I can manage. Go away so I can do them myself."

"Aha. *Them*. Your legs." Max nodded sagely. "Hairy, are they?"

"Maaaax..." she wailed. "For heaven's sake..."

He grinned at her distress. "Please. Allow me."

Without giving her time to do more than sputter, Max knelt beside the tub and rolled up his sleeves, reaching in and grabbing the squirming leg that had no place to hide. "Watch that ankle," he ordered.

Peta whimpered. "What the hell do you think you're doing?"

"You are about to see the amazing dexterity of Max Wolfe in action."

As he pulled her leg from the opaque bathwater, he wondered if she was going to see his cock in action too.

Never had a woman's leg, all shiny and dripping, caused such an instant and hot reaction. He clamped down on the arousal that flooded him, and carefully squirted a large dollop of shaving cream on her leg.

He smoothed it over her skin.

Peta's breath caught in her throat, and he raised his head at the sound.

Their eyes met.

His hands continued their work, stroking, caressing, spreading the foam over her skin. There was nothing businesslike about his touch, or her reaction.

A little moan crept from her mouth, and her gray eyes darkened. Jesus, she was lovely.

Hidden from the chest down by the milky bathwater, her shoulders gleamed at him, and he began to sweat as he realized that all her secrets were just a tug of the facecloth away. The one she was clasping to her breasts like it was a shield.

He swallowed and picked up the razor. "Don't move," he whispered.

Peta didn't answer, just licked her lips. Was she afraid? Did she think he was going to nick her skin? Did she trust him? Was she as aroused as he was? Christ, he'd been in a lot of beds and done a lot of wild things, but shaving this woman's legs was stoking some fire inside him to a higher temperature than he could ever remember.

The razor slicked through the foam, leaving a trail of smooth skin behind it. Max whisked it clean and continued his work, making sure he carefully shaved every single square inch.

Then he released her heel and watched as her leg disappeared beneath the water again.

"Now the other one."

"Um, that's my bad ankle."

"I know. Here..." He folded a towel and rested it on the side of the bath. "Put your heel here, and let me take it from there." Let me take *you*.

His jeans were strangling him now, but he bravely continued, trying not to make matters worse by letting his eyes roam to where the water was now lapping around that wet facecloth.

She obediently raised her leg. A lot more thigh showed this time, as she was sliding her leg out to the towel.

Beautiful white thighs. Rounded and womanly, and just perfect for fitting around him as he filled her.

His hand shook, and he let himself enjoy the pleasure of sliding some shaving cream onto that delicious patch of skin above her knee.

"Um, Max? Just the lower leg, please."

Fuck.

He quickly turned to his task, before he came in his jeans. All this shiny scented skin was overwhelming.

Her ankle was purple and blue and some other ugly colors, but the swelling had gone down. "Your ankle looks better today," he mumbled, trying to keep his mind on his job.

"It feels good," she moaned. Yes, she definitely moaned.

He finished shaving, and rinsed the razor, putting it carefully out of reach. But he left his hands on her leg. "Now. Is there anything *else* you need shaved?"

He couldn't resist the urge to touch her, to feel her, and he let his hands slide over her softness up past her knee to her thigh.

Her eyes were wide, staring at him, and he wasn't sure of her expression. For once, his skill at reading a woman seemed to have deserted him.

Was it heat he saw there? An unfulfilled sexual longing? The dark pupils were dilating now, all right, but seeing as his hands had slipped all the way to the water and a little beneath, he doubted it was from a concussion.

Could it be desire? Or nerves? Or embarrassment?

Shit. He didn't know. He knew what he wanted it to be, and with other women, at other times, he'd have pursued those wants, and made sure of his conquest.

But Peta was different. He held back, just softly running his fingers over the inside of her thigh. He was amazed that the water in the bath didn't just evaporate from the heat he felt his body generating.

"I'm quite handy with a...razor," he said quietly.

Her eyes never left his face.

"You have only to ask." *Please ask. Please say something, anything. Gimme a clue here. Before my cock self-destructs and I can never raise my head again.* The words "premature ejaculation" raced through his brain as the zipper on his jeans crushed painfully into his balls.

Peta licked her lips and he saw the water move as she dragged in a breath. "Umm...er...I think...I'm fine, Max."

Oh I think you are too, darlin'. Very fine.

"Well, okay then." He slowly released her leg, slithering his wet hands over her skin and watching in fascination as goosebumps appeared in response to his touch.

He couldn't resist the slow smile that crossed his face. "You look good wet." He raised his eyes to hers once more. "Very good."

She swallowed.

He lowered his voice even more, letting a little of his heat come through. "Very good indeed."

He moved away from her then, making sure the towels were where she could reach them.

He thought he heard her sigh as he left the bathroom.

Chapter 8

For the rest of that day, an uneasy awareness percolated through Peta's quiet house.

She realized that both she and Max had crossed some invisible boundary at that moment in her bathtub when, with his hands around her thighs, their eyes had clashed.

It was as if there was some sexual pot simmering somewhere, and every move Max made, every sound, damn near every breath echoed like church bells in her newly-sensitive ears.

She'd never been as aware of him as she was now.

Peta hunched over her keyboard and tried to drag her thoughts back to the book she was editing, the contract she was trying to negotiate, and the hundred and one other things she should be doing.

Instead of lusting after Max Wolfe.

The man himself was waiting for Phoebe, standing by the window and finally hissing with relief as a car pulled up outside.

Was he that anxious to get away?

Peta stifled a sigh. He hadn't seemed that way when she was wet and naked. Oh dear.

Phoebe's voice sounded in the hallway as Max opened the door and let her in. A gust of icy air came with her.

"Yes, yes, it's cold. Yada yada. Haven't got time to talk about the weather." Phoebe bustled into the living room and grinned at Peta. "Well, you look a damn sight better than last time I saw you. Max taking good care of you?"

Peta simply couldn't meet his eyes. "Yes, thank you, Phoebe. We're managing very well indeed."

"Good. Wish I could say the same."

Peta frowned. "What? What's the matter?"

Phoebe paced. "It's that dratted Sandra Dean. That's what's the matter. I called her last night and *told* her to get her ass in early because she was going to have to open the office."

"And?" Max was resting on Peta's table. Much too close to Peta for her own peace of mind.

"And that annoying girl never showed up." Phoebe frowned. "I got there and found the place dark as pitch. Had to do it all myself."

Peta wrinkled her brow. "Well, Phoebe, it was a miserable snowstorm...maybe her car's stuck somewhere. Cut her a little slack, would you? She's only been with us a month or so."

"Hmph." Phoebe snorted eloquently. "If she thinks she's going to make it to two months, she'd better shape up. Luckily, nothing too important came in, just these emails..." And she passed a folder over to Peta.

"Here you are, Max. Go. Run your errands and stuff. But remember..." Phoebe hollered through the open doorway as Max shrugged into his new jacket. "I expect that edit finished by the end of this week. No later. No excuses."

"Yes, Ma'am," he grinned, poking his head in and waving. "I'll be back, as the Terminator says."

Phoebe snickered. "Oh go away, Arnold."

Peta pasted a weak smile on her face and nodded at the door, where Max wasn't any more. He'd sure taken off in a hurry.

"So." Phoebe settled her backside into a chair and helped herself to a cup of coffee from the carafe Peta and Max had been sharing. "You go to bed with him yet?"

"*Phoebe!*" Peta's mouth dropped.

"Oh come on, dear. You've been hotter than the sidewalk in July for that man ever since he strode into our offices. And he's been sizing you up pretty good for just about as long."

Peta was, for once, lost for words.

"So it's a natural assumption. Put two people in the same house, let 'em get to sniffing around each other, and see what happens."

Peta's eyebrows rose. "You set this up."

"Did not. How could I possibly know you were going to do something as idiotic as drive that little peanut of yours off a bridge? And on the same night Max's apartment collapsed? I'm good, honey. But I'm not *that* good."

Peta's mind whirled. "But...but..."

"Oh yeah, there's that British confusion. No wonder you lost the war."

"What war?"

"The one we won." Phoebe grinned.

Peta threw up her hands. "I give up."

"So did they."

"Phoebe...be serious." Peta leaned across the table. "Did you deliberately move Max in here so that he could...that we could...well, you know..."

Phoebe narrowed her eyes. "Let's just say I hate to see an opportunity to make two people happy slip by."

Peta chewed that over in her mind for a moment or so. "And you think it would make us happy?"

Phoebe snorted. "To judge by the URST in this room this morning, oh yeah."

"URST?"

"Didn't I teach you anything? You know, what we look for in a manuscript? Un-Resolved Sexual Tension?"

"Oh right." Peta's mind tried to follow Phoebe's conversation. "*That.*" There certainly was plenty of "URST" around the house today.

"So if Sandra doesn't show up, I'll be there all day, I guess," continued Phoebe, dismissing Peta's sex life from the conversation and returning to her professional business. "I'm going to dinner with Struthers tonight, but nothing else is on the schedule."

"Struthers? Again?" Peta smiled, knowing how much Phoebe enjoyed her dinners with the town librarian. The fact that he was an elegant and still-attractive man in his late fifties didn't hurt either.

Peta liked him. He was erudite, very intelligent, and made her laugh.

"Well, have a good time," she said.

Phoebe snorted. "I intend to. Now. Let's see what we have here." She delved into the file folder and turned the conversation back to the efficient operation of Mayfield Masterpieces, even though its business was being conducted largely from Peta Matthew's dining room table under the watchful gaze of Mr. Peebles.

* * * * *

While Phoebe and Peta explored the mysteries of the publishing world together, Max donned his sunglasses and took off for town. The bright sun was dazzling against the heavy snow, piled along the sides of the road by the plows that had finally caught up with the weather.

He blessed Phoebe's all-wheel-drive, and wondered if he might swap his own two-wheel drive SUV for something with this kind of traction.

He hadn't considered it up to now, since it was unlikely he'd be around Mayfield for more than a few months, but something was changing. Something was starting to whisper quietly to him that this might not be a bad place to stay for a while. Time unspecified.

It was unsettling, and Max fidgeted, jumping at the blast of a horn from behind him as he lingered a second too long at an intersection. Damned impatient drivers.

He drove past the small police station and noticed an unusual amount of activity outside the normally tranquil building.

There were even a couple of state police vehicles parked there, along with a large black van. He frowned, then passed by, looking for a spot near the insurance company. It was time to check in with them and figure out what the hell he was going to do about his stuff. The stuff that had probably been completely ruined by the plaster which had crushed it and the snow that must have fallen on it through the gaping hole in the roof.

Once again he blessed his lucky stars that he'd had such a narrow escape. And also that he'd had the foresight to take out a small personal items policy. It was part of his nature to be financially cautious, and this time it was certainly going to pay off.

When he emerged from the office some forty-five minutes later, he'd discovered that it wasn't going to pay off very well.

Max sighed and headed for the bank.

Fortunately, his Internet "interests" provided a nice income, although Jasmine must have gotten the surprise of her life when she saw herself featured prominently on a porn site.

He couldn't resist a little chuckle. Served the bitch right. She owed him big time for fucking him, and then firing him without a word. And he was quite happy collecting. Whatever scruples he had didn't extend to hardhearted witches who seemed to think that the world existed solely for their own pleasure, and fuck everyone else who got in their way.

And speaking of which...

"Hello, darling. Not playing nursemaid today?"

Christ, he must have been distracted. Diana Stiles had crept up on him without his even knowing it.

"Good morning, Diana. Lovely day, isn't it?"

Diana laughed. "Dear God. Max Wolfe talking about the weather. What has this world come to?" She glanced down at his pants. "With the operative word there being 'come'."

Max felt his temper rise. Suddenly, Diana's blatant intentions seemed...sordid. "I'm sure you're busy. If you'll excuse me, I have errands to run."

Diana hung on. "For *her*, I suppose, hmm? Fetching pillows? Bandages? *Tea*?" There was an edge to her voice that Max couldn't miss.

"Yes. Thanks for reminding me."

He detached himself from Diana's arm and stepped over a convenient pile of snow. Diana's skirt was way too tight to allow her to do the same, and she pouted. "You have my number, darling. Call me anytime you want some real fun. I won't even ask you to make tea..." Her lips curled in what was supposed to be a smile, but looked more like a snarl.

Max managed a stiff grin and put even more room between them. She was practically turning his stomach. He wondered what had ever possessed him to think she was attractive? Christ, he'd fucked her. What had he been thinking of? Or, more to the point, what had he been thinking *with*?

Max shook his head. God, how things had changed. How *he* had changed. A year ago he'd have gone along with Diana's naughty little ménage. But come that Christmas party, he hadn't been able to. When the other guy had shown up, Max had left. Whoever he was, he was welcome to her. He knew, even then, that it wouldn't be worth it. And if Peta had ever found out...well, perhaps that was what had held him back.

A cheery voice hailed him, dragging him from his thoughts.

"Hallooo Max..."

Okay. There were some drawbacks to small town life. And one of them was crossing the street towards him, hand extended.

Edward Sharp.

With the wide, gleaming smile of men who are used to public interaction, Edward strode carelessly through the snow, and shook Max's hand. Clasping both of his around it, Edward managed to convey the impression that his day was complete thanks to the happy chance that had brought them together.

He looked and acted like just what he was. A politician.

Max restrained the urge to vomit.

"Good to see you, Max, good to see you. So how are you today? How are you?"

He also had a bad habit of repeating himself, in case one missed the pearls of wisdom first time around. Or ignored them. Which, reflected Max as he withdrew his hand from Edward's grasp, probably happened a lot.

"Fine, thanks, Edward. And you?"

"Well, run off my feet of course with this damned snowstorm. Had to roust the entire Town Works Department out of bed to clear it. Damned snowstorm."

Edward looked personally affronted, as if Mother Nature had deliberately set out to piss him off with her "damned snowstorm".

"I can imagine," answered Max.

"Heard about Peta's accident. How's she doing, do you know? Nasty thing, that, eh? She still in hospital? And you too, building collapsed on you, huh? I told Mrs. Lee to get that darned place inspected. But noooo...damn fool woman. We've got the finest building inspector here in Mayfield..." He waved his hand around with pride. "But does she take advantage? Nooo. Damn fool woman."

Max swallowed. No wonder Edward managed to continually get himself re-elected as Senior Town Councilman. No one else could get a word in edgewise.

Edward fell into step beside Max, seeming quite content to go wherever he was going. "You know, Max old buddy, been meaning to ask you..."

Max cocked an eyebrow, having learned not to interrupt Edward when he was in full swing.

"The election's coming up soon. I know I can count on your support—" He grinned in an "I-know-you'd-never-consider-voting-for-anyone-else" kind of way. "But the thing is, you see, the campaign is costing a goddamned fortune."

He frowned, allowing a wrinkle to appear between his nicely-tended eyebrows. "A goddamned fortune."

"It is?" Max gazed at the man next to him. He figured Edward for about forty or so, well-built, dark hair without a touch of gray in it, and extremely well-dressed. Rumor had it that he got a manicure and a facial weekly, but went out of town to do it. Vanity—thy name is "candidate".

"Oh absolutely, absolutely." Edward paused by a snow bank, and Max realized he'd stopped too. Damn. He really hated this kind of thing.

"Now I know it might be a bit forward for me to suggest this, but I'd welcome campaign contributions from *anyone* at this point." He raised a pair of dark brown eyes to Max's face and gave him a very nice imitation of a rather sad cocker spaniel. "*Anyone.*"

"I see," said Max.

He began walking again, and Edward hurried alongside. "So if you wanted to get involved in something meaningful, something that will deepen your attachment to this lovely town of ours, won't you give it a thought? Something meaningful, you know."

"Yes, I see." Max was noncommittal and repeated himself. Shit. It must be catching.

"I can tell you're a man of the world," Edward's friendly grin and nudge offered the conclusion that this was something that Edward felt himself to be also. "With all those ladies buzzing around you like bees. Bees, they are. And nice ones too. Of course, being a married man I wouldn't know about that..." The grin changed to more of a leer.

Max curled his lip. "Quite." God, now he was picking up Peta's phrases. That had been too *Brit* for words. "And how is Mrs. Sharp?"

"Oh good. Good. She's in Florida. Be back in time for the election of course. My wife is my staunchest supporter." Edward assumed the expression of a man who is staunchly supported by his wife.

"Well, anyway, think about it, would you Max? It's a great chance to get involved in the affairs of Mayfield. Such a fine place, don't you think? Such a fine place."

"I'll give it some thought, Edward." *About two microseconds worth.*

They had arrived at Phoebe's SUV and Max pulled out his keys.

"Well, I'll let you go on then. I expect you have lots to do. Where you staying? You got a roof over your head, have you?"

Max sighed. "Indeed I have. For the time being I'm staying with Ms. Matthews. It's worked out well since she needs some help and I need a room."

"Really?" Edward's eyebrows flew up towards his elegantly coiffed hair. "Well, how about that? How about that?"

"How about *what*?" Max's control was growing weaker by the minute. He wondered if burying a politician headfirst in a snowbank was a Federal offense.

"Well, you and Peta. Peta and you. In the same house too. Fancy that. In the same house. Lovely girl, handsome man...you're a sly one, Max."

That just about did it. Max opened the car door and turned to Edward.

"Edward, Ms. Matthews has suffered a nasty injury to her ankle. It's my pleasure to be able to help out in any way I can. The present situation has worked out well for us both. That's all there is to it."

Edward prudently stepped back a little, obviously sensing the fury that Max knew was boiling right behind his eyes.

"Umm, of course. Of course. Wouldn't dream of suggesting anything else, Max. Good Lord. Good Lord. I mean Peta...well, it goes without saying, doesn't it? She's charming, but let's face it, not your sort of woman at all, is she?"

"Goodbye, Edward." Max slammed the car door shut on Edward with a sense of relief, and drove off, not caring very much whether the tires *accidentally* sprayed a little slush up onto the perfect crease of Edward's pants.

He was fucking furious. He hated being hit up for money, disliked politicians on principle, and was blindingly mad at Edward's assumption that Peta wasn't his kind of woman.

No wonder the world was screwed up. Politicians were so fucking stupid. And so fucking *wrong*.

Chapter 9

Edward's eyes narrowed and the public smile he'd perfected in front of his mirror disappeared from his face as he watched Max Wolfe's taillights disappear down Main Street.

He bent to brush the spattered slush off his pants. *Fucking asshole.*

He turned and re-traced his steps down the sidewalk to "Diana's Den", the small knick-knack store owned and operated by Diana Stiles. It was pretty quiet over the winter months, but in the summer did a land-office business selling junk to tourists who wanted to be reminded of their vacation by useless pieces of clutter.

The bell dinged softly as he walked in, and seeing Diana with a customer, he dug up his best "aren't-I-charming" grin.

"Well, well, good morning Mrs. Hendricks. Finding some new treasures, are we? Finding some new treasures?"

The woman at the counter blushed and smiled back. "Hello, Mr. Sharp. Fine job your boys did on the roads. I'd have hated to miss out on this little piece here. Thanks to you I could come over and pick it up."

Edward stared at the amazingly ugly gnome that was glaring at him from the counter as Diana rang up the sale.

"Well, good for you. Good for you. Glad you're happy with the way the town's run. I'm sure I can count on you next month?" He held out his hand and Mrs. Hendricks blushed and giggled as she put hers into it.

"Oh, Mr. Sharp. Of course. You bet. Chuck and I would never consider anyone else." She accepted her package from Diana with a word of thanks and tittered her way out the door, making the bell chime once more.

"Stupid cow," grumbled Edward.

"Didn't get any contributions this morning, Edward?" Diana's cool voice cut through the silence in the store.

"Not a fucking penny."

"Aw, darling. You sound upset." She crossed the store, turned the sign in the window from "Open" to "Closed" and latched the door. "It's almost lunchtime. Would you care to join me...for a bite?"

Edward's eyes met hers.

Diana Stiles was one hot piece of ass. Her blue eyes gleamed, and she licked her full lips as she tugged a couple of pins free and let her blonde hair fall over her shoulders.

"In the back?"

"Well, certainly not in front of the window," she laughed. "Although if the rest of the town knew what a great fuck you are, it might help your campaign chest..."

Edward growled as she took his hand and led him through the small opening into her back room.

She pushed him down on the old sofa and tugged him free of his shearling jacket. He smiled as her hands fell to his belt and he watched her eagerly pushing his pants down around his ankles. He was already hard, waiting, willing to go along with whatever happened next.

It would be good, he knew that. Diana's cunt was always hot, wet and ready.

She stepped back and licked her lips. "Oooh, Edward. So nice and hard. You really have a great cock, you know that?"

Edward's chest swelled. "Yeah, yeah. I do, I do," he agreed.

Diana's hands pulled her skirt up, and revealed her pantyhose. She kicked off her clogs and let the front of her skirt fall back down, hiding her body as she shimmied the hose down her legs in a little seductive striptease.

Edward pouted. "I wanna see your pussy, baby, your pussy..." he moaned.

"Oh, you will, Edward. If you're a good boy."

Edward licked his lips. "C'mere. I'll show you how good a boy I can be..." He reached for her.

Diana let him pull her towards him, and he forced her closer, making her lean her hands on the back of the couch. He scrabbled for the zipper at the back of her skirt and let it drop, revealing her from the waist down.

Impatiently she kicked it away. "Do it, Edward, do it. You know how I love it..." She shoved her pussy at him, kneeling astride him.

Edward bent his head and "did it".

He buried his face in her mound, finding her pointy little clit right away and sucking on it for all he was worth.

Her moans drove him on, and he tongued her cunt, spreading her juices around and pulling on her folds with his teeth.

"Oh God, yeah, just like that," she breathed, pushing her pussy into his face.

Edward continued, enjoying the wild feel of her mound writhing against his mouth and her bare thighs next to his.

His cock began to ache. "Fuck me, Diana, fuck me for chrissakes..."

"Not yet," she moaned.

"Yes, now, bitch..."

He wrenched his mouth away, wiped his lips with the back of his hand and roughly grabbed her hips, pulling her downwards towards his cock.

"Oh all right. Spoil sport." With a little moue of disappointment, Diana grabbed the hardness beneath her, positioned it exactly at the right spot and plunged downward, taking Edward's breath away.

"Fuck, yeah," he breathed, forgetting to repeat himself.

She moved, spreading her thighs wide and taking more of him deep inside her as she raised herself and lowered back down.

He moaned.

The back door to the little room opened and a cold draft disturbed the two on the couch.

Edward froze. "*Shit*...Diana?"

Diana turned her head and stared at the newcomer. "Oh it's you," she said casually.

The man was solidly built, carrying two large boxes and had an apparent disdain for the weather since he wore a light t-shirt with his scruffy jeans and the short sleeves showed off several tattoos circling his muscular arms.

His face showed no expression as he watched the couple fucking on the couch.

"Well don't just stand there. Put the boxes down, and close the damn door. It's cold," complained Diana.

The man's face eased into a slight smile as he followed her directions. His buzz cut hair gave him an air of almost military hardness, and he strode purposefully through the room to stand behind Diana.

"Come on then, you know what I want." Diana had never stopped moving on Edward's cock.

"Yeah, hurry up, man, hurry up," grunted Edward.

The man unzipped his pants, and tugged a condom from his back pocket.

He sheathed his cock and stood close behind Diana, letting her back rub him and arouse him to his full length.

"Oh God, I want some of that," she moaned.

"You'll get it."

He slid his hands beneath her sweater and found her breasts, pulling and pinching them and making her cry out as she leaned into his palms urging him on.

Her hands slipped behind her, and Edward felt her smearing her juices around and up between the crack of her buttocks. "Come on, come on...I need it. Christ, I need it."

"You ready?"

She grunted.

"She's ready," hissed Edward, gritting his teeth.

The man knelt awkwardly and grasped Diana's ass cheeks, pulling them wide and exposing her tight pink anus.

He rubbed it. Hard.

Diana sobbed with pleasure and stilled for a moment. "Oh yeah, oh yeah," she cried. "More. Please..."

Edward took his turn with her breasts. They were full, luscious, and probably silicone, but he didn't care. He bit down hard on a rigid nipple.

"Jesus *Christ*..." Diana yelled. "I'm gonna come..."

The man's cock found its target and he thrust fully into her ass, moving in and out and setting up a rhythm that exactly matched Edward's.

Edward could feel the fucking thing moving against his cock inside Diana's cunt. A thin membrane was separating them, and with Diana's heat and the other man's cock rubbing his, it was an exquisite torture he couldn't withstand.

"I'm gonna spew," he grunted.

"Go ahead." The voice was rough, and came from behind Diana.

He did. With a huge groan, Edward came, firing spurt after spurt of come deep inside her. He felt her reaction.

Her body quivered around his cock, and she sank her fingers into his shoulders. "Christ, yeah..." she moaned.

Her orgasm shook her, fierce and savage, and with a harsh sound the man behind her came too.

Edward could sense the shudder in the man as he released himself up Diana's ass.

"Oh Jesus." She moaned, coming again at the second assault. "Oh *Jesus*..."

"God, that was...that was..." sputtered Edward. His mind reeled, and he barely registered the man pulling away from Diana and tossing the used condom into the trash.

"Yeah, not bad," he said.

Both Diana and Edward turned weakly and stared at him. "*Not bad?*"

Mike Dean shrugged and pulled up his jeans.

* * * * *

It was well past lunchtime when Max finally returned to the house on Acorn Street, and he was prepared for a lecture from Phoebe on his lateness. Shrewdly, he'd stopped in at the market and picked up an assortment of munchies with which to placate her.

It had worked. She was smiling at him over a mouthful of potato salad. Peta was tucking in to a shrimp salad sandwich and peace reigned.

Max congratulated himself.

"Mmm. Good." Phoebe wiped her mouth. "Bless you, Max. I was getting hungry and I know Peta has to keep up her strength."

Peta, whose mouth was overflowing, simply nodded.

"So what's up in town? Anything new?" Phoebe reached for the container of potato salad, stared at it for a moment, and then put it back down with a sigh. "Better not. Struthers is taking me out for a quick bite and I can't fill up the way I used to."

Max grinned. "Again? Seeing rather a lot of him, aren't you?"

"Not as much as I'd like," grinned Phoebe back.

"*Phoebe!*" Peta choked a little and grabbed for her soda. "You naughty thing."

"So what if he's a bit younger? Still a fine figure of a man, if you ask me. And bright, too." Phoebe pulled some grapes towards her and leaned back with a contented sigh. "It's good to find a man whose brains probably match his...um..."

Peta blushed.

"I'll take your word for it, Phoebe," chuckled Max. "But to answer your previous question, Mayfield is recovering nicely from the storm. The roads are almost down to bare pavement, and Edward Sharp is already out trolling for donations." He knew his mouth was turning down and couldn't help it.

Fortunately, his feelings were echoed by his fellow diners.

"Oh damn. He's after money, I suppose. He hit you up?" Phoebe's eyebrows rose questioningly.

"Yup."

"Give him any?"

Max was insulted. "Good God, no. I'm not that stupid."

"Good. A lot of folks are, though. He's been Senior Town Councilor for several years now. Does a reasonably good job of it too."

"So why does he need money? Seems like he's pretty much guaranteed of a win next month," said Peta.

Phoebe leaned forward confidentially. "Well, rumor has it..." She glanced around and lowered her voice. "Rumor has it that his wife is about to divorce him. Sheila left for Florida before Christmas and told a few folks she wasn't coming back. He's been living off her money, you know. He may look and act and dress wealthy, but it's all hers. Nothing of his. He'll lose a bloody fortune if she goes through with her threat."

Max considered this interesting piece of news. "I suppose the position doesn't pay much?"

"Nope. This is a small town. We've got our priorities straight. Most of the town budget goes to the services we need, not the politicians we don't."

Max thought back to the police station. "That reminds me," he said. He grabbed a chip from beneath Peta's straying hand. He smiled.

She frowned.

"There was a hell of a lot of *something* going on at the police station. Lot of vehicles, a couple of County Mounties, big black van. Didn't hear anything else, though..."

Peta raised an eyebrow. "Something to do with the storm, do you think?"

Max crunched thoughtfully. "Could be. I don't know. And when Edward grabbed me, I wasn't about to hang around long enough to find out."

"Can't say I blame you," said Phoebe approvingly. "You know that the word around town says Edward's having a...thing...with Diana Stiles?"

Max gulped down his chip. "Really?"

Phoebe nodded. "Yes, really. I got it from Doris down at the hairdresser's. She says it's why Sheila is threatening to divorce him."

Max sipped his soda. Edward was not unattractive, he supposed, and as such, a likely target for Diana's sexual appetites. He grimaced.

"Well, they're welcome to each other," said Peta. Her tone was quite sharp.

"Indeed." Phoebe grinned. "Now. What are you two going to get up to this afternoon?"

Max coughed. "Phoebe, you've left enough work here to keep us both busy until bedtime, I should think." He attempted a casual smile.

"Right, right. Max is right. There's a lot of work to do," added Peta. She tried to push away from the table, but Max was there before her.

"Stay. I've got it."

Phoebe chuckled. "My, you've got him well-trained."

Peta snorted. "Certainly. If you don't mind being addressed like a dog. Sit, stay, beg, roll over..." She trailed off, realizing what she was saying.

Fortunately, she was spared Phoebe's response as Max came back into the room.

"Well, dears, I must be off. Got to see if Sandra's shown up yet. Damn the girl. I'll be in the office if you need me. And then home. Max, you need the car any more today?"

Max shook his head. "Nope, all set, Phoebe. You're an angel. I talked with the guy over at the garage and he's gonna run my car over here tomorrow morning. So I won't have to bother you for yours. You've got your wheels back."

Phoebe grinned. "Excellent, young man. Like to see a little initiative there, don't you, Peta?"

"Yes. Quite."

Max suppressed a snicker.

"Oh but that reminds me," added Peta, frowning. "What about my car?"

Max glanced at Phoebe and back to Peta. "Well, honey, I'm afraid the news is not so good there."

Peta bit her lip. "Total loss?"

Max nodded, and Phoebe crossed the room to give Peta a hug. "Don't you worry about it, sweetie. We'll figure something out. I have to run. Behave yourselves...no, don't see me out, Max. I know the way."

Phoebe grabbed her keys, her bag and her coat and whirled herself out of the house. Both Max and Peta winced as they heard her tires spinning in the driveway.

Silence fell as Peta reached for her laptop and pulled it back in front of her on the table.

"Interesting," mused Max.

"What is?" answered Peta, busily loading a new disk into her drive and clicking her mouse.

"The geopolitical situation in the Lesser Antilles?"

"Oh yes, right..." mumbled Peta. "What?" She looked up.

Max sighed. "Never mind. I'll leave you to your work. If you need me, just yell. I'll be upstairs. My laptop is up there, along with Branulf the Muscularly Challenged and his erstwhile babe, Morriae the Thick Headed."

"Ah. You're still editing *Sword of My Passion*, are you?"

Max nodded. "Sadly, yes. I can't wait to find out if he does more than smolder at her dove-white breasts..."

"He hadn't better or we'll have to switch genres, and the release is already being promoted as a historical, not a bodice ripper." She turned back to her monitor.

"It could sure use some bodice-ripping," grumbled Max as he climbed the stairs. "Come to think of it, so could I."

Chapter 10

Unaware that Max was entertaining visions of ripping her bodice, Peta worked steadily for the rest of the day. It helped take her mind off the man upstairs and the fact that just being in the same room with him raised her "URST" levels into the danger zone.

Certainly he was delectable. And of course she'd love to just tumble him right into her bed and have her way with him. Or let him have his way with her. Or discuss ways they could have each other.

She wrenched her mind off Max and back to her work, only to find herself doing the exact same thing just about every ten minutes or so. Drat the man. Even when he wasn't in the same room, he was disturbing her.

Finally, the light faded, and Max reappeared, still looking delectable. Even more so since he'd obviously been running his hands through his hair, which had rumpled it to a soft mess.

Peta sighed and told her twitching fingers to be still.

"If I have to read about one more heaving bosom, I'll 'heave' myself."

She grinned. "Editing getting to you, is it?"

"I don't mind *editing*." Max pulled out a chair, twirling it around and doing that essentially guy-type thing of sitting on it backwards. "It's just the twaddle I have to edit that bugs me."

He crossed his arms on the back of the chair and leaned his chin on them, studying Peta. "Do women really like that stuff?"

She chuckled. "You bet. Heaving bosoms, pulsing hearts, knights on white horses. They go for it in droves."

Max shook his head. "Makes no sense to me. It all stops short. He's about to kiss her, and then, *wham..* He gets attacked by marauding Vikings."

"In a medieval historical?"

"Well, by somebody who could just as well be a marauding Viking. I doubt if anyone reading that drivel would care about historical accuracy anyway. *Hysterical* accuracy is more like it."

Peta smiled patiently at him. "Max, don't dismiss it out of hand. It pays the bills, which, I might point out, includes your salary."

Max pursed his lips in distaste. "Right. I forgot. Fourteen trembling bosoms a week covers my grocery bill. I'll make a note." He stood up and stretched. "Speaking of grocery bills, I'm hungry."

Peta closed her laptop. "Yes, now you come to mention it, so am I. How about beans on toast?"

Max stared at her. "What?"

"Typical British meal when you can't think of anything else. I have beans, there's bread, we can poach an egg and stick it on top if you'd like?"

"And you eat this...stuff?"

There was a distinct pause between the words "this" and "stuff". Peta could clearly hear the original word he'd been planning on using, and it wasn't "stuff".

"Well, of course." She raised a defensive eyebrow.

"Um. How about we call out for a pizza?"

About to argue the point, Peta realized that she probably should humor him. He was, after all, taking care of her. And actually, pizza sounded a lot better than beans on toast right now. "All right. You've convinced me."

Max headed for the phone, muttering something that sounded suspiciously like "thank God".

They chatted companionably over their pizza, discussing non-personal things like their work, books, movies, and generally avoiding any topic that might have brought up the undercurrents that seethed between them.

Peta found herself fascinated by Max's hands. They were strong and masculine, but with fingers that were long and shapely. She swallowed a large chunk of pepperoni as she caught herself wondering what he could do with them, besides spread shaving cream on her legs.

She coughed, and decided enough was enough.

"Max, this was great. Really. Thanks for thinking of it. But it's been a long day. I think I probably should turn in."

"Okay."

Well, damn. That was too easy.

Max helped her out of her chair and picked her up, stopping for her cane on the way. "I'll bring you your pain pills when you're settled," he said. He carried her up the stairs to her room and lowered her onto her bed. "Just give me a shout. Can you manage from here?"

Peta wondered what would happen if she said no. But she knew she couldn't risk it. Couldn't face the possibility that all his teasing and innuendoes were just that. Teasing and innuendoes.

No, it was better to hold on to her fantasies of wild monkey sex with this man, than have him turn her down. Or worse, agree, and then watch him flit off to the next little chickie that caught his eye.

"Thanks, yes. The cane makes it all much easier. If you want to leave the pills here..." She nodded at the table.

"You won't take 'em." Max's answer came right back, smoothly and quite accurately. She wouldn't have taken them.

She bit her lip. "Go away now."

He grinned. "Gotcha, babe. Can't hide from old Max." He turned to leave the room. "Don't waste too much time, okay? I'm just going down for water and the pills, and I'll expect to see you in that bed when I get back. None of that face-creaming or hour-long night time ritual stuff women seem to love. You need rest."

Peta narrowed her eyes, and although it was on the tip of her tongue to ask where panty-creaming stood in his overall categorization of things, she held back. "Thank you, Max. You're *so* acute."

Accepting the sarcasm with a snicker, Max left.

Ten minutes and two pain pills later, Peta was alone.

He'd given her the pills, watched steadily as she swallowed them with a grimace, and tucked her in efficiently, simply wishing her goodnight.

Well, *bollocks*. She'd found no excuse to ask him to stay and cuddle her. Or do other nice things to her. And he'd seemed to be anxious to leave.

As she slid into sleep, Peta sighed. Her bed was lonely, in spite of Mr. Peebles's presence.

She wanted Max.

* * * * *

In fact, he'd waited outside the door until he heard her breathing become deep and regular, and then taken himself and his painful stiffy off to his room. He wondered if anyone had died from "URST" and if so, what the coroner's report listed as cause of death.

He might well be the first, since he was harder than iron, and had run out on Peta like a damn rabbit rather than the wolf whose name he bore. He sighed. There was nothing for it. He'd have to take care of matters himself.

Again.

He kept his shower quiet, a challenge in the little bathroom which seemed designed to be exactly two inches narrower than his elbows, but the warm water eased his muscles and his soapy hand reached for his cock. He shivered a little as his hand encircled his hard-on.

He wanted Peta with a craving he couldn't recall feeling before. No two ways about it. And he just might be able to have her, too, since she'd developed a certain "heated" look in her eyes whenever he got near to her. A bead of pre-come emerged from the reddened and swollen head, and Max closed his eyes, lost in visions of Peta. Her ankle was healing nicely, and he knew of a few positions that wouldn't put any pressure on it at all.

He'd take her in a chair perhaps. His hand moved at the thought and a bolt of electricity slid up his spine. Let her just slide down on him at her own speed as her knees rested either side of his thighs. He moved his fist faster, lost in his vision of their heated joining. A split-second vision of Peta's eyes blurring as she orgasmed on top of him was enough.

Max came with a shudder and a long, drawn-out groan. *Shit..* This was not good. Not good at all. It was no substitute for the real thing.

And he still wanted the real thing.

As he slipped beneath the covers, he grimaced. The bed was cold, that fickle cat had deserted him, and he had no excuse to prowl the halls tonight. He had to sleep in his own lonely bed.

And he hated it.

* * * * *

Max's heart very nearly stopped on the following morning, as he marched down the hallway to check on Peta.

She wasn't there.

With a fierce frown he ran down the stairs, two at a time, only to be brought up short by the sight of her sitting quite comfortably in her own kitchen with a mug of tea at her side.

"What the fuck?"

"Good morning, Max," she answered. At least she had the courtesy to look tired too.

"What the hell are you doing down here? Why didn't you wait for me? Or at least shout? You could have fallen or something—" Max realized he was babbling and shut his mouth with a snap.

"Oh, don't be such a fusspot. I'm fine. Really. The ankle is heaps better this morning, and I managed perfectly well with the cane. Stop complaining."

Max clamped down on his temper and struggled to get his heart beating again. He busied himself with the coffeepot, since tea was the last thing he'd wanted this morning. Peta's teapot sat proudly next to her, and sneered at him.

"I'll grab the paper," he said. "*I'll spank you silly if you scare me like that again,*" was what he meant.

The fragrance of coffee was a soothing balm to his soul, and Max tossed the newspaper in front of Peta and went to pour himself a cup.

A choking sound whirled him around, and he ignored the spilling coffee.

"Max—" gasped Peta.

"What?"

"Look...look at this..."

Max looked at the newspaper. The banner headline said it all. "MURDER IN MAYFIELD". He shrugged. "It happens everywhere, babe. Sad, but true."

"No, Max, you don't understand. It was *Sandra.*" Peta's horrified gray eyes met his, and Max felt a chill run over his flesh.

"Sandra as in Sandra Dean? *Our* Sandra?"

Peta nodded. "Listen to this." She turned back to the paper. "The victim has been identified as Sandra Dean, aged twenty-eight, a recent newcomer to Mayfield and current employee of Mayfield Masterpieces."

She glanced up at Max. "Oooh, nasty way to get our name out there. Phoebe'll be doubly upset, I'm sure."

"Go on," said Max. He sat across from her, a frown on his face.

She turned back to the column. "Ms. Dean's whereabouts on the night of the fifteenth are being traced, and authorities are seeking her ex-husband for questioning. She was brutally strangled..." Peta's voice tailed off and she gazed at Max. "Oh God," she whispered.

He pulled the paper over and continued reading. "Brutally strangled, sexually assaulted, and her body dumped in a corner of Meachem's Field, where it was discovered yesterday by a citizen walking his dog. Lieutenant Frank Summers would give no further details of the crime, simply stating that the investigation was "ongoing". When asked if residents of Mayfield should be concerned for their safety, he responded that all citizens should take normal precautions. He saw no immediate need for alarm within the community."

Max raised his head and whistled. "Poor Sandra."

Peta's eyes were filled with tears. "Oh, God, Max. How could someone do such a thing? I scarcely knew her, but she seemed so nice."

Max quickly scanned the rest of the article, but other than a couple of repetitive quotes from Edward Sharp about the effectiveness of the Mayfield Police Department, and a request for information from anyone who might have seen something, there was little else in the way of details.

"Do you know Mike Dean?" His question snared Peta's attention from her mug, and she raised troubled eyes to his.

"No. Can't say as I do. I heard Sandra mention him once, briefly, and of course her divorced status was listed on her employment forms. Do you think it was him?"

"I haven't a clue. But I'm sure the cops will go after him first. A crime like this – an ex-husband...it's sort of logical."

"I suppose," said Peta sadly. "What an awful waste of a life, Max. She was so young."

"I guess that explains all the activity at the P.D. yesterday, that big black van must have been the Forensics crew," mused Max.

Peta tilted her head. "Crime fan, are we?"

"Not really. Just fascinated by what will drive a human being towards that kind of violence. And of course I watch all those shows on TV."

"Well, I think it's terribly sad. Even though she'd only been here a couple of weeks, I feel rotten about it. I wonder if there's family we should notify?"

Max shook his head. "Let the authorities take care of it, Peta. It's their job."

"I'd still like to do *something*, though. Makes one feel very helpless in situations such as these, doesn't it?"

Max thought that one over. "Look, we're bound to have Phoebe on our doorstep any minute. Perhaps you two could arrange a service for Sandra or something?"

Peta looked impressed. "Max! What a brilliant idea. Of course. I doubt that there's anyone else around to do it." She grabbed for pencil and paper and started making lists of things to do.

She'd actually gotten to number three when the doorbell rang.

"That has to be Phoebe," sighed Max, getting up. "You got enough tea in that pot for her, or shall I make more coffee?"

Gnawing on the end of her pencil, Peta shook her head. "Better do coffee. Phoebe's not convinced about tea yet. I'm working on her."

Glad to see that Peta's spirits were returning, Max headed to the front hall to open the door.

It wasn't Phoebe.

It was the police.

Chapter 11

"Hey, Peta. It's the law, babe. You pay tax on all that tea of yours?"

Peta frowned at Max as he re-entered the kitchen, followed by Lieutenant Summers. "Hello, Frank, nice to see you. Ignore Max here. He has a misplaced sense of humor."

Frank Summers grinned. "No problem, Peta. We've heard it all before."

Max snorted. "Coffee, Lieutenant? Sorry, no doughnuts this morning, but I can whip up some beans on toast if you want."

Both Frank and Peta ignored him.

"How's Linda and the baby?" Peta turned her back on Max along with Mr. Peebles, who was investigating the Lieutenant's boots.

"Just fine, thanks. Little tyke is growing faster than weeds." Frank cleared his throat. "Actually, Peta, I'm here on official business. And I'm glad I caught *you*, Mr. Wolfe. Seeing as you're next on my list."

"What list is that, Frank?" Peta's question was full of curiosity. What on earth could the police want with her?

"We're attempting to find out exactly where Sandra Dean was the night she was killed."

Peta gulped. The horror of such a murder was still too new, almost too unreal for her to accept it. "How can we help?"

Frank referred to a small notebook. "Well, we know she was in the Red Barn earlier that evening. And I noticed from your accident report that you were on your way home from there. So I figured I'd see if you remembered anything in particular about that night. Did you see Sandra there?"

"*You* were there?" Max's question slid into the silence that followed.

Peta continued her theme of ignoring Max. This was one area she *so* didn't want to get into, given her reason for going there in the first place. Which was, of course, Max.

"I was only there for a few moments, Frank. I didn't order a drink or anything. I may have said hello to a couple of folks, but I honestly can't recall seeing Sandra there."

Frank nodded. "Yeah, that pretty much bears out other witness statements." He took a small photo from his pocket. "How about this guy? Did you see him there?"

Both Max and Peta leaned towards the black and white snapshot. A man stared back at them, expressionless, holding a board with numbers on it in front of his chest. It was the typical mug shot, so beloved of television newscasts and post office bulletin boards.

"I know him," muttered Max.

"Yes, I do too," added Peta. "He makes deliveries around town, doesn't he?"

Frank nodded. "Yep. But did you see him at the Red Barn that night? Either of you?"

Peta sighed. "No. No, I can't say that I did, Frank. But the place was crowded, as I recall." And with one rather nubile woman who was clinging to Max in an extraordinarily affectionate way. Truth to tell, Peta couldn't remember much else.

"This is Mike Dean, isn't it?" asked Max.

Frank paused. "Well, yeah."

"So he did time?" Max pursued his train of thought doggedly.

"Um, yeah."

"For violent crimes?"

Peta wanted to kick Max. He was starting to sound like Columbo or somebody. "Does that matter?"

"Well," said Frank carefully. "We aren't allowed to discuss past offenses publicly, of course, but I can assure you that there was no violence concerned. Just a simple business with some bank notes that weren't—ahem—legal."

"Counterfeiting, huh? Well, well." Max stroked Mr. Peebles absently. Mr. Peebles tolerated it with his usual disdain.

"Did you find Mike yet?" Peta had to ask the question that was trembling on her tongue.

"No. We're still looking. Which is why I'm here verifying information and the sheriff is checking into all his known haunts."

"Any evidence that leads you to think Mike might have done it?" Max barked out the question.

Frank frowned. "I'm sorry. I'm not at liberty to discuss ongoing investigations."

"Frank, we're not the press. We're friends of Sandra's. Or would have been if she'd been here longer," said Peta. Max was getting closer to being kicked every time he opened his mouth.

Frank sighed. "Sorry, yeah. But truthfully, we don't have much to go on. We haven't heard back from the State Forensics lab yet. There was nothing in the way of evidence around where the body was dumped thanks to the snow, which got pretty messed up, and nobody seems to have seen anything useful." Frank turned his head.

"And that brings us to you, Mr. Wolfe. You were at the Red Barn that night, I understand. A Miss..." He checked his notebook again. "A Miss Tuesday March has verified that information."

Peta stared steadily at Max. For once, his hazel eyes avoided hers, and he cleared his throat. "That's correct, Lieutenant. For the record, we left at sometime after ten, I guess, and not long after that my ceiling caved in."

Frank chuckled. "It's okay, Mr. Wolfe. We're not looking for an alibi here. Just your recollection of Mr. Dean's presence."

"To be honest, I don't remember seeing him there, but as you said, the bar was very crowded."

And doubtless Miss Tuesday March's boobs were blocking your vision, thought Peta nastily.

Frank sighed. "Well, thanks. It was worth a shot. Sorry to have bothered you."

"Not at all, Frank. Anything we can do to help, you know that." Peta staggered to her feet, and Max was immediately at her side with an arm around her, helping her pull away from the table.

Frank's eyes narrowed slightly. "How's the ankle? You were damn lucky, you know."

"I do know. And Max here is a big help. But it's getting much better, thanks." Peta grimaced. "It seems Sandra wasn't so lucky."

123

Frank shook his head. "A horrible thing. Truly horrible. Makes one wonder what can drive someone to do that to another human being."

Max made appropriately sympathetic noises, and slid his hand to Peta's waist, encouraging her to lean on him.

She was being driven to commit some crime on Max's person, and it would definitely be sexual in nature. She wasn't sure if it was in violation of city ordinances, however. But murder certainly was. And if Max didn't take his hands off her, Lieutenant Summers might have another killing on his hands.

The motive however, would be quite clear. "URST".

* * * * *

After listening to the hundredth sigh from Peta, Max gave up and threw in the towel. They'd worked throughout the day, spared Phoebe's presence by the disarray at the offices of Mayfield Masterpieces, where she was currently holding the fort with all the determination of a knight under siege.

Apparently she'd been fielding calls from the media, making sure that Mayfield Masterpieces was spelled correctly if she was quoted, and fending off questions about Sandra Dean from anyone who passed the building.

It was a dreadful situation, and Phoebe was responding like an old war-horse hearing the bugle sound the charge.

"Come on. "

"Come on where?" said Peta, looking up from her keyboard.

"Out. We're going out to grab some dinner. The snow's cleared, the restaurants are open, and we need a change of scenery."

"Oh."

It wasn't the raging enthusiasm he'd hoped for, but then again, he'd managed to avoid any discussion of Miss Tuesday March for the entire day, so he told himself to count his blessings and take Peta to dinner. Perhaps a nice solid plate of lasagna would mellow her out and ease her mind.

If not, he'd get her drunk. Anything to stop the worrying he could see was going on in her active brain.

In a surprisingly short time, they were pulling up to the crowded parking lot behind Cary's Café.

"Oh lord, Max. Here?" Peta's lips tightened.

"Sorry, babe. It's the best food around, the best plowed parking lot, and they serve liquor. Can't be too choosy. Besides, I'm just not in the mood for a super-sized burger and fries tonight."

He lifted her from the car and carried her to the front door, where an exiting customer held it open with a smile.

Max noted that she was now slipping her arms quite comfortably around his neck every time he picked her up. Apparently, she was getting used to it. Good. So was he.

An attentive hostess seated them right away, thanks to Peta's injury, and surrounded by the hubbub of the full restaurant, Peta finally smiled.

"It's called 'cabin fever'," she said.

"What is?"

"This." She nodded at the crowded room. "You can bank on it, after every snowstorm. A couple of days indoors and people fall over each other to get out and see four different walls."

Max chuckled, then jumped as a finger poked him in the back.

"Hey you two." It was Phoebe. "Glad you decided to get out. Good for you. Max, have you met Struthers?"

Max stood and shook the older man's hand. "Yes, Phoebe. You introduced us a while ago. Good to see you. You leaving? Coming? You eaten yet?"

"We're on our way out," answered Struthers in his usual smooth voice. "Lovely meal, too."

"Join us for a minute or two? I'm sure it'll take a while to get our orders in," said Peta.

Chairs were rearranged, and the table for two became a table for four in next to no time.

"So, what do you think?" Phoebe leaned towards Peta.

"You mean about Sandra?"

"Well, of course I mean about Sandra. It's all anyone's talking about tonight."

Struthers stroked his chin. "Very, very sad. A real tragedy. Haven't had anything like it around these parts in years."

Max nodded. As the conversation turned to the ins and outs of the murder investigation, he looked at Phoebe's companion.

Struthers must be in his late fifties, mused Max. Quiet, yet amusing, Max could see how Phoebe was charmed by the man. His eyes laughed when he did, and he was very intelligent, knowing exactly when to shut up. Which was right about now, since Phoebe and Peta were talking intensely about Sandra and her killer.

"Any theories, Max?" asked Struthers, quietly.

Max shrugged. "Well, the ex is always the most obvious suspect. And it seems that it was a crime of considerable savagery. I'd guess some kind of passion would have to be involved. Nothing neat or arranged."

Struthers grinned. "You like those TV shows too, do you?"

Max grinned back. "Yup. I have to admit, they've lured me in." He gazed around the room. "You have to wonder about people's motives. *Why* kill Sandra? Was it sex gone wrong? Did she piss him off? What made him snap and strangle her?"

"Can't imagine," answered Struthers. "Standard answer would be temper. She didn't seem to have much in the way of worldly goods, so greed wouldn't work. I suppose revenge is a possibility, but who on earth would carry a grudge that far?"

Max sighed. "I don't know. I really don't know."

"What don't you know?" A voice jarred on Max's thoughts and he looked up to see Cary Stiles leaning over his shoulder.

"Oh, hello Cary." Peta would be pissed at this interruption.

"Good evening, all. Having a good time? Food all right?"

"Hello, Cary. Yes, lovely meal. Struthers and I are just leaving, and these two are about to order." Phoebe nodded at him, and Peta gave him that royal nod that Max assumed passed as an effusive greeting in her native land.

"Good, good," said Cary. "You folks need anything, be sure to call me, you hear?"

Max tried to be civil. "Thanks. We will."

"Well, come on, Struthers. Time to be off. Oh, and Peta…" Phoebe was pushing away from the table and Cary held her chair for her.

"I'm going to dump another load of flea-market stuff at your place, is that okay? I'll make time later in the week to go through it all."

Peta willingly agreed. "Sure. The back door to the mudroom is unlocked. Just put it in there."

Farewells were said, and in a surprisingly short space of time given the crowd, Max and Peta were tucking into enormous portions of lasagna, bread sticks, a nice red wine, and a huge antipasto.

They were spared any more of Cary Stiles' charm, since, after a lingering and soulful gaze at Peta, his work had demanded his attention.

Max was glad to see him leave. Damned nuisance. Drooling over Peta like a dog over a bone. Max's conscience gave him a karate chop. Well, damn, sure he was doing the same thing, but it was *different*. His conscience sniffed in disdain. He mentally told it to go fuck itself.

"This is sooo good," mumbled Peta.

"Mmm. Beats the hell out of beans on toast any day."

Peta wrinkled her nose at him. "Don't knock it til you've tried it," she said, around a mouthful of salad.

"I'll save that treat for some other time, I think," he chuckled. "By the way, does Struthers have a first name?"

Peta sipped her wine, and then watched as Max topped up her glass. "Funny thing, that. I've never heard one. He's always been Struthers, as long as I can remember. I'm sure he has one, but you know how these things work. Once you're introduced as something, that's how you stay in people's minds."

Max nodded. "Yeah. I know what you mean."

"Names can be funny things, can't they? Like, for example, take the name 'Tuesday'. Now that's something that ought to be outlawed. Calling a girl that."

Max choked on his lasagna.

"And the image it presents...well. I ask you. *Tuesday*.. Of course there was Tuesday Weld. She was a pretty little thing. Not much in the way of assets, though. Do you remember her?"

Peta's innocent grin didn't fool Max for a minute. This woman was on a fishing trip and damned if he couldn't see her rod and bait quite clearly. It was pointing directly at him.

Of course, if she licked her lips once more like that, there'd be something pointing at *her*, too.

He pretended to think. "Can't say as I do. I'm not much of a one for old movies. "

"Ah."

Peta giggled. It was an unusual sound, coming from her, and he was charmed. He wondered how many glasses of wine she'd had, and cast a surreptitious glance at the bottle. Not more than two, he calculated. But perhaps she was one of these people who got drunk on a couple of glasses of wine.

In the old days, he'd have called her a cheap date. Now, she was just — delightful.

"You're a randy little devil, aren't you, Max?"

"Am I?" His lips curved in a smile, unable to resist the impish mischief peeking out from her gray eyes. It was good to see her enjoying herself. Even if he did have to pull the knives out afterwards.

"Oh yes. And you can get away with it, because you're so bloody gorgeous." She blinked. "Please tell me I didn't say that out loud."

Max looked smug. "Too late. You did. You think I'm gorgeous."

Peta blushed. "Damn. I think it's time to go home."

Max couldn't have agreed more.

Chapter 12

The glow of the porch light welcomed Max and Peta home as he carried her carefully to her front door.

Peta was happy. She was in no pain, she was in Max's arms, and *he* was about to take her into her own home. And close the door behind them. It was the stuff of fantasies, dreams and some very hot images that she'd tried to stifle.

All to no avail. He only had to walk in the room and she felt her hormones stir, and when he touched her—well—they went from stir to high-speed blend in half a second.

Just like they were doing right now.

He was still grinning at her unwise comment, having looked at her in the car a couple of times and shaken his head. "Gorgeous, huh?"

"You're not going to let me live that down, are you?"

"Nope." His grin had widened, and was still there as he fumbled with her keys and her weight.

She kept her hands around his neck and let him fumble. The hell with it. She was enjoying herself.

One hand cautiously slipped to the back of his head and she permitted herself the luxury of running her fingers through the hair that tumbled over his collar. It was longer than fashionable and she'd kill him if he cut it.

Soft and silky, it fluttered around her hand, and she stared at the mix of colors, not realizing that he'd paused at her touch.

"Peta," he whispered, tugging her close.

"Mmm?"

"I like it when you do that."

"Me too," she answered idly. Her hand kept up its stroking move and she watched it until her vision was blocked. By Max's face.

"Perhaps you might like this too..."

And he kissed her.

Catching her by surprise, Max's lips met hers, warm and sweet, sending a shiver of pleasure through her body. She couldn't keep herself from responding. It was, after all, what she'd craved since he first walked into her office at Mayfield Masterpieces.

And it lived up to every expectation and then some.

He just brushed her mouth at first, holding her tightly in his arms. She slipped her other hand more comfortably around him, and felt his tongue as it licked at her lips.

"Open for me, Peta," he murmured.

She obliged. Parting her lips she let him in. Eagerly and willingly, she welcomed him, tasting wine and Italian food and Max. Sweet, sweet Max.

He was tentative at first, moving around her mouth, learning her, just flicking his tongue against hers as if in encouragement. She flicked back and suddenly his kiss deepened.

With a groan he slid her down his body, carefully lowering her to her own feet, but never allowing their lips to separate.

His hands came up to her face and cradled it, moving it, angling it so that he could plunge deep. She shuddered as his touch became more demanding, his tongue darting around hers, coiling and teasing her.

She touched his cheek with her palm, loving the slight roughness, the raspy stubble that grew there.

He smelled good. Like leather and man and heat. It was an intoxicating combination, and on top of the wine, just about knocked Peta off her feet.

She rocked back and gasped as she inadvertently put her weight on her injured ankle.

"Damn. This is no place to do this." Max wrenched his mouth away from hers, opened the door and picked her up again, carrying her inside and kicking the front door shut behind him with his heel.

The darkness of her hallway surrounded them as the light from the porch faded into obscurity. By mutual consent, they gravitated back into each other's arms, lips meeting lips, sighs echoing sighs.

The kiss heated up, and Peta moaned as Max's hands tugged her hips against him. His mouth devoured her, and she offered herself up willingly. This was *Max*. She was finally getting a good taste of the man of her dreams, and it was everything she'd wanted and more.

Her brain struggled to assimilate the information while her body just struggled. She wriggled against him, feeling his cock against her through the layers of their clothing.

In that instant, Peta knew that *this* would be the night. This would be her chance to fulfill her fantasies. So what if it was a one-night stand? So what if he left her tomorrow for someone else? She'd have this night to remember, and to judge by the hardness she was grinding herself against, it would be a hell of a night.

Max drew her breath into his mouth and gave it back, making her dizzy and sending her blood pressure skyrocketing. Trying to absorb all the sensations of this fabulous kiss was overloading her poor brain, and finally, she just gave up and surrendered.

She let the moment take her. The moment — and Max.

His hands were everywhere, stroking, seeking, brushing her backside and her sweater. She muttered in distress as he finally pulled back.

"Peta," he rasped. "I want more. I want you."

"Oh heavens, Max, you idiot. Can't you tell I want you too?" Peta was tempted to smack him. How polished a seducer was he if he couldn't sense by her actions that she was hot, ready, and wanted it *now*, please.

Right now. Right here. On the hall floor, up against the hall wall, anywhere at all would be just fine. As long as it was within the next five seconds.

But Max would have none of that. He shed his leather coat, tugged Peta free of her parka, tossed both jackets towards the hallstand and swept her up in his arms once more.

Peta noticed the pile of clothing out of the corner of her eye and chuckled to herself. The usually dexterous and smooth Mr. Wolfe had missed his target. Good. Perhaps she was rattling him as much as he was rattling her.

She couldn't see his eyes as he carried her up the stairs to her room, but she could feel the heat of his body against her palm where it lay at the back of his neck. Her own flesh was rapidly approaching boiling point, and her legs were aching. Not from the injury this time, but from the need which flooded her. The need to spread her legs wide and welcome Max home.

He laid her down on her bed, letting her legs dangle free over the edge, and followed her, lowering himself between her thighs and resting his weight on her breasts. She loved it and reached to pull him even closer.

His lips returned to hers, fiercely now, his tongue a live thing that felt as if it had been waiting for the chance to dive into her mouth and settle down there.

"Max," she moaned, gasping for breath but unwilling to stop his kiss.

He moved away slightly, and she almost cried.

"Are you sure you want this, Peta?"

Was she sure? Was she *sure*? She was writhing beneath him in a dreadfully wanton display of raging lust and he was asking if she was sure?

Peta snorted. "If you can't tell, then I want to know who you are and what you've done with Max Wolfe."

"Just checking," chuckled Max.

His hands flew to her sweater and began undoing the buttons up the front.

She watched him, loving the gleam in his hot hazel eyes, the way he determinedly freed her from the clinging folds of her clothes, and feeling the wetness between her legs as her need grew.

"Damn, how many clothes do you have on, for chrissake?" He'd stripped away her cardigan and found her thermal shirt beneath. "Is this a test or something? Undress the woman before the poor guy explodes?"

Peta giggled. "Yep. You have to want me badly enough to find me."

"Oh no problem there, darlin'," he muttered, unsnapping her jeans. "No problem there at all. I want...I..."

His voice trailed off as he finally revealed her bra. "Oh, yeah. I want *these*."

He lowered his head and licked her nipple through the thin silk.

Peta groaned at the feel of it, the hot pleasure of his touch on her sensitive breasts. "God, Max..."

"So good, honey, so good," he muttered. He kept his head lowered and offered the same attention to the other peak, bringing her nipples to an almost painful level of arousal and wetting the fabric of her bra.

He moved back a little and just looked at them. "Lovely, Peta. "

"Er...they're not Tuesday's breasts, you know, Max," said Peta. She couldn't help her reaction. She knew she wasn't overly well endowed in the mammary department.

"That's okay. Today's will do just fine."

"No, no, I meant — "

His hands found the latch between the cups and opened it, baring her, and driving all thoughts of witty repartee clean out of her head.

She'd loved his touch through the silk. She loved his touch to her naked skin even more. She could feel the heat now, the movement of his tongue as he found her nipple and played with it, sucking it between his lips and letting it pop back out again.

He seemed fascinated by them, moving from one to the other, bringing each to the heights of arousal and then transferring his attentions to the other one. Peta was dizzy from his touch. Her cunt was beginning to ache and each and every swipe with that tongue of his was echoed by a dart of pleasure deep in her belly.

It seemed hours before he raised his head and grinned at her. "Sweet," he said.

"More," she answered.

His eyes flared and he slipped her bra away from her, returning to her jeans and shoes and easing both away from her, taking care not to hurt her ankle. She realized he could probably whack the bloody thing with a hammer and she wouldn't feel it.

Her pain right now was one of need, an overwhelming almost violent desire to get Max and his cock inside her.

His hands slid down her thighs, pulling her panties down with them and leaving her naked on the bed.

And damn him, he was still dressed.

"Max," she whispered. "You too."

He smiled, a hot and sensual smile that did wonderful things for his mouth and her heart.

"Help me?" he asked.

Sure. Gimme some scissors, a knife, a machete. She'd have those clothes off him and his body stripped bare in ten seconds or less.

"Of course." Peta sat up and found herself nose-to-chest with Max. Nose to a very nice chest. Which was presently covered by a sweater. Not satisfactory.

She wanted the real thing.

Tentatively, she slipped her hands beneath the wool and found skin. Blazing hot and hard skin. Swallowing, she moved her hands up, indicating that he should get the damned thing off. It was nice and soft, and a very pretty shade of ecru, that would be a perfect match for the carpet she wanted to see it lying on. Or anything else, for that matter, as long as it wasn't on Max.

He obliged, tugging it the rest of the way up and over his head, letting it drop to the floor.

And there it was. That fabulous, wonderful chest of his, firm and hard, and just dusted with some glittering hairs. Exactly the way she liked chests to look. His nipples were flat brown disks and she eagerly explored them with her fingertips, brushing them at first, then growing more bold as Max responded with a slight shudder.

"Am I...is that...do you like that?" she asked. It was risky, but she let her eyes meet his.

Oh goodness. Yes. He certainly looked like a man who "liked" it.

His cheeks were flushed, his lips a little apart, and he had a predatory look in his eyes that was not dissimilar to the animal whose name he bore.

"You really are a wolf, aren't you Max?" said Peta.

"Only with you," he growled back.

She grinned and reached for his pants. They were tighter than tight across his cock, and she carefully unfastened them and spread the fly apart, revealing his briefs, which were struggling to contain that part of him she wanted more than anything.

"Oh dear. It looks most uncomfortable, Max. Let's see what we can do about it." Gently, she eased the briefs away from him, leaning down and pushing both them and his jeans lower onto his thighs.

His cock nearly took her eye out as she released him, and she moved her head aside with a gasp. "Bloody hell,

Max." The wine had loosened her tongue and she said the first thing that came into her mind. "It'll never fit."

Max grinned tautly. "Oh yes it will. Like it was made for you, babe."

She stared at him. "Are you sure?"

"Not a doubt in my mind."

She returned her gaze to his cock, and wondered again at its size. It seemed enormous to her, although she admittedly had little to compare it against. It jutted towards her from its nest of sandy hair, and she couldn't stop herself from reaching for it.

"Do you mind if I...?"

"Peta," sighed Max. "I don't mind *anything* you do. I am yours. Use me as you wish. But..."

She looked up again as he paused.

"Be gentle with me?"

She snickered. "Right. Of course."

And strangely enough, she was gentle with him. Fascinated by the ridges and veins of his cock, Peta explored it, running her fingers over its silky hardness and then discovering his balls beneath. She'd never had the chance to get quite so familiar with a man's personal parts, and she took full advantage of it.

Only when a little groan from Max distracted her did she look up.

"Honey, you're killing me here. How about you let me play for a while now? Fair is fair."

With a smooth move, Max pushed her backwards onto the bed and took over. And God, did he take over.

Suddenly, she was surrounded by his heat, and the feel of his naked body next to hers. She felt her cunt begin to weep hot tears as he swept his hands over her, and she bit back a cry as he found her nipples once again. My goodness, did he like to play with her nipples.

And she had no objections, either, come to think of it.

When he slid his hand over her belly to her mound and gently tugged her curly hair she nearly flew off the bed.

"Max," she yelled.

"What?" he muttered. Apparently he could speak with his mouth full.

Peta gulped. She'd never imagined herself so hungry for a man that the words would come easily to her lips. "Fuck me, Max, please just fuck me."

Chapter 13

Fuck.

There it was again. A sound. Someone yelling.

He froze in place, surrounded by the clutter he'd been so anxiously sorting. There were hats, and oddly shaped bowls, and more than one set of salt and pepper shakers. He glanced around him, cursing the low light but knowing that it was all he had.

He had to make the best use of it.

He waited, patiently, scarcely breathing, knowing this was his last chance tonight to find it.

No more noises disturbed the silence. He returned to his task. Cautiously he lifted something wrapped in newspaper. It was a rather ugly vase of some sort.

His temper was rising now along with his eagerness, his heart pulsing with the thrill, the challenge, the knowledge that he was fooling them all.

He had to find it.

It had to be here somewhere. It had to.

He knew approximately what size it was, and yet there were so many things that could have come close.

He found a box of books and eagerly bent to examine each and every one. Carefully, he pulled them out, riffling through the pages in the dim light, trying to make out the titles.

Another sound stopped him.

Shit. It sounded like someone was fucking. And doing a good job of it too.

His cock stirred.

He checked the last book — useless. He wanted to throw it at the wall in frustration, but knew he couldn't.

Carefully, quietly, he replaced the junk back to where it had been, as best as he could remember. His mind blurred as his anger transferred itself to his cock, which pressed against his fly.

Why not?

He had a condom. No tell-tale evidence. And what a kick.

A distant moan broke the silence, as whoever was getting off let the world know about it.

The sound was enough.

He unzipped his pants and sheathed himself in the darkness, excited now by his own touch and the feel of the latex as he unrolled it over his hardness.

He had to strip off one glove to grasp himself, and he carefully folded it, tucking it into the pocket of his jacket.

He looked around him again as he began to stroke.

Junk. Nothing but junk. No square box that held the answer to all his troubles and all his dreams.

His anger and his cock rose simultaneously. The thrill of the forbidden, the sense of danger, the frustration at yet another dead end, all contributed to a hell of a hard-on.

Fuck them all, he thought, as he quickened his strokes.

I know what I want. I just have to find it. And if anyone gets in my way...

Visions of her eyes as he fucked her and choked her swam through his mind, exciting him and tightening his balls.

He was coming. Here, in the gloom of a house not his own, when someone else was only a floor away, fucking, not knowing what he knew...

Assholes. Ignorant assholes. All of them.

He'd show them.

Like he'd shown Sandra.

Nobody, but NOBODY, got in his way. Not this time. Not for this special quest of his.

This time he was going to win. To triumph in his hunt, to claim what was rightfully his, and fuck 'em all.

On that thought, his balls clenched and his teeth smacked together as he bit back his cry.

He came, shooting hot and hard into the condom. Emptying his balls and his anger from his body in a gush.

He smiled to himself, then stilled, heart pounding, as another sound made itself known.

"Mrreeeooowwlll."

Chapter 14

Max Wolfe suckled on Peta Matthew's nipples like they were the last nipples on earth.

He loved nipples. He loved the way they plumped and hardened in his mouth, and the way the merest flick of his tongue could bring shivers and sighs to the woman attached to those nipples.

But Peta's nipples — well, they defied description. Especially since they topped a set of breasts that seemed to have been made to match his oral dimensions. They fit his mouth perfectly.

Every little move he made brought a response to her writhing body, and he could smell her arousal as it built beneath him.

He could have spent hours just playing with her breasts, but his cock was reminding him that there was work to be done and he'd better get to it. Very shortly, too, or the help might just go on strike. A very explosive strike.

With a little pop he released her nipple, leaving it with a last wet lick.

"Oh, Max," she moaned.

Two of his favorite words. "Yeah," he answered. "Oh yeah."

For a second he wondered at himself. Where had his gift for sensual conversation gone? He should be filling her ears with down-and-dirty talk about what he was going to do to her and how he was going to do it. Getting her so hot and bothered that she'd be halfway to her orgasm before he got his cock anywhere near her.

But somehow, with Peta, conversation wasn't necessary. He didn't have to talk her, or himself, into a state of heightened sexual awareness. His was so heightened right at this moment it might need oxygen.

He slithered down her body, feeling her heat against him and the pounding of her pulse through her skin.

She widened her legs in welcome and in invitation.

He answered both with his mouth, just grazing her thighs with his lips and then letting his tongue flick across her wet and swollen folds.

"Oooh," she cried, "Bloody hell..."

He grinned, keeping his tongue busy and finding the little bud of flesh that sent her into shivering waves of pleasure. Even while fucking she was always the Brit.

"Yes, Max, there, oh please — *there*."

Hmm. So that was the spot, was it? Max filed the location for future reference, continuing his exploration. He inhaled her scent, sweet and tart and all her. Her taste was the same. Unique and seductive, he let her juices run over his tongue as he pushed it through her flesh and found her cunt.

"Oh...oh...there too," she moaned. "Yes. My God. *There*..."

Max was elated. The woman was a screaming mass of hot spots, and he was finding every one of them. He'd bet there were a few she didn't even know she had.

After this night was over, she would. It was a promise to himself that Max intended to keep.

But right at this moment, he had another need. His control was deserting him, he knew his cock was leaking tears of frustration, and if he didn't get inside her within moments, he was going to come like a volcano, all over her comforter.

He withdrew from her and reached for his pants pocket, pulling out the condom he'd carried around with him since the first day he'd moved in with her. He'd just known that the moment would come when he'd need it.

And that moment was now.

"Peta love," he whispered. "Look at me."

She pushed herself up on her elbows and squinted at him, her eyes hot and gray and unfocussed.

"I want you. I want your cunt around my cock. More than anything."

He tore the foil wrapper with his teeth as he kept one hand on Peta's flesh.

"Yes, me too..." she stuttered, watching as he removed the condom and tossed the packet aside.

"You too what?" he asked, noting her gaze as it fell to his hands. Slowly, agonizingly slowly, he unrolled the condom down his length, clenching his teeth in an effort to retain control of his wayward cock. Just knowing she was watching him excited him in a variety of new ways. It was erotic, and thrilling and—oh hell.

"I want you inside me." She stared at his sheathed length.

"You mean like this?" He slipped a finger into her and pulled it out again, spreading her honey over her searingly hot skin.

"No, not like that, well, yes, that's good, but no..."

Max grinned. Well, perhaps it was more of a feral snarl. Grinning seemed beyond him at this point.

"So what do you want inside you, Peta? My tongue?"

"Yes. No. I don't know. Just fuck me, Max, for heaven's sake."

"Fuck you with what, Peta? Say it. Tell me what you want."

Her eyes remained fixed on his cock. "I want *that*. And I want it *now*." She glanced up at him. "Please."

"Okay, Miss Manners, since you asked so nicely..." His humor was wasted.

Peta sagged back onto the comforter and widened her thighs even more as his hips settled between them.

Slowly, carefully, he positioned his cock between her legs and rubbed the head against her.

She moaned.

He felt rather like moaning himself as her heat burned through the thin shield and seared him.

He pushed further, breaching her soaking cunt and entering her, savoring each and every millimeter, and listening to her pant beneath him.

"Oh God. Oh Jesus. Oh God—"

Good. She'd reached the religious stage. Of course, he'd reached it, waved at St. Peter and passed it several minutes ago.

"Open your eyes, Peta," he commanded, and as she did so, he sank home.

Peta screamed. "Maaaaax," she wailed. "Oh fuuuuucckkk..."

Oh fuck indeed.

Max's breath caught in his lungs. She boiled around him, tight and silky, and her cunt accepted him like a long-lost friend.

Her eyes never moved from his as he pressed himself deep, and her tongue slid from between her lips as she gasped again.

He wanted her. He wanted all of her. He wanted to bury himself inside her till his eyelids hit her clit.

He slid one hand under her thigh and lifted her leg, resting her healthy ankle on his shoulder. She was totally open to him, and now he could claim what he knew, somewhere deep inside, was his. All *his*. Only his.

He pushed further, and the sobbing cry that answered his move told him he'd found her deepest places.

He was truly lost inside her. His balls were against her buttocks, their hair tangled together, and Max wondered in amazement at the feelings that flooded him.

He wanted to stop and examine them. To look at them clinically and compare them with all the other women he'd fucked. To find out why this was different. Why his balls were as hard as rocks, why his pulse was beating so loudly in his ears and why his breath had left him as he'd claimed her.

But nature demanded otherwise.

He pulled back and thrust home again, more forcefully this time, encouraged by her moans and the way her hands scrabbled on the comforter.

A grunt of pleasure broke from his own throat, and surprised the hell out of him. Something about this woman, the way her body grabbed for him and held him tight, reached places inside his own body that had never been touched before.

She panted now, harsh breaths that he forced from her lungs with the pounding of his cock. Low growls were coming from her throat, and her head was tipped backwards, neck muscles taut, lips pulled away from her teeth.

She looked almost savage, passionate, and as desperate as he was to finish it.

He stroked her with his hands, fucked her with his cock and devoured the sight of her, smothering himself in the experience. His nostrils filled with the scent of Peta and sex, and his mind spun as his balls hardened even more and the electric tingle started to spark at the base of his spine.

He was coming. And not a single thing in this world could stop him. He wanted her there too. He wanted to share it, to shout and scream along with Peta.

His body was brushing hers, but was it enough?

He took no chances. He dropped a hand to her mound and found her clit, letting his own weight push his fingers against it as he pistoned his hips into her.

She went rigid beneath him, just as he felt his cock swell and his heart stop.

He exploded.

So did she.

Their cries mingled, their bodies heaved, and Max felt the bed shake with the massive orgasm they'd combined to produce.

Her cunt clamped around him like a fist, matching his spurts with its clenching and releasing and dragging him into the most amazing come of his life. His cock throbbed as he filled her, and it seemed to fuel her own orgasm as she shuddered around him once more.

He could feel her calf muscle like a solid bar against his neck, so tightly did her body spasm.

Slowly, almost painfully, the moment subsided, and Peta's body softened against his.

She struggled to catch a raspy breath, as Max regretfully withdrew his now-satisfied and exhausted cock.

Gently he eased her more fully onto the bed, pulling the comforter back and resting her head on the pillow.

She turned her head and looked sleepily at him. "Bloody brilliant, Max. Bloody brilliant."

He grinned and left her, taking care of the condom and making sure there were blankets available if they got cold during the night.

Yeah, right. With the heat they'd generated, he doubted it would be a problem. But somehow, he wanted to make sure she'd be all right.

It was an odd feeling, thought Max. He had no desire to pull his pants on and leave. No wish to rid himself of her scent, or get the hell out of her room as fast as he could.

In fact, he couldn't wait to slip in beside her and take her in his arms. Perhaps give her a little while to rest up and then start all over again.

He lifted the comforter and lay down next to Peta, sliding himself around her and tucking her into his body.

She sighed.

He smiled.

She snuffled, and sighed some more. Then snored.

Well, hell. She was sound asleep.

* * * * *

Light filtered through Max's eyelids and a heavy weight rested on his belly. Something soft was flickering at his cock.

He lay still and savored the sensation. Memories of fucking Peta flooded his mind, and he sighed with pleasure. He couldn't remember waking up in a woman's bed before, let alone waking up and wanting her all over again. It wasn't his style.

But this feeling, this...this...warmth, was new. Special. Something to be relished.

"Oh, honey, yeah," he sighed, as his cock responded energetically to the soft touch. The very soft touch.

The almost silky soft touch.

He opened his eyes. "Oh fuck."

Mr. Peebles was sitting on his stomach, and expressing his displeasure at this display of lassitude by flicking his tail.

Right over Max's now fully-aroused cock.

A low chuckle from the door attracted his attention, and he moved his head to see Peta standing there, cane in one hand, robe clutched around her in the other.

"I see Mr. Peebles is a very effective alarm clock," she grinned.

Max grinned back. She looked delectable. Her hair was all over the place, her robe should have been burned years ago, and he wanted her so badly he ached with it.

"C'mere. I can think of a better way to wake up."

Peta hesitated and clutched her robe more tightly as her eyes dropped. Good God above, they'd fucked themselves blind and yet she was still shy. Max's mind whirled to find the right words.

"I need a morning cuddle," he said.

"Oh. Oh all right," she smiled. Leaning the cane against the bedside table, she awkwardly levered herself back onto the bed, next to Max, who promptly grabbed her and tugged her so that she was almost on top of him.

"Good morning."

She smiled at him, gray eyes wide, with a hint of embarrassment lurking in their depths. "Hullo yourself."

"You all right? I didn't hurt you last night?"

She swallowed. "*Hurt* me? Good lord, no. I feel fine. Just great. Marvelous. Better than I have in a long time, in fact."

She did, too, realized Max. She was glowing, and her skin was heating up as his nimble fingers found the tie on her robe and tugged it away from between them.

He sighed as he felt her naked breasts pressed into his chest.

"Now *this* is what I call a morning cuddle."

"Mmm," she answered. In a delightful little move, she dropped her head to his shoulder and tucked it under his chin, charming him and making his heart turn over.

"I hate to sound cliché or anything, but, um, was it good for you?" Peta's question was hesitant.

Max growled and slipped a free hand up her robe to caress her buttock.

"Well, I hope that was a yes," she sighed. "Because it was fabulous for me. But of course, you'd know that. I'm sorry if I wasn't quite up to your standards, but believe me, I had a lovely time. Thank you."

Max blinked. She was talking like they'd had a damned tea party last night instead of mind-altering sex.

He opened his mouth to challenge her when the phone rang.

"Oh *bollocks*," said Peta, slithering from his grasp.

He couldn't have put it better himself.

Chapter 15

"Peta? Hello, Peta? It's Phoebe," said the phone in Peta's hand.

For a few moments, Peta's mind blanked. *Phoebe who*? Her mind whirled with thoughts of the naked man reclining next to her and what she'd like to do to him, and it took all her concentration and then some to recall who and where she was.

"Oh Phoebe, yes. Hello." It was Phoebe, her boss. *That* Phoebe.

A stray hand crept to her naked breast and played. She batted it away, trying to concentrate on her conversation as she sprawled on the bed, far too near Max for comfort. Near enough for pleasure, but not for chatting on the phone.

"You're up early?" Not the most scintillating of questions, but it was the best she could do given the circumstances.

"The office was broken into last night."

Peta sat straight up, forgetting that Max held one of her nipples, and she grimaced as he accidentally tugged it. "*What*?"

"The office. I came in early this morning to try and get some of the grunt work out of the way, and I found it like *this*..."

Peta could hear tears trembling in the older woman's voice. "Phoebe, did you call the police?"

Max was behind her now, supporting her, frowning and tipping his head in query.

"Yes, they're on their way."

"We'll be right there, Phoebe. Don't touch anything. Don't worry, just wait for them, okay? Wait outside for them."

"I'm outside now. In my car. I didn't want to go back in there. Can you come over?"

"Of course. I just said we would. Give us a few minutes. Stay put, okay?"

"Okay. Thanks, dear, I'm sorry..."

"Don't be silly," scolded Peta. Max was gone, shrugging into his clothes. "We'll be there shortly."

Phoebe had hung up.

"The office was burgled last night," said Peta. She too reached for her clothes.

"Anything stolen?" asked Max.

"I don't know. Phoebe took one look and called the police, I guess. She's there now in her car waiting for them. Max, can we..."

"I'll meet you downstairs. Dress warm. And hurry."

Peta breathed deeply. Max Wolfe was a whirlwind in bed, which she'd expected, but he seemed to be such a caring man in other ways, too, which caught her by surprise when she allowed herself time to think about it.

And time was one thing she didn't have right now.

Grabbing a warm sweatshirt, she picked up her cane and stumbled from the room.

The flickering lights on the tops of two police cars greeted them as they pulled up outside the offices of Mayfield Masterpieces.

Situated in a remodeled store, the small company looked onto the street and the nicely-painted door was ajar, with snow on the doormat marking the passage of heavy official boots.

"Phoebe?" Peta called out as she and Max walked carefully inside.

"Back here, Peta," came the answer.

Following the sounds, Peta and Max made their way through the reception area to the larger room behind, and Peta gasped as they entered.

There was chaos everywhere.

Two officers were moving slowly around, making notes in their ever-present books, and Phoebe herself was sitting at her desk talking to Lieutenant Summers.

"Oh Peta, Max. Bless you both for coming," she said, catching sight of them as they stood, open mouthed, looking at the mess.

"My God, Phoebe. Who on earth would do this?" Peta couldn't grasp it. Couldn't get her mind around the fact that someone would wreak havoc in such a dreadful way.

"I don't know," moaned Phoebe. "I was just telling Frank here, we've nothing of value."

"They didn't take the computers," noted Max.

Peta caught an expression of surprise in Frank's eyes as he glanced at Max.

"Good observation. No they didn't. And as near as Phoebe can tell, not much else is missing, either."

"Peta, check the data file, will you? See if our hard copies are in there?" Phoebe nodded at a filing cabinet whose drawers hung askew.

Making her way carefully around the paper on the floor, Peta did as she was told.

"They're all here. Nothing's missing. Every single one's here..." She ran her hands over the data storage file, as familiar with its contents as she was with her own kitchen cupboard. More so, probably.

Phoebe sighed and sagged. "Well that's a relief. Those disks are the most valuable things we have, Frank."

The Lieutenant chewed on his pencil. "You don't keep cash around, do you?"

"No, Frank, no cash," answered Peta. She thankfully eased down into the chair Max had pulled out for her, and took comfort from his presence behind her. "All our transactions are done on-line, either bank transfers or PayPal, or whatever."

"Our entire livelihood is pretty much virtual," added Phoebe. "Those disks over there are our original hard copies of each book we publish, on a month by month basis. We've got backups on our hard drives, of course, but it would be a great loss if someone had stolen those." She nodded at the file.

"So what were they after?"

Max's question dropped into the room like a lead balloon, bringing a frown to Frank's face and a worried look to both Peta and Phoebe.

"I wish I knew." Frank eased himself off the desk. "There were a lot of boxes dumped out, books thrown around, it seems they were looking for something. But God knows what." He sighed. "Phoebe, about all I can do for now is have one of my guys dust for prints. Can you all drop by later and give me samples of your fingerprints? We're bound to find them all over the place, and I need to be able to distinguish between those that belong here and those that don't."

Three nods answered him, and Phoebe passed him a bunch of keys. "These are my spares, Frank. Take them, and I'll lock up in a minute, when I leave. It's all yours until you tell me otherwise."

Shortly thereafter the "authorities" left the scene, promising to return with a fingerprint kit.

Phoebe sighed. "I suppose I'll just lock up then, and leave it. Can't start tidying up until the guys are done with their 'dusting' stuff."

Voices sounded in the front office, and Max moved quickly to the door. Peta noticed him frown and followed, with Phoebe right behind her. All three moved into the reception area, closing the door on the disaster within.

Edward Sharp and Cary Stiles were standing on the doorstep, looking rattled and uneasy, and both trying to push forward at the same time.

"Peta, are you all right?" Cary's smooth tones flowed through the room.

"I saw the police here, Phoebe. What on earth happened, eh? What happened?" asked Edward repetitively.

Peta closed her eyes and drew a deep breath, wishing they'd both go away. Far away. Like Australia or someplace. She didn't need this right now.

Max didn't need it either. He wanted to check the place out, make sure it was locked, get Phoebe settled, and then take Peta home. They had some unfinished business to attend to.

Cary won the battle of who was going to get inside first, pushing past Edward with a grunt. He immediately moved towards Peta.

Peta stepped back, right up against Max's chest.

"Peta, my dear, are you all right? What happened? The police...I was so worried." His handsome face creased in a frown as he stared at her, and held out his hand.

"How kind, Cary."

Max noted her frosty tones with a certain amount of male pleasure. It was, after all, his chest she'd plastered herself against, not Cary's.

Realizing that his hand was still waving uselessly in the air, Cary stuck it in his pocket. "Well, we don't see emergency vehicles rushing around town too often," he paused. "Until recently, that is."

His gaze rose to meet Max's. "Until all these newcomers started showing up."

The implication was quite clear, and Max caught the little hiss as Peta sucked in a breath through her teeth.

"Cary, you're being absurd. Someone broke in last night and trashed the office. Probably some kids out for a spree or something. Nothing was stolen, as far as we can tell, and other than the mess, no harm was done. I'm sure Phoebe appreciates your concern, but there's nothing you can do here."

The dismissal was firm, unsubtle, and Cary's eyes narrowed as he took in her stance against Max's chest.

"I see." His tone of voice said as much as his raised eyebrow. "And I suppose you can account for *his* whereabouts last night, can you?"

Max flinched, struggling to hold on to his temper. Only Peta's warmth against him stopped him from taking Cary by the ear and teaching him some manners.

Peta's next words surprised him. "Yes I can. All night. *All* night, Cary. Do I make myself clear?"

The veneer of charm dropped from Cary Stiles' face for a second or so, letting a cold light shine from his eyes. "Oh yes. *Perfectly* clear." He leaned forward, lowering his voice so that only Peta and Max could hear. "But don't come crying to me when *Romeo* here dumps you and moves on."

He turned on his heel and stalked out before Max could choke him. And choking him was the first thing on the list of the things Max wanted to do to Cary Stiles. Followed by some rather intense discussion in which fists would be involved, and probably concluding with a well-placed boot to the balls.

"That shit," he breathed.

Peta shivered a little. "Did you see his face, Max? I've never seen somebody get so cold all of a sudden."

"My, my. Cary left rather quickly, didn't he? My, my..." Edward turned from his conversation with Phoebe as the door slammed behind Cary.

Max sighed, letting his muscles relax a little. Cary might have gone, but Max wouldn't forget. Wolfes were known for their ability to carry a grudge.

"Thanks for coming by, Edward," said Phoebe.

The door opened again, and Struthers poked his head in. "Everybody all right? Anything I can do?"

"Oh Struthers," said Phoebe. "How kind. Just a bit of a burglary, that's all."

A frown crossed Struthers' face and he moved to her, taking her hand in his. "Nothing too valuable missing, I hope? Good heavens," he looked around the room. "What is this town coming to? Murders? Robberies?"

Edward's chest swelled. "Our town has the finest police force in the county, Struthers. The finest. I'm sure they'll have things well in hand."

"He seems to be taking all this quite personally, doesn't he?" whispered Max into Peta's ear.

"It is *his* town, you know. In his own mind, anyway."

"Of course we do," soothed Phoebe. "Struthers, would you mind terribly following me home? I'm really feeling a bit shaky at the moment."

Struthers paused. "My pleasure, dear. But..." he glanced at Max and Peta. "I say, would you two mind very much keeping an eye on the library for an hour or two?"

Max met the man's eyes. Clearly Struthers was caught in a dilemma. He wanted to take Phoebe home, but didn't want to neglect his duties.

"Excellent notion, Struthers. Excellent," said Edward, glancing out the window. "Look, Phoebe, leave your car here. Go with Struthers. I'm sure Peta and Max can handle the library this morning. And I'll formally declare this afternoon an early-closing..." he nodded outside. "If this keeps up, doubt that anyone is going to be doing much traveling anyway. If it keeps up."

They all looked outside. The gray skies were spitting ice pellets, and Peta winced, knowing how miserable driving would become if it went on for any length of time.

"I'd better go alert the troops. Sand, salt, that sort of thing. Muster the troops." He headed for the door. "Let me know if there's anything I can do to help, won't you, Phoebe? Anything I can do?"

Peta sighed as he left. "You know, he's got a good heart under all that bluster," she said.

"Yes he does. Yes he does." Max couldn't resist it.

"You, Max Wolfe, are a bad man." Peta's grin was genuine and relaxed for the first time since they'd arrived at the office, and it warmed Max's heart.

Phoebe was gathering her belongings together. "Well," she sighed, "I'll be off then. Struthers will drive me home. Will you two be okay at the library?"

Peta chuckled. "Phoebe. This is me, remember? The book queen?"

Struthers laughed. "I have no concerns, Peta. None at all. Now if you can get Max here into some *good* reading —"

Phoebe snorted, but he ignored her. "Like Clancy, or Deighton, or something...just check the fiction section. Plenty of good stuff there."

Struthers held the door for Phoebe and the two headed out. But Phoebe couldn't resist taking a parting shot. She turned her head and grinned at them both over her shoulder.

"I'd also suggest the Kama Sutra. Reference section, aisle three. Fourth shelf from the bottom." It was a stage whisper that crossed the room quite clearly, and made Peta's face burn.

"Good to know," chuckled Max.

Bloody hell. As if they needed a reference book on sex. Peta snickered to herself as she and Max locked up the office and headed towards the library. Max could probably have written it, or at least given the author a few pointers.

"What's that enigmatic little grin for?" Max bent his head down and his hazel eyes met hers as they strolled carefully through the sleet.

Peta blinked. He should get those damned eyes licensed as dangerous weapons. One glance and she was creaming her panties. She jerked her thoughts back to his question. "I was just wondering at Phoebe's precise knowledge of the whereabouts of that book."

"Oh," said Max sagely. "I thought perhaps you were wondering what was in it."

"Certainly not."

"Pity," answered Max.

"Why?"

"I thought it might be — *interesting* — to find out..."

Chapter 16

"Fucking *Christ*."

The explosive comment followed the slamming of Diana Stiles' shop door, almost knocking the bell onto the floor.

"My, my, Cary dear. Such a temper. " Diana strolled to the window and looked out, sighing. "I don't think it's worth even opening today. Look at this. Sleet, ice, people aren't going to bother to come out at all."

"I don't give a shit about your fucking store." Cary growled as he paced.

"Well, fuck you too. So what was going on down at Phoebe's? I saw the police there."

"Some kids trashed the place, I guess. I don't know. Who cares?" He ran his hand through his carefully arranged hair.

"Pity," said Diana. "I'd rather hoped somebody had strangled that bitch Peta and put her out of *both* our misery."

Cary snorted. "If you think you're going to get your claws back into Max Wolfe, you can forget about it. He's fucking her, Diana. Damn near came right out and said so."

Diana's mouth hardened. "Oh really?"

"Yeah, *really*," sneered Cary. "Looks like your legendary sexual *skills* weren't enough for him, huh?"

Diana glared at her brother. "Like you? You never even got into that bitch's pants, Cary, let me remind you. She turned you down flat. Now you'll never know what that little British cunt feels like, will you?"

Cary's hand lifted, and Diana pinned him with a glare colder than the ice falling outside the window. "Don't even think about it," she hissed.

Sagging, Cary let his hand fall back to his side. "Fuck it all, Diana."

"Still can't come up with the cash?"

The question hung between them, as Cary leaned against the counter with a sigh. "Nope. I'm in big trouble, sis."

"Sorry. Can't help you."

"Can't? Or won't?"

"Look, Cary. You've got the fucking gambling problem, not me. You're the one who went out on a limb with those new restaurants when I advised against it. Everything I have is tied up in this place. You know it and I know it."

"So what am I gonna do?"

"Sell that goddamned house, for chrissake. I've told you time and time again."

Cary shook his head. "Can't. Mortgaged to the hilt. I'd lose more on that deal than I've lost to Vincenzo."

"Well, in that case, don't come whining to me. I've got my own troubles, and I don't need yours." She stared at him coldly.

"You are such a fucking piece of work, sister dear. No wonder Wolfe doesn't want your ass any more."

"Get out." Diana's tone was vicious. "Get the *fuck* out."

"I'm going. Sometimes I think Vincenzo is a nicer person to deal with than you. He only breaks a guy's legs. He can't hold a candle to you."

"Don't let the door hit you on the way out." Diana winced as the door slammed behind her brother once more.

The curtain separating the store from the back room moved slightly, and Diana checked the locks and turned out the lights. Business was over before it had begun.

She stepped through the curtains.

He was waiting.

The expressionless face of Mike Dean watched her as she moved towards him, her fists clenched.

"Lose the skirt," he growled.

"What?"

"The skirt. Lose it. We both know your pussy is naked under there. Don't make the mistake of playing with me. You're hot right now, and I want to fuck. Lose the skirt."

With narrowed eyes Diana reached for her zipper, lowering it slowly.

"Drop it and come here."

She licked her lips at his harsh command, and stepped out of her skirt as it fell to the floor.

"Lose that shit too." He gestured at her garter belt.

She pouted. "But I like it."

"I don't. Get your ass naked. Now." His hands dropped to his fly and he opened his jeans, letting his cock fall free.

Diana stripped off her garters and stockings, never lifting her eyes from his cock. "Okay."

Mike stood still, letting her approach, waiting, watching, only his arousal showing his readiness.

"Now what?" Diana finally met his unblinking stare.

"You're a fucking bitch, you know that?" His question required no answer. "Put your hands on the back of the couch."

Diana bent over, resting her palms along the worn fabric.

Mike raised his hand and brought it down hard, the sound of the slap ringing throughout the small room, and almost knocking Diana off her feet.

She moaned. "*Christ*, Mike —"

"Shut the fuck up." Mike's hand came down again, leaving another bright red mark on her buttock.

"Owwww..."

Roughly, he dragged her snug sweater up her body, pulling it to her neck and over her arms, effectively muffling her head in the fabric. "I said shut up."

A mumble came from inside the wool.

Mike slapped her again, making her hips rock and squirm. "You love it and you know it. Now shut up and take it."

The low light glistened between Diana's thighs as her juices ran from her cunt. Her buttocks were reddening beneath Mike's hard punishment, and her legs were widening, as if bracing herself for the next blow.

It came, fast and savage, and was followed by several more stinging slaps.

Diana sobbed beneath the fabric and her fingers clenched on the back of the couch. "You son of a bitch, fuck me..." she growled.

"Not yet," he shot back. "When I'm good and ready, not before."

He reached out an arm to her desk and grabbed a large paperclip. With an efficient move he reached beneath her, grabbing her clit and pulling it hard.

"*Jesus fucking Christ*," she cried.

Mike pushed the paperclip roughly over her clit, extending it out and away from her flesh. He grabbed two more and treated her nipples to the same hard grip.

Diana sobbed and moaned at the harsh pinches.

"You like that, *Miss Stiles*?" Mike stepped away and surveyed his handiwork.

Diana's breasts dangled free, their nipples protruding and red as the paperclips held them fast. Her clit was gleaming between her legs as she shuddered.

"You like the way I make you feel. Go on. Say it." Mike struck another hard spank on her buttocks.

"Yes, *yes*..." sobbed Diana. "Oh fuck me, *YES*..."

"You didn't ask nicely, *Miss Stiles*," hissed Mike, rubbing his cock over her reddened ass cheeks.

"*P...p...please*—" Diana's moan was barely discernible through the tangled folds of her sweater.

Mike calmly reached for his back pocket and removed a condom, sheathing himself. "Maybe I will. How'd you want it? Up the ass? Hmm? Up the cunt?"

"I don't fucking care. Just *do it*..."

"When *I'm* ready, bitch. Not before. You want it here, maybe?" Mike shoved his hand into Diana's cunt. The force behind it pushed her onto her toes and forced her smothered head down onto the back of the couch.

"*Aaaaggh*," she screamed. "Yes, *more*...do me. Do me *NOW*...I'm fucking *coming* for chrissake — "

Mike wrenched his hand out of her and swiped the juices over his sheathed cock. "You asked for it."

He grabbed her bruised ass and spread her cheeks wide, thrusting at the tight hole his actions revealed.

With one quick movement of his hips, Mike Dean shoved his cock deep into the willing and waiting ass of Diana Stiles, pounding into her until she screamed and sobbed and shuddered beneath him.

He'd never even removed his boots.

* * * * *

"Did you hear something?" Peta paused on the library steps, resting her hand on Max's arm.

"Like what, honey?" Max was busy watching for icy patches, making sure Peta didn't slip, and wondering how many people were in the library at this time of day. He'd never done it in a library.

A flock of blue jays swooped past. "Oh, it must have been them," laughed Peta, watching as they squabbled noisily. "It sounded almost like a scream."

"If you say so. Come on, let's get inside and out of this mess." Max pushed the heavy door open, and they walked into the soothing quiet that seems to be part and parcel of any public library.

"Gosh, I wonder if anyone's here," whispered Peta.

"Why are you whispering?" Max whispered back.

"Have to. It's the law," she answered with a grin.

"Hellooo..." Max's call echoed to the tall ceilings and round the shelves of books that ringed the hall.

There was no answer.

"Well, that settles that," said Max. He closed the door behind them and clicked the lock.

"*Max*. What are you doing? Suppose someone wants a book?" Peta's eyebrows rose in horror. "Or wants to return one, or something?"

"Then they're out of luck. Let's face it, Peta, it's a shitty day. Nobody's going to be out driving around in this muck. They've all got their books or their videos or whatever. We're closed. Too bad." He unbuttoned her coat and tossed it aside, following it with his own. "It does mean one thing, however..."

Breathlessly, Peta stared at him. "What's that?"

He grinned. "It means we have the library to ourselves. We can—browse—to our heart's content. Uninterrupted."

Peta's lips curled up in a rather naughty little grin. "Oh yes. We can, can't we? I didn't think of that."

"Oh I did," said Max. He pulled her against him and rubbed his hips against hers, letting her feel the cock that was hardening by the second beneath his jeans.

"Hmm. I have a feeling that your definition of 'browsing' and mine might differ slightly," murmured Peta, rubbing back.

"Perhaps we can work on establishing a mutual 'definition' of browsing," murmured Max. He dipped his head to hers and ran his tongue around her ear. She shivered in his arms and the little move stoked his inner fires.

God, she touched him. In all the right places and some that felt new, excited, and almost surprised at the sensation.

"Where would you like to start?" Her breath was hot on his neck as she spoke.

"What?"

"Browsing. Where would you like to start? Fiction? Non-fiction? Reference? Or—" She bit back a groan as Max let his tongue trace her neck. "Poetry?"

"Oh *definitely* poetry," he murmured.

"It's...it's this way," she stuttered.

With a sigh, Max let her walk away from him to the far corner of the room. She was still limping a little, but seemed to be able to put weight on her ankle. Max felt foolishly pleased. As if he himself was responsible for her healing.

She disappeared between two tall shelves, and Max glanced around. There. The light switches. He quickly shut off most of the lights, leaving only the essential ones in the front reception area, and a few high on the wall.

"Er, Max?" Peta's voice came from the shadows. "How am I supposed to browse if you turn off the lights?"

"Oh, I'm sure we'll think of something, babe," he grinned.

"Well, you're not making it very easy."

"And you're making it very hard," he quipped. It was the truth, too. Something about the quiet, musty aroma of thousands of books added to the silence which surrounded them was turning him on. Big time.

Of course, it could just be that he was alone with Peta. Memories of their night together lurked in his mind, and he wanted more. Much more.

He trod quietly over to find her, the worn carpet softening his steps and muting the sounds of the outside world. She was at the end of a long aisle of books, idly thumbing the titles, running her fingers over the spines and smiling.

She certainly loved her library.

"Pick one," said Max, making her jump.

"One what?"

"I don't know. Any one. Poetry. I've never been much for poetry. If it doesn't rhyme with 'Nantucket', I probably haven't heard it."

Peta laughed. "There speaks the literary whiz who's editing manuscripts. Shame on you, Max."

He closed in, cornering her against the wall, beneath one of the small lights that dotted the room. "Go ahead, pick one. Read something to me."

Peta sighed and reached out, pulling a volume at random from the shelf and letting the pages fall open in her hands.

"Oh...I...er...maybe not this one," she muttered.

"No, go ahead. I promise I won't laugh." Max was in front of her now, lightly resting his hands on her hips. Not too close, but not too far. He could see her chest rise and fall as she sucked in air, and felt the slight shudder that went through her as he touched her.

She held the book to the side, catching what little light there was. "Ahem, this is by Sarah Teasdale. It's...it's a love poem, Max."

"That's good," he said. "Go on, read some of it."

"Are you sure?"

Max lifted a hand and brushed her hair away from her neck, just brushing his lips against the skin he revealed. "Oh yeah, I'm sure. Read, honey."

Peta cleared her throat again. "Okay," she said. There was a definite quaver in her voice.

Max felt his cock harden even more as her scent surrounded him, that wonderful smell that was so uniquely her. He let his hands wander, just barely touching her, but keeping her aware of his presence.

"*I am not yours,*" she began, voice halting and unsure. "*Nor lost in you.*"

Max slithered his hands down to her waist, brushing her breasts.

"*Not lost, although I long to be...*"

He unsnapped her pants and slid the zipper down, the ratcheting sound punctuating her words.

"*Lost as a candle lit at noon, lost as a snowflake in the sea...*Max, what are you doing?"

Max dropped to his knees in front of her. "Just adding an interactive component to the poetry. Go on."

Peta drew in a raspy breath. "*You love me, and I find you still a spirit...*"

He eased her panties down, dragging them to her thighs along with her jeans.

"Oh heavens, Max..."

"Shhh. Don't stop. Keep reading."

"But suppose someone comes in?"

"They won't. I locked the door, remember? Keep reading."

She shivered beneath his hands as he caressed her belly and leaned forward, running his tongue over her navel.

"*A spirit beautiful and bright, yet I am I, who long to be*...oohhh..."

Max's tongue headed south. He found her mound and the wet softness beneath.

Peta gulped. "*Lost as a light is lost in light.*"

He thrust his face into her, hungry for her taste, needing the sweet juices that were liberally coating her flesh. She was hot to his touch, and her moan let him know that his "interactive component" had hit just the right spot. He smiled against her clit and touched it with the tip of his tongue.

She gasped.

"Read on," he growled.

"I...I...*Oh plunge me deep in love*..."

Max plunged. Deep. His tongue worked her, flicking from her clit to her cunt and back, darting like a mad thing, and making her pant.

"*My senses leave me deaf and blind.*" Her voice was getting harsh as Max kept up his movements, sliding his hands behind her and cupping her cool buttocks in his hot palms. Deaf and blind he could manage. Quite well, to judge by her response.

"*Swept by the tempest of your love*...good grief, Max," she choked.

"That's not in there," he said. "Stick with the poetry." He lowered his mouth to her again, feeling her tense beneath his hands.

"Max, I'm going to...to..."

"I know. I want you to. Keep reading."

"But there's only one more line," she stuttered. Her hips thrust towards him, and her thighs hardened as she fought to spread her legs wider than her hobbling jeans permitted.

"Doesn't matter. Go on." Max felt like a man possessed. His senses were one hundred percent focused on the woman he held, and what he was doing to her. He liked oral sex as much as the next guy, but had often admitted that he preferred being on the receiving end of things. Until now.

Until Peta.

He couldn't get enough of her. Her taste, her scent, her hot honey, which flowed liberally now, soaking her thighs and his lips. She was sweet and different, and all Peta, and he knew he'd never tire of her. Of this. He was addicted already, and she hadn't even come yet.

But she was damned close.

"*A...a...taper...in...the...rushing...wind*...oh God, oh God—"

Max pushed her over the brink and she fell apart, sobbing for air, and coming around his face as he sucked her clit and felt the savage twitching of her cunt as she came.

He buried his face in her, sharing the moment, filled with pride as her body responded. She whimpered and shuddered in his hands as her orgasm rolled over her, her buttocks clenching and her thighs trembling as she let herself go.

He held her, waiting, letting her ride out the tremors as the earthquake inside her body subsided. Then he brushed light kisses along her moist skin, licking her, nibbling on her, soothing her.

He slowly pulled away, and tugged her clothing back up around her, standing at last in front of her, as her eyes opened and blearily tried to focus on his.

Max grinned. "I've suddenly realized something—"

Peta blinked.

"—I *do* like poetry, after all."

Chapter 17

Mike Dean sprawled on the couch, watching Diana as she struggled back into her clothing.

"Christ, pass me a tissue will you? I'm all sticky."

Mike didn't move. "Get it yourself."

"Jesus," muttered Diana, reaching for the box herself. "How can you be like that?"

"Like what?"

"So damn...damn...*cold* about everything."

Mike shrugged. "About what? You like a good rough fuck. So do I. Doesn't mean I have to do the lovey-dovey thing afterwards."

Diana winced a little as she rested her bruised backside on the desk. "Yeah, but with all this other stuff going on? Your ex-wife was just strangled, for chrissake..."

"So?"

"But...she's — she *was* — your wife."

"Yeah. My mistake. She liked it rough, but other than that, we had nothing going. I got out, she was okay with it. What's the big deal?" Mike could have been discussing the weather.

"She's dead. Fucking stone cold dead. Strangled. And I'll bet the cops are looking for you." Diana's voice changed slightly. "Did you do it?"

Mike snorted. "Shit, no. She was my ex, remember? What would I want to strangle her for? And if the cops want me, they'll just have to find me. " He snorted. "They ain't smart enough to look *here*, that's for sure."

Diana chewed her lip. "And yet you came to Mayfield after you got out of jail, right? She was here..."

"Sure she was. We met, we talked. We even fucked once for old times sake. But I had no interest in her, and she had none in me. So she's dead. Tough. Happens to us all eventually."

"Jesus Christ, you're a fucking piece of work, you know that?" Diana shook her head.

"And that's why you like me around, remember? You, and that piece of political crap, Sharp." He allowed a small, cold smile to cross his face. "Who else you gonna get for a three-way, *Miss Stiles*? Don't seem to be too many folks around here who'd do that and not let on about it."

Diana narrowed her eyes. "And are you planning on *letting on about it*?"

Mike rose to his feet. "Dunno." He raised an eyebrow at her. "If the time is right and there's something in it for me. Who knows."

"Mike, you wouldn't...I...I..."

"You'll what? Make it worth my while?" Mike curled his lip. "You ain't got enough cash to buy my silence, *Miss Stiles*. Now Sharp, on the other hand..." He moved to the back door and grabbed his jacket. He turned. "Don't sweat it. Wouldn't do me any good to go broadcasting it around town."

Diana released a sigh of relief. "Where are you going?"

"What's it matter to you? I got someone to see. But I'll be back, as that big guy says in the movies. I like your ass too much. I like the way you fuck. Not many women can take it like that and give it right back. Next time you're gonna suck me off, you got that?"

Diana sighed. "Sure. As long as you can get it up again and fuck me with it, I'll stick it in my ear if you want. I like the way you fuck, too, Mike, if it's of any interest to you."

"It's not."

Mike closed the door behind him, leaving one rather sticky and exhausted woman alone. A smile spread over her face as she lifted her skirt and rubbed her hands over her buttocks.

* * * * *

There was a not-dissimilar smile of satisfaction creeping over the face of Peta Matthews at that same moment, as she curled up on the welcoming lap of Max Wolfe in the Mayfield Library.

They'd found the large and very comfortable chair customarily occupied by Struthers, and had settled themselves into it with a minimum of fuss and bother, fitting against each other like two halves of a puzzle.

Peta sighed. "Max, I don't know quite what to say."

Max nuzzled her hair. "About what?"

She snorted. "You know very well about *what*." She sighed. "About what you just did to me. I've never...I mean no one's ever..."

Max pulled back. "You mean no one's ever gone down on you before?"

Peta could feel the color spreading across her cheeks, and she lowered her gaze, unable to meet the question in his eyes. "Not like that. Not the way you do. Did. And *never* in a library."

Max grinned. And there it was again. That gigawatt smile that lit up every circuit in her body, and made her heart thump madly.

She had to turn away, before she did something monumentally silly, like smother him with kisses or fall in love with him or something.

Bloody hell. Where had that thought come from?

In an effort to distract herself, Peta turned idly to the desk and noticed the dull glow of the monitor. Struthers' computer was on. The screen was dark, but the system was up and running.

"Max, look. The computer's on. I wonder..." She leaned over and grabbed the mouse. Sure enough, as soon as she touched it, the screen flickered to life. "You know, there's something I've been wanting to do, but with all the stuff going on, and work too, I haven't had the time."

"Yeah, me too," murmured Max, stroking her back.

"Well, yes, of course. Um, that too, but hang on a sec...let me see..." She clicked through to the Internet access and located her favorite search engine.

Intently, she typed in a few letters as Max rested his chin on her shoulder and watched. "Mike Dean, huh?"

"Yes, just a minute...here it comes..." A screen full of links appeared.

"Are we trying to play Miss Marple here?" Max's chin dug into her skin as he spoke.

"Certainly not. Well. Maybe. Just a little. I'm naturally curious."

Max chuckled, jiggling her on his lap. And that other hard thing that was pressing into her thighs and severely distracting her. She sighed and returned her thoughts to the screen, narrowing her search.

"Here we are. Mike Dean. A mention in the paper that he'd been sentenced...oh look. Three to five years. A plea bargain. Yeah, forgery, just like Frank said."

"What's this one?" Max pointed at a link lower on the screen from a federal site.

"Umm...let's see...oh wow. Charges of aggravated assault dismissed." She narrowed her eyes and read the public report of an incident at the Federal Penitentiary. *"Michael S. Dean was cleared of the charge of aggravated assault when another inmate came forward with an eyewitness account of the incident. Dean's sentence will not be affected by this matter. He is currently scheduled for release on..."*

"Hmm. Tough customer." Max's words echoed Peta's own thoughts.

"Yes, absolutely. Tough enough to kill Sandra, do you think?"

"If she pissed him off, yeah. I wouldn't doubt it," said Max thoughtfully. "Why don't you put those nimble fingers of yours to good use? Check out Mr. Cary Stiles?"

Peta snickered. "For what? Arrogant handsomeness?"

"You think he's handsome?" Max's head jerked.

"Of course. He works hard at it too. Doesn't mean I like him for it."

"He's not *gorgeous*, huh?"

Peta sighed. "I knew I wasn't going to live that down." She typed in the name and hit enter. Another couple of searches later, and she'd reduced the links to those related to their Cary Stiles, not Cary Stiles the landscape gardener from Florida, or Stiles Cary, the well-known porn star.

"Here we go," muttered Peta. "Owner of Cary's Cafés. Recently awarded local Businessman of the Year...yeah...yeah..." She scrolled down the screen. "Hmm."

"Hmm?" Max leaned over her shoulder.

"Hmm, as in apparently Cary had a hard time getting a couple of permits here. Look..." Peta pointed at the Town Meeting rosters she'd located. "He wanted a certain building that wasn't zoned for restaurant operation. But look, see here? The matter was suddenly settled. In Cary's favor too."

"Bet that cost him a pretty penny." Max's tone was thoughtful.

"Good God." Peta straightened in Max's arms. "I don't believe it."

"What?"

"This photo. *Café and Capo*. Hell of a caption."

They both stared at the grainy image on the tabloid website.

Peta read on. "*Seen enjoying each other's company at the local Eagle Feather Casino last night were noted restaurateur Cary Stiles and Mario Vincenzo, both of whom were trying their luck at the baccarat tables. An unusual pairing, since Mr. Vincenzo is currently the target of a federal racketeering task force investigation. Perhaps Mr. Stiles was looking for some new recipes for 'Capo-ccino' to add to his menu?*"

"Wow," said Max.

"Wow, indeed." Peta closed the screen and leaned back against Max's chest. "So where does this leave us?"

"Cuddling in Struthers' chair?"

"Quite." She tried to focus, but it was damned hard when Max kept brushing against her ear like that.

She sighed. "Okay. So we have Mike Dean, who seems quite capable of murder, and is the most likely suspect. And of course we know that the murderer is never the most likely suspect, right?"

"Right," answered Max. He bit her neck and licked the small mark.

"Ooooh," groaned Peta. "Max, cut it out. Let me think here."

It was Max's turn to sigh. "You're no fun."

"Hmph. You didn't think that an hour ago." She turned and smiled at him.

He pressed a quick kiss on her lips, making her dizzy. "That's right. But you're like Chinese food. An hour later and I'm hungry again."

Peta glanced at her watch. "Look, give us a little longer and then we'll go home, all right?"

Max shifted slightly beneath her thighs. "I guess I can survive. But if I die from unrequited lust, it's all your fault."

Peta hesitated. "I—I could 'requite' it, if you want..."

Max bit his lip. "I know, honey. I know. But I'd rather wait until the *requiting* can take place in slightly more romantic surroundings."

"You would?"

"Well, no. Yes. Hell, I want to fuck you, sweetheart. For hours. I want to be inside you so bad I'm hurting with it. I don't see a comfortable place around here, and although I'm so ready I could take you right here and now, it wouldn't be enough." He licked her earlobe. "For either of us."

Peta swallowed, held captive by the heat she saw in his eyes. She wanted the same thing too. Her body ached at his words, and her mind swam from the images he'd conjured up.

"Oh Max," she sighed, and kissed him.

Max kissed her back. Their lips met and moved and searched and each found what the other was looking for. The heat and the taste and the sensation that told them both something special was happening.

Stunned, they drew apart.

Max watched Peta's eyes as she opened them and met his gaze. He knew he probably looked the same. Like a deer caught in the headlights.

He cleared his throat awkwardly, unsure of himself for the first time he could remember.

Peta shifted on his lap, and drew in a deep breath before turning back to the screen.

"Well, uh, I suppose we should turn this off for Struthers," she said.

"Wait up a minute," said Max. A few words had caught his eye. "What's this?"

Peta clicked around. "It's Struthers' request list. You know, if someone comes in and wants to reserve a book? Or get one from the Library Net?"

"Got it. Check this out..." He pointed at one particular entry.

"Hmm." Peta struggled with the unfamiliar program. "Got it. Here it is. Oh, this is interesting..."

She leaned forward, brushing Max's arm with her breast. He struggled manfully with himself, torn between the urge to cup it or read what was on the screen. His curiosity got the better of him, however, and he followed Peta's cursor as she traced various links.

"The King James Bible. Someone's been doing some research into antique books." She clicked some more. "Edward Sharp. He's been requesting reference material on the '*he*' Bible."

"Bibles are gender-specific?" Max was puzzled. In his experience, books were pretty much sexless. Excluding Playboy, of course, which didn't really qualify as a book. Unless one made it past the centerfold to read the articles.

"No, but this one is special. The first King James Bibles were printed—if you want to call it that—in 1611 or so."

Max watched as Peta slipped into lecture-mode. Her eyes were intense and focused, and he was charmed as she reeled off facts and figures. This was, indeed, one very bright lady he was cuddling.

He backed off a little from his thoughts, wondering why they were making him slightly uncomfortable. Not for the obvious reason, either. His fascination with Peta went far deeper than his cock. It went to places untouched by a woman's hands. Places that he never realized were so sensitive. Emma Hansell had sparked a couple of them to life, but Peta seemed to have set a huge blaze going.

He wasn't too sure if he liked it or not.

"It was bound in leather..." Her voice pulled him back from his contemplations and he struggled to follow her narrative.

"About sixteen inches across by ten inches or so, and it was called the 'he' Bible because of a misprint in the first 50 copies. Oh, Max look...there's a photo of one of them."

Peta pointed and sure enough, the page from the Old Testament that had been scanned into the website featured a glaring error in Ruth, Chapter 3, Verse 15. Highlighted, of course, for those whose biblical knowledge didn't include a familiarity with the Book of Ruth.

People like Max.

"Instead of saying 'she went into the citie', the original had been printed to read 'he went into the citie'. The error was found and corrected," continued Peta, *"and another one hundred and fifty were printed with the right word. Those are known as the 'she' Bible."*

"Logical. Flawlessly logical."

"Thank you Mr. Spock." Peta clicked on, ignoring him. *"The estimated worth of the 'he' Bible is in the range of one to two hundred thousand dollars. In a recent auction at Sotheby's, one sold for over four hundred thousand dollars. Wow."*

"Wow is right. That's a whole lot of cold hard cash for one book."

"Yes, but Max. Think how rare they are. Only fifty known copies in existence. Printed in the time of King James, for God's sake. I know you Colonials think that anything that happened before 1776 is ancient history, but in fact, life was raring along quite nicely long before the Pilgrims landed in Plymouth. King James followed

Elizabeth the First, and was the first monarch to unite both England and Scotland under one flag—"

"Er, thank you, Miss Matthews. Will there be a quiz later?"

"Max?"

"Yes?"

"Sod off."

Correctly interpreting this to be the British version of "fuck you", Max subsided, and considered the information they'd uncovered. "So Edward Sharp has a fascination with old books, does he?"

Peta wrinkled her nose. "Apparently so. He's certainly asked Struthers to dig up plenty of reference material. It would seem that several copies made their way across the Atlantic too...here's one for sale at an American Collector's site...hmm...it's a steal at a hundred and sixty-five thou."

Max grimaced. Peta's definition of a "steal" differed from his. For that kind of money he could pick up a really smart little Ferrari. Or a nice house, come to think of it.

Now why should he think of that?

"Oh, and for the modest sum of three hundred dollars or so, you can buy an actual page from a 1611 Bible. Now *that's* nice..."

Max grinned. When shopping on the Internet, most women would be rooting through pages of over-priced lingerie. But not his Peta. She was slobbering over some ratty old paper from four hundred years ago.

She was one special woman.

And the realization scared the crap out of him.

He reached over and shut down the system. "Let's go home," he said.

Peta slid from his lap as he stood, and her eyes stared at his. The gray turned stormy as his hand held her close.

"Forget the books, forget the suspects and the hell with motives. Let's just go home."

She licked her lips. "Okay."

Chapter 18

"I got your message." The air was cold around him, sleet falling hard now, making the earth slippery and gray and turning the remaining snow into ugly piles of discolored slush. It was nearly dark.

"Yeah. So I see."

He swallowed his distaste for this practically subhuman man. If only his brains matched his muscles. "So what did you want?"

"I want to know what you talked to Sandra about."

He feigned ignorance. "I'm sorry? I don't know what you mean?"

"Yeah you do. Don't fuck with me." Mike Dean came nearer. *"You were after something. She told me."'*

"She did, huh?" Well, damn it to hell. This certainly threw a wrinkle into his carefully laid plans. Fortunately, he'd come prepared.

"Yeah. She did. Told me you were after a box or something. A special kind of box." Dean circled him.

"Oh, that box." He took comfort from the feel of the knife handle in his pocket.

"Yeah. THAT box. Seems you wanted it pretty bad too. So I'm figuring..."

Good God. Dean was actually thinking. This must be a first.

"I'm figuring it's gotta be pretty valuable. If you wanted it bad enough to fuck Sandra for it."

"Perhaps I just wanted to – er – fuck Sandra, as you so eloquently put it?"

Dean snorted. "Nah, she ain't your type. She likes it rough. Far rougher than you could manage."

A haze of anger filled his mind, and his bile rose. What an arrogant and ignorant prick this man was. He deserved everything he got.

"Now if you was to tell me what you're looking for, perhaps I could help. And then perhaps we could split it. Or..." Dean let his voice trail off suggestively.

"Or what? You'll practice some of the delightful tricks inmates pick up behind those high walls, I suppose?"

"Yeah. I could always see how you like it up the ass. Or I might just drop a few words in some official ears. Like the ones that have a hat between them. A cop hat."

"I see. This would be a...what's the word...a shakedown, right?"

"Got it in one."

"No." His anger flooded him and strengthened him. If Dean thought he would ever, EVER share what was rightfully his, then Dean was stupider than he looked. Which would be hard. He suppressed a chuckle. Once again someone was underestimating him.

"No?"

"Correct. The answer is no. Not only won't I even consider sharing with someone who has to pick his knuckles up off the ground to scratch his knees, but I refuse to be intimidated or scared by your threats. What I want is none of your business. And it will stay that way."

Dean's face tightened into lines of anger. "Gonna take the consequences, then, are ya?" Dean neared him, menacingly, fists clenched. "Perhaps I can change your tune."

"*I doubt it, you incompetent fool. I've come too far and waited too long to let someone like you get in my way...*"

His hand flew up from his pocket and the knife caught Mike Dean by surprise. He staggered as the vicious blade sliced through his jacket and into his chest without stopping.

Dean gasped and coughed, looking down as the blood seeped slowly from the wound.

"*You fucker,*" he grunted. "*You dirty little motherfucker. I never figured you for this kind of shit...*"

"*That's probably a big part of your problem.*" He twisted the knife, driving it even higher into Dean's ribcage and pushing him backwards towards the tarpaulin spread on the ground behind him. "*You don't figure all the odds, Mike. You're too stupid to live, as they say.*"

Dean's eyes glazed and he stumbled, gasping a hoarse cough as his falling weight wrenched the knife through his organs. He collapsed.

The blue tarp contrasted quite nicely with the snow, and the blood on Dean's clothing provided a rather impressionistic splash of color.

The killer sighed, sparing but a moment to appreciate the collage. It was damned annoying. Now he had to dispose of the body. Again.

Chapter 19

"This is some weird kind of ritual, isn't it?"

Max's question brought a smile to Peta's face as she concentrated on what she was doing. "Absolutely. Miss one step and you're in big trouble."

Max grunted from his position as observer, seated at Peta's kitchen table.

She continued. "Now after you've put the boiling water in the pot, you swirl it around, like this." She swirled. "Then you dump it out, like so." The water was dumped.

Max sighed.

"Now, the pot is nice and warm, so we can begin. Here's the tea—" Peta showed him the contents of the elegantly decorated tin she'd pulled from a cabinet.

"That's not tea. No bag. Tea comes in bags."

She chuckled to herself. Max was so...so American at times. "No it doesn't. Be quiet and watch. Making a good cuppa is a very valuable skill. One spoonful per person and one for the pot." She carefully measured three spoons of loose tealeaves into the "nicely warmed" pot. "And *then*, making sure the water is boiling, we pour it in."

Peta carefully removed the kettle from the top of the stove and filled the pot with boiling water. She smiled, put the top back on, and carefully brought it to the table, setting it in front of Max with a smug grin.

"There."

Max raised an eyebrow. "Do we get naked now, and dance around the table? Wait for the next full moon and bury it beneath a rowan tree?"

Peta chuckled. "No more paranormals for you, I think." She sat down, making sure the cups, the milk and the sugar were all within reach. "No, no chanting or burying. We let it steep."

"For how long?"

"Until it's ready."

"Ah." Max sighed again, but she caught the hint of humor in his eyes. She snuggled a quilted cover over the pot.

"What's that?" asked Max curiously.

"A tea cozy."

"Tea what?"

"Tea cozy. It keeps the heat in the pot while the tea steeps. Very important."

"Uh huh." Max shook his head. "You ever hear the term obsessive-compulsive?"

"Honestly, Max. Once you've had tea made like this, you'll never go back to bags again."

"Right." His expression gave him away. One hundred percent skeptic.

Peta toyed with her spoon. "So who do you think did it, Max? Any theories?"

"It's bugging you, isn't it?"

"And it's not bugging you?"

Max ran his hands through his hair and stared absently at the teapot. "Well, yeah, I must admit I'd like to know who's behind it. Such a savage murder. It screams out passion and hatred, and maybe insanity, I don't know."

Peta looked at him. Her heart quivered as she noted his rumpled hair, and the thoughtful look in his eyes. His shoulders were so strong, and yet his hands could be so gentle. And his mouth...well, she blushed just thinking about what his mouth could do to her body.

"Perhaps it was someone she met at the bar? A stranger? A date she picked up...or just some guy she took off with and let him get a bit too rough?"

"What?" Peta summoned her mind back from delightful sensual areas of exploration and tried to focus.

"Sandra's killer. If there was any kind of motive I'd be a lot happier."

Peta snorted. "So would the police most probably."

"Money is a good motive, you know. And we've found out that Cary Stiles might well be in debt to some rather unforgiving gentlemen with multisyllabic continental names..."

Peta nodded, and stood. "Bickies with our tea, I think," she said. "Go on, Max, I'm listening. Dr. Watson to your Holmes." She cocked an eyebrow at him. "Elementary, dear Watson," she quipped.

Max smiled. "Well, we're assuming it's someone we know. That's probably stupid, but bear with me here."

"All right." Peta put the "bickies", which apparently translated into a plate of cookies, on the table and moved to Max, carefully kneeling down on the floor between his legs.

He gulped. "Uh...what are you doing? "

She'd slid her hands along his thighs and was just resting them there. "Letting the tea steep. Listening to you as you expound your amazingly acute observations on murder. Relaxing...go on. You were talking about Cary?"

Max swallowed as she settled herself comfortably. Very comfortably.

Peta was in her element. She had Max distracted with the talk of murder and mayhem, and she herself was about to distract his brain out of his ears. She hadn't spent one summer researching male genitalia for nothing.

Her hands slid to his fly, and she heard his breath catch as she let her fingers rest on his zipper. A rather solid bulge was distorting the fabric.

"Max. You're not talking."

"Uhhh..."

Peta snickered to herself. She'd actually rendered the great Max Wolfe speechless. Or at least her fingers had as they slowly tugged the zipper down and released the swollen flesh beneath. It thrust between the two halves of his fly, still confined by his underwear, but more than ready to come out and play. Peta licked her lips.

"So Cary might need money, yes?" She asked the question as she pushed Max's pants down around his hips, making him wiggle in the chair so that she could free him. He may have been speechless, but it was a quite willing wiggle.

"Yeah," he breathed. "Yeah. Cary might have needed...ahh—"

She held him. Held his hard cock, ran her hands over it and took a good long look at this good long piece of manhood that Max wielded like some medieval sword on the women he conquered.

"Keep talking, Max," she urged. Payback. Pure poetic payback. She grinned as she lowered her mouth to him.

"I...shit, Peta...oh lord—"

He was smooth as silk between her lips as she bent to him. She'd ached for this moment, ever since he'd rendered her totally useless in the library. Wanted the chance to show him what it felt like, to turn to jelly in someone's arms and lose oneself in their touch.

Now was her chance. "You're not talking," she whispered. Her breath spread over his slick cock.

"You're right," he rasped.

She risked a look up at him beneath her eyelashes and her heart thumped at the expression on his face.

He burned.

His eyes seared her with fires that she'd personally stoked, his hair was mussed, a delightful color was sweeping across his cheeks, and those wonderful Wolfe lips were slightly parted.

Yes, there was no doubt about it, she was turning him on. And of course the ramrod hard cock in her mouth was a dead giveaway too.

"Peta..." His hand went to her head, and she paused, wondering if he was going to stop her. But no. He simply ran his fingers through her hair, and rubbed her scalp beneath it, neither pushing her nor holding her in place, but just resting his hand alongside her head as she moved on him.

Peta felt a swell of pleasure flood from her loins to her lips. Max tasted wonderful. Uniquely him, all man, with a dash of soap and fabric softener thrown in to the mix.

She couldn't help but smile around his cock as she traced the long veins down to its base with her tongue.

Max moaned.

"Christ, babe," he muttered.

"How come you're not talking to me, Mr. Holmes?" she grinned, letting her lips dot light kisses along his length.

"Because that's not my *pipe* you've got in your mouth, Dr. Watson," gritted out Max. "You don't have to —"

"Oh but I *want* to, Max. Do you mind?"

"Mind?" The retort gushed out on a large exhalation as Peta's tongue found a particularly sensitive spot. She returned to it again and again, making Max's hips squirm.

"No, I don't...I don't...oh sheeeiiittt," gasped Max. "D'you know what you're doing to me?"

Peta didn't answer. She was too busy setting up a rhythm between her hand and her mouth, and spreading moisture over as much of Max as she could swallow at one time. And, surprisingly enough, that was quite a bit.

She let her other hand delve between his thighs and find his balls. He jerked as she caressed them, gently rolling them around over her hand.

Peta slipped her mouth off him for a moment. "Is that nice, Max?" she inquired politely.

Max groaned.

She'd take that as a yes. She returned with renewed enthusiasm to Max's cock, playing and loving it with her mouth and her hands. She did all the things she'd read about, invented a few more, and when she found that particularly sensitive pressure point behind his balls, Max gasped out loud.

"Peta...too much...I'm gonna come, honey—" His voice was harsh as he fought to hold himself back.

"That's okay, Max. You made me come. Now it's my turn." She blew a breath over the very tip and licked at the small bead of pre-come that oozed from the tiny eye.

He choked. "Peta, shit, Petaaaa..."

Max was in the very throes of ecstasy. The thought flashed through his mind that this phrase, used extensively by the many romance writers whose work he'd edited, actually meant something when a woman's mouth was clamped firmly around one's cock.

He pulled her head away, amazing himself as he did so. He wanted Peta. He loved her mouth on him, and would happily have come right then and there, but things were changing for him. Superstud Max Wolfe wanted more.

He shivered as the realization flooded him, and promised himself some time to figure it all out. Later. Right now, there was only one thing he wanted.

"Sweetheart," he said. "I want to be in you when I come." He reached down to his pants pocket as she leaned back with a question in her eyes.

Pulling a condom out, he passed it to her. "Please. Put this on me."

He knew his voice was rough, harsh even, since he was fighting tooth and nail to hold on to his orgasm. Her touch as she unrolled the latex sheath damn near sent him over the edge.

But something held him back. Some need, some desire, something from way down deep inside him that was telling him not to erupt into this woman's hands, but into her body, where he belonged.

Belonged. That was a novel concept. "Now take your jeans off, honey. Everything. Ride me, Peta."

"What, here? In the kitchen?" Peta sounded scandalized, and a painful grin slid over Max's lips.

"Afraid you'll shock the tea cozy?"

She narrowed her eyes and stared at him, then dropped her hands to her belt. His heart rate soared as she kicked off her shoes, stripped her jeans, and slid her panties down with them.

He could smell her, see her moisture shining between her thighs, and even though he was milliseconds away from coming, he still wanted to devour her, taste her, cover her with licks and kisses and get her naked skin against his.

Blushing, Peta looked at him helplessly, the erotic picture she made as she stood there, naked from the waist down, burning his retinas straight through to his balls.

He opened his arms, holding them out and beckoning her to straddle his lap.

"Uh, Max? Is this going to work?"

"Oh yeah, babe. It'll work. C'mere."

Carefully, Peta spread her legs and eased herself onto his lap. "Put me inside you, sweetheart," he growled as her heat singed his thighs.

"All right," she whispered. The intent look in her eyes as she reached for his cock and positioned it at the opening of her cunt nearly undid him.

He bit his lip, allowing the small pain to keep him from exploding as her hot wetness began to slide down over him.

"Ah, God, yeah," he sighed.

"Oh Max," she whimpered. "This is...this is amazing."

"Isn't it though?" he answered. His hands slipped behind her, grabbing her buttocks and positioning her just exactly where he wanted her. She settled all the way down on him, resting on him for a moment and apparently examining the sensations she was experiencing.

"You fill me, Max," she breathed.

"I know," he answered. "I know."

Her feet touched the floor either side of the kitchen chair, and in response to a slight movement of his hands, she rose a little then sank back down.

Max moaned. "Oh yeah, just like that, babe. Oh God."

Peta rode him. Max's mind blanked, and he lost himself in her. She was loving him with her cunt, experimenting, playing, tightening her muscles around his cock as she moved.

It was heaven. Bliss. Beyond description. Max couldn't think at all — he could only feel.

She took him so deep that he swore he could feel her womb as she pressed down on him.

Knowing her movements would make him come within seconds, he slowed her with one hand on her hip and slid the other between their bodies to find her clit.

A gasp told him he'd been accurate. He toyed with it, slicking her moisture around and holding her motionless, watching the sweat break out on her lip as she tried to obey, tried to fight the urge to move on him.

Their breath mingled and their eyes met, gray staring into hazel. For one blinding moment, Max could see himself, as if reflected by Peta's soul.

He looked—strange. Soft, hot and passionate, and he barely recognized the Max Wolfe staring back at him. A shiver took him that had nothing to do with her cunt or his cock. This was something else.

His fingers worked her, making her shudder and shake and she moaned as she rested her forehead against his.

"Max...I..."

"Let it go, babe. Come for me. Come now..." He pushed harder against her clit as she gave up the battle and ground her hips against him.

He was so primed for orgasm that the first inner twitchings of her cunt were enough.

His buttocks clenched painfully and he cried out as the final dam broke and he spurted his come deep inside Peta.

She sobbed in his arms, trembling with her own orgasm, and feeding his with the thousand minute inner fingers that were running up and down his cock like little lightning bolts of pleasure.

Their world shook as their bodies merged and melded into one throbbing and screaming moment of release.

Peta's hands were digging painfully into his shoulders, and he realized he'd clamped his own fingers deeply into one of her buttocks. He slowly eased the pressure, letting her put her weight down fully on his lap.

Once again he leaned his forehead against hers and closed his eyes. Flooded with feelings he couldn't explain, Max rested there, content, holding his woman. Their skin was stuck together from the heat they'd generated, and she was panting a little as the tension left her and she leaned into his embrace.

"Are you all right?" He asked the question cautiously, hoping she wouldn't ask him the same thing. He wasn't sure if he was all right. Or ever would be again.

"Flat out knackered," she mumbled.

Max frowned, and was about to ask for a translation when their world rocked again.

Literally, this time.

Chapter 20

"What the dickens..." Peta pulled herself up with a quick jerk, almost leaping off Max's cock as the house shuddered around them.

That had been one hell of a loud crash outside.

She struggled with her panties, cursing the weakness that still sent trembles through her limbs. Her ankle was aching, her thighs were sticky, and she'd never felt better. She cursed whoever or whatever it was that had destroyed the moment.

"Wait for me," called Max, as he disposed of the condom and hurried to pull his own clothes back into place.

Together they staggered to the front door and opened it, unsure of what they'd find outside.

Darkness had fallen, and the sleet had changed to snow, coating the roads and the slush with a fresh veneer of white.

A snow plow, bearing the logo of the Mayfield Department of Public Works, was angled drunkenly up on one snowbank, tangled with two cars and an unfortunate dumpster.

The driver was out of the cab, and staring at something on the sidewalk in front of Peta's house.

He looked up as Peta opened her door. "Christ, call the cops and an ambulance, will you? I think I hit this guy..."

Max dashed for the phone as Peta carefully made her way down the steps. He was at her side again within moments.

"The cops are on their way," he called, as he followed Peta to the dark mass sprawled in the snow.

"Oh Mary Mother of God..." breathed Peta.

It was a body. A man's body, lying face down in front of them with blood staining the whiteness around him.

"I swear I didn't see him until it was too late, so help me," gasped the driver. "I was just doing the regular plowing, and he staggered out in front of me. I couldn't stop in time. Oh shit...is he hurt bad?"

Max bent down, and Peta held her breath as he touched his fingers to the man's neck.

He glanced up at her and shook his head. "Nothing. I can't feel anything."

Sirens sounded, and two police cars pulled carefully alongside, lights flashing and radios blaring. Frank Summers leaped from the first one.

"You guys all right?" he barked.

"We're fine," said Max. "It's this guy. Snowplow hit him, apparently..." He nodded at the man lying at their feet.

Frank walked carefully around, and leaned over, doing the same thing Max had just done—searching for a pulse.

"Oh fuck," he breathed. "Doesn't look good." Gently he eased him onto his back.

The wide-open sightless eyes of Mike Dean stared at the snowy sky. A pool of blood stained the front of his jacket and the handle of a knife could clearly be seen protruding from his chest.

Peta swallowed. And swallowed again. And then rushed behind the nearest shrub and heaved up everything in her stomach and down to her toes. The image of Dean's body, all bloody, and that knife—Peta retched again.

A hand was rubbing between her shoulder blades. "You okay, babe?"

"Shit, Max, go away. Please just let me be sick in private..."

The hand kept rubbing. "Take deep breaths, honey. It's okay."

Peta swallowed and grabbed a handful of snow, rubbing its harsh coldness over her face and into her mouth.

The shock of the icy crystals brought her out of her nausea. "Sorry, Max. I've never seen anything like that..."

He hugged her and she took comfort from his touch. "I know, love. I'm sorry. If I'd had any idea..."

"Don't be silly. I'm fine now. It was just the shock. Come on, Frank will probably have questions."

Squaring her shoulders, Peta turned back to the street, unaware of the look of awe in Max's eyes. It was time to find out what the *fuck* was going on.

Frank had men everywhere and more cars were arriving. Yellow cordon tapes were appearing, and the body lay undisturbed on the sidewalk, as police scurried around securing the scene.

Max and Peta crossed carefully to Frank's side.

"Nasty business, this," said Frank.

"Murder usually is, isn't it?" answered Peta acerbically.

"Well, we don't get too many, that's for sure." Frank frowned. "And Mike Dean, too. So soon after his ex-wife."

Max frowned as well. "Does this get him off the suspect list for her killing, Frank?"

The Lieutenant sighed. "I suppose we'll never know, now."

An officer hurried up to Frank. "Found some blood further up the street," he said curtly, and Frank nodded at Peta and Max.

"You two would be better off out of this. Let us do our job and I'll stop by in a while."

Peta agreed. She was shaking a little now, and realized that the street had filled with onlookers. The last thing the police needed was a crowd, and already Frank's men were attempting to herd people back into their homes.

"We'll be here if you need anything, Frank," she said, turning to Max. He took her hand without a word and led her back indoors.

She sat at the table and shook. She couldn't stop. Tremors rattled her from her teeth to her kneecaps, and she was barely aware of Max as he moved around the kitchen.

A cup of steaming tea appeared in front of her along with a curt command. "Drink this."

Obediently, she lifted the mug, finding that she needed two hands to stop it from slopping all over the place. She winced as the boiling sweet liquid burned her lips. "Ack, Max...that's...that's awful. How much sugar did you put in it?"

"Dunno. And I had to nuke it, too. You need hot and sweet right now, Peta. It's the shock that's making you shiver. Drink it, babe."

She took a shuddering breath and swallowed, letting the heat flood down her throat and warm her belly. Max was right. It did help. Good old tea—better than Valium any day.

As the shaking eased, she raised her head and stared at Max. His brow was furrowed, and his eyes worried as he stared back at her.

"I don't like this, Max. I don't like this at all. What the hell is going on?"

Max sighed and ran a hand through his hair. "Looks like someone's got it in for the Dean family, married or not," he said.

Peta's thoughts ran wild as Max prowled her kitchen. Unable to sit still, it seemed, he opened and closed cupboards, fussing around, fidgeting with crockery and doing God-knew-what.

The smell of bacon finally penetrated her contemplative fog, and she stared as Max plunked a plate down on the table in front of her.

"Eat," he ordered. Putting another plate down, he pulled out the chair next to her and sat down.

"What's this?"

"Peanut butter and bacon sandwiches."

"You're joking." Peta poked at the creation on her plate.

"The Colonial version of beans on toast. Protein and carbs. Eat."

"Er...Max..." Mindful of the state of her stomach, Peta looked cautiously at Max's offering.

"It could be worse."

"It could?" For the moment, Peta couldn't see how.

"Sure. If I was Elvis, that would be deep fried and have bananas in it too."

Peta closed her eyes, but the scent of the bacon had awakened her taste buds and she realized she was hungry. Tentatively, she took a bite and chewed.

She glanced at Max to find him watching her as he devoured his own sandwich. He licked his lips and grinned. "Well?"

"Um...not bad, actually. Not bad at all." And it wasn't. The crunchy bacon blended nicely with the peanut butter and Peta found she'd finished it off with no problems at all.

"Want another?"

"Er, no. Not right now. I'll take another cup of tea though. Perhaps with only one lump of sugar this time..." She smiled at him.

Max poured the tea and it dawned on Peta how comfortable this was. Being here with Max, sitting around the table, eating, having tea. Just like any ordinary couple. Any ordinary *married* couple.

Oh *bollocks*. She was in trouble. Very big trouble. Marriage and Max might begin with the same letter but that was just about all they had in common. Peta closed her eyes against the hurt that pinged within her heart.

"Look, try not to think about it, all right?" Max's voice sounded worried.

If only he knew what she *was* thinking about. But then again, perhaps it was better he didn't. He'd probably be out the door so fast even Frank's speediest cop car wouldn't be able to catch him.

She grimaced. "Can't help it. It isn't every day someone winds up dead practically on our doorstep."

"Well, there is that," agreed Max.

A loud pounding on Peta's back door made them both jump, and Peta gripped her cup as Max went through the mudroom to see who it was.

Diana Stiles erupted into the room, practically hanging off Max's neck. If his face was anything to go by, he wasn't exactly enjoying the experience.

Peta sighed. *Just* what she needed. This was probably going to call for a couple more pots of tea.

* * * * *

Max had a hard time hiding the distaste he was feeling as Diana threw herself into his arms.

"Max, how awful for you. I came as soon as I heard."

He staggered back into the kitchen, only too aware of Peta's eyebrows as they shot up her forehead. Diana was clinging to him and she was no lightweight.

He managed to detach himself.

"A body. And outside your door too. How dreadful for you, you poor thing."

"Quite," said Peta.

"Oh, of course, yes. Hello Peta. Terrible, terrible thing," said Diana dismissively. Pouting a little as Max deposited her in her chair, she continued on regardless. "Did you see it, Max? What happened?"

Max beat a strategic retreat to Peta's side of the table and poured another cup of tea. Diana looked at it like it was about to bite her. "What's this?"

"Tea," snapped Peta.

Max tried to hide a grin. "The British version of penicillin, Diana."

Peta wrinkled her nose at him.

Diana frowned at the byplay. "So anyway," she pushed the cup aside. "Tell me what happened?"

Max sighed and sat down, away from Diana's reach, just in case. Nothing wrong with being cautious. The fact that he was nearer Peta helped too. "We thought a snowplow had hit someone. We were, sadly, wrong."

"I don't understand." Diana pursed her lips in a little moue of confusion.

"Hellooo..." Frank Summer's voice echoed from the front door.

"In here, Frank," called Peta. "Come on in."

"Sorry to intrude — oh, hello Diana."

Diana turned her megawatt smile on the Lieutenant. "Hello Frank, dear. I just dropped by to find out what was going on. All the sirens and lights...I was worried..." Her gaze flew to Max and left everyone in the room in no doubt as to who had been occupying her thoughts.

Max, faced with three pairs of eyes, did something he didn't think he was capable of doing. He blushed.

"Well, Diana," said Frank, clearing his throat. "It's not good, that's for sure."

"An accident, was it? I saw the snowplow on the bank."

Frank's gaze fell to his hands. "No. This was no accident. Mike Dean was murdered."

Max was astounded at the effect these words had on Diana. She blanched pure white and her hand started to shake.

"M...M...Mike D...Dean?" The words were little more than a whisper, and even Peta was leaning forward as if she, too, sensed this woman's shock and horror.

Frank's eyes narrowed. "Yes, Mike Dean. Did you know him, Diana?"

Diana swallowed with difficulty, and Max noted the tears that filled her eyes. He flashed a glance at Peta, and they shared a moment of unspoken communication. Diana *had* known Mike Dean.

"Yeah," Diana whispered. "Yeah, you could say that I knew him."

Frank reached for his notebook. "Diana, I'd like to ask you some questions, if you don't mind. Would you like to come down to the station with me? Or will you be okay doing it here?"

Max stood. "Look, Peta and I can give you guys some privacy if you want," he said.

Diana waved her hand. "No, no. It's okay. It doesn't matter who knows now, I suppose."

Frank cleared his throat. "Can you tell me how you knew Dean and the nature of your relationship with him?"

Diana bit back a sound that was half a laugh and half a sob. "Relationship?" She twisted her hands. "I don't think you could call it that, Frank. We just...used each other." She looked down, hiding her eyes. "For sex."

The last two words were whispered, and the other three had to lean in to catch them.

Frank sighed. "Okay. Fair enough. When did you see him last?"

Diana raised her head. "Today. He came by my store today. We...we...um...spent some time together, and then he said he had to leave. He had to see someone."

Frank was writing notes furiously in his book, and Max was listening intently. He wondered who else, if anyone, had been present. He knew, first hand, what Diana liked. And thank God, he didn't. He was a one-on-one kind of guy. Correction, a one-on-Peta kind of guy.

"Did he say who he was going to see?" Frank paused in his writing.

Diana shook her head. "No, he didn't. Mike didn't...talk much."

Frank turned to Peta and Max and took their brief statements about the actual incident. Neither of them blushed when asked to recount what they'd felt when the snowplow had skidded off the street.

As far as Frank and Diana knew, they'd been having tea and heard the crash. It was a masterful job of flat out lying, and Max was proud of both himself and his woman. *His* woman. Yes, his woman. He rolled the words around his brain and tucked them away for the time being.

Frank stood. "Well, I guess this'll do it for now." He looked at Max, in a man-to-man sort of way. "We found blood evidence further up the street that suggests Dean was dumped from a moving vehicle and staggered this far, only to get hit by the snowplow."

Peta sucked in a breath. "Could he have survived, do you think, Frank?"

Frank shook his head. "I doubt it. He was on his last legs. The Doc says the knife wound was deep and high, catching the heart and the aorta. He'd bled out internally, but the snowplow opened up the wound."

Peta swallowed and Max rested his hand comfortingly on her shoulder. Diana sniffed loudly, but he couldn't give a shit. It was Peta who had the whole focus of his attention.

"Terrible thing for Mayfield. Two killings. Just terrible." Frank nodded at them all and left.

"He's starting to sound like Edward Sharp," mused Max absently.

"Oh *GOD*," squawked Diana. "*Edward.*"

"What about him?" said Peta, tilting her head.

Diana's color returned with a vengeance, flooding her face from chin to forehead.

Max sighed as the coins dropped into place within his brain. "Edward was your third, wasn't he, Diana?"

"Your third? I don't understand..." Peta's comment brought a painful twist to Diana's lips.

"You wouldn't," she said snidely.

Max's grip on Peta's shoulder tightened, but he spoke to Diana. "He was the third man in your—games?"

Diana nodded. "And Mike made some comments...said some things. He said he wouldn't tell, but that I didn't have enough money to buy his silence, and do you think he...could he have threatened...oh my *GOD*. Do you think Edward did it? To shut him up?"

Max blinked. The idea of Edward Sharp killing a man was too absurd for words. "I doubt it. Dean looked like he'd only been stabbed once. Edward would have repeated himself and done it at least twice."

"*Max!*" Peta's shocked exclamation rang around the room. "That's in very poor taste." He glanced down and saw the minute twitch at the corners of her lips as she clamped them together to suppress a giggle.

"I wouldn't put it past Mike to try blackmail, though," said Diana. "He was capable of just about anything. But he said he didn't kill Sandra."

"You *asked* him?" Peta's eyes widened.

Diana gripped her hands tightly again. "Yeah. I asked him."

A tap on the back door preceded Frank Summer's head as it peeked around the jamb. "Hey folks, just wanted to let you know that the front area is cordoned off for a while — even though the snow'll probably obliterate anything useful, the lab boys asked us to keep it secure. You all okay with using this door for now?"

"Certainly, Frank, no problem," sighed Peta. "Just let us know when it's all clear?"

"We won't be going out again tonight anyway," added Max.

Diana's face hardened and her shoulders slumped. "Frank," she said abruptly. "Do me a favor? Are you going back to the station?"

"Yep. Need a ride?"

Diana stood, shooting a long and rather sad glance at Max as he stood protectively next to Peta. "Yes please. I'm done here."

There was a world of emotion in those simple words.

Max found himself pitying her. She'd been hit hard, tonight. She'd lost a playmate and been plunged into questions about people that went way beyond their ability to satisfy her sexual needs.

For a self-centered woman like Diana, the knowledge that Dean was dead and Max himself no longer available must have rolled over her like a ton of bricks. Not to mention the fact that nasty things like blackmail and murder had intruded on her private life.

"Goodnight, Diana," he said.

"Goodbye, Max." She stood and followed Frank from the room, totally ignoring Peta.

Chapter 21

Peta's thoughts tumbled over themselves as Diana closed the door behind her. She watched as Max busied himself around the kitchen, rinsing dishes, putting them in the dishwasher, and passing a few comments to Mr. Peebles who had ventured out from wherever he'd hidden himself during all the commotion. A small portion of a "bickie" was exchanged.

She tried to grasp the whole picture, but visions of Diana, Mike Dean and Edward Sharp plagued her. She frowned.

"You're frowning," said Max unnecessarily. "Still can't get Dean's murder out of your mind?"

Peta shrugged. "Of course not. It's horrible. But..."

"But?" Max sat down and brushed her hair away from her cheek. "What else is going on in that inquiring mind of yours?"

Peta bit her lip. "I can't help but wonder."

"About what, honey?"

"Well, you know. What Diana said. About...about her and Dean. *And* Edward."

"Ah. Yeah. The old three-way."

Peta knew she was blushing. "I consider myself reasonably intelligent, Max. It's not a new concept. But finding out that someone you know is actually *doing* it, well, it sort of throws one for a loop, you know?"

Max snorted. "I suppose."

"Have you...?" The words were out before she could bite them back. She cursed at herself silently.

Max raised an eyebrow. "Have I what? Been in a three-way?"

Peta nodded. Damn her curiosity. Now he was going to think she was some sex-obsessed busybody.

He shook his head. "Not like that." He ran his hands through his hair. "Look, honey, I'm no boy scout. I've had my fair share of fun, and yeah, I've even played with a couple of women at the same time. But I've never shared a woman with another man. Not my style." He looked away from her. "Between you and me and Mr. Peebles, it's the reason I never followed up on Diana's invitations."

"She wanted you to...to..."

Max nodded. "Yep. And I'm sorry, but accidentally touching another guy's...well, it's just soooo *not* my thing."

Peta considered that. A little spark of pleasure ignited inside her. She discovered that she was rather glad. Of course, that was followed by further considerations—like having Hugh Jackman on one side of her and perhaps Mel Gibson on the other. Oooh...

"I don't like that look."

"What look?" Peta blinked at Max.

"The one that says you're thinking hot thoughts, and I may not be included."

"Oh. *That* look." She grinned. "I was just thinking about catching a movie soon."

Max stood and stretched. "Yeah, right. I know you better than that, honey. It wasn't a movie you were thinking about catching. It was some movie star, or maybe even two, wasn't it?"

Peta blushed. "Certainly not."

"Hugh Jackman?"

She felt the hot blush deepen in her cheeks and hid her face in her hands. "I don't like this. You know me too well."

Max chuckled. "Lucky guess. At least your mind is off the bad stuff. I can deal with Mr. Jackman."

"You can?" Peta wasn't sure what he meant.

"Sure. I'll just put me there in your fantasies, instead." He leaned over and picked her up. "Just one of me, though."

Peta slipped her arms around his neck. "That'll be more than enough for me, Max."

And it was true. Max was everything she'd ever wanted, and then some. He'd burst into her life, upset her ordered world, shown her that sex could be a transcendental experience when done right, and made her go and do the stupidest thing she'd ever done. Fall in love with him.

Sighing, she snuggled into his chest. "Max, let's go to bed. I want to forget all this. We're alive. We're healthy. Pretty much. Life is so...so uncertain at times. Think about Mike. He got up this morning, not knowing it was his last day on this earth." She sighed again. "Take me away from it all, Max."

"You bet, babe." He dropped a gentle kiss on her lips, and held her high against him. "Tonight's for us."

* * * * *

It was a promise that he fully intended to keep, realized Max as he shouldered open Peta's bedroom door. He was going to give her the best night yet, and drive all the rest of the world from her mind. Tonight she would be thinking only of him.

The room was cool, as always, and the drapes were still open. He carefully lowered Peta on the bed, told her to stay put, and crossed the room to draw the heavy curtains closed. The darkness fell, and along with it the strange silence that accompanies a winter storm. No cars passed, no horns honked — it was as if they were in a world apart. Alone. Just the two of them.

Peta shivered. He hoped it was from arousal, but to be on the safe side...

"C'mon, babe. Into the shower with you. You're cold."

"I...but..."

"No buts." Max busily removed her clothing, noting the goosebumps on her skin. "You're shivering, and I know I'm good, but something tells me that we need to warm you up before we get to the *warming up*, if you catch my drift."

She chuckled and shivered again. "You're right. It is cold in here." She agreed with eyes wide as she watched him strip.

"Okay. Let's go." He herded her into her little bathroom and turned on the faucets. "Grab a few towels, will you? We'll need them after our shower."

"Um...*our* shower?"

Max looked at her. "Yeah. Our shower. You've never showered with a guy before?"

She shook her head, and Max couldn't help the large grin he could feel spreading over his face. This would be a night of firsts for her.

"You'll love it. So will I. Someone to scrub my back for me." Peta snorted, then choked as he added "...and my front."

Not waiting for her response, he hit the shower lever, and stepped in, holding out his hand to her. "Come on in, honey, the water's fine."

Peta looked nervous, intrigued, and uncertain. "My hair...just a minute..." She reached into her cabinet and pulled out a clip, twisting her gorgeous chestnut mass into a lump and securing it. "There."

"Okay. Cool. Now come here." Max knew it was more of a command than an invitation, but hell. He wanted her in front of him, all soapy and wet and hot beneath his hands. His cock did too. It was making its approval of that plan quite plain to anyone who bothered to look.

And Peta looked. She licked her lips and Max couldn't stop the groan that seeped from his lungs.

"Now, babe, before I explode here." More horrible thoughts of those two frightening words "premature ejaculation" danced through his mind, and he breathed with relief as she put her hand in his and carefully stepped under the stream of water.

She sighed in pleasure. "Oh God, Max, that feels good. I didn't realize how cold I was."

Max snickered. She hadn't realized how hot she was, either.

He reached for her liquid soap and squeezed a liberal amount into his hands. "Now let's take care of some personal hygiene here," he mumbled, losing track of his thoughts as his hands touched her skin.

The soap bubbled to soft foam and he caressed her arms and shoulders with it, making her giggle as he shoved his hands beneath her armpits for good measure.

Not to be outdone, Peta squeezed more soap out and began to work on him. She lathered his chest, paying particular attention to his nipples and distracting him.

He lowered his hands and worked on her breasts, loving the little gasp she made as he brushed the hard points at their tips.

"Mmm, nice," he breathed. "So nice."

Peta worked on, letting her palms slide down to his waist and smoothing the soap over his belly. "Yes, it is," she answered absently.

The scent of flowers spread through the room with the steam from the shower, and filled Max's nostrils. It was mixed with her own particular scent, the one that screamed her name when it sneaked into his brain.

He pulled her closer, squishing their soapy bodies together. "Oh, Peta, love, damn, you feel good like this. All naked and slippery. Especially here..."

He slipped his hand down past the softness of her belly, rubbing lather into the curls on her mound.

Her hips jerked forwards into his touch. "Oh hell, Max, the things you do to me," she breathed.

"Oh, hell, Peta, we haven't even started yet."

His hand slipped around behind her as she massaged the ridges of his spine. They were closer than close, his cock nestled against her stomach, slithering around in bliss amongst the soapy foam.

He found her buttocks and kneaded them, letting his fingers roam wherever they wanted. And they wanted all her secrets. He found her cleft and followed it, pressing a little, intruding a little, and making her squirm.

"Max," she sputtered, trying to pull back.

"Relax, babe. I'm just touching you, nothing more," he soothed. And of course, he lied.

His seeking fingers found their way between her buttocks to the tight ring of anal muscles. He rubbed it gently, making her shudder.

"*God*," she stammered.

"Yes?" he answered, grinning.

"Max, for pity's sake..." She writhed as he found her sensitive nerve endings and played, rubbing, teasing, pulling away and then returning. His cock was on fire, but he ignored it, knowing that this was new territory for Peta and that she was awakening to some totally unexpected sensations.

His hands continued their play as he rubbed himself against her breasts, letting the soap slide between them and heighten their pleasure. Daringly, he let one fingertip press against her. "Relax, Peta. Just relax. Trust me."

Peta sighed with pleasure. "I do, Max. I do."

He felt her tensions subside, as she accustomed herself to this new feeling. Slowly, he let his finger penetrate her.

She shuddered. "Bloody hell."

"Feels good?"

"It feels...I can't describe it," she breathed, grabbing onto his shoulders and digging her fingertips into them.

Max smiled, satisfied. She'd warmed up, all right. *These* shivers weren't from the cold.

Her hands slid down his back to his own buttocks, and she let her fingers squeeze and knead them, bringing a surge of heat through Max. Like his cock needed any more.

"You have a great arse, Max," she murmured, then gasped as he moved his finger around a little.

"So do you babe," he answered.

Her fingers strayed.

"Um, Peta?"

He felt her chuckle through her breasts where they were plastered against his body. "Sauce for the goose, Max, sauce for the goose."

Jesus fucking *Christ*. She was doing the same thing to *him*. Her fingers found him and rubbed, right on his anus. He was torn between wanting to jump about four feet into the air and coming on the spot.

Fortunately, he did neither. He simply froze.

She continued her exploration, cautiously caressing him with soapy fingers. He couldn't help it. He moaned.

"You moaned."

"Did not."

"Did too," she chuckled.

"Well, fair is fair. You moaned too," he smiled.

"Do I take it that *this*—" she pressed against him again, "—meets with your approval?"

"Honey, anything you do meets with my approval. Um, well, let's amend that. If you've got a butt plug around here anywhere, you can just put it away again."

Peta laughed and pulled away from him, smiling at him over the lather that dotted her nose.

Max's heart stopped as he looked down at her face. It shone with pleasure and joy and reflected the passion he was feeling. Something inside him shifted, realigned itself and settled down again, leaving him hot for her, but unsatisfied, as if just taking her, fucking her, and making her cry out as she came wasn't enough. Would never be enough.

The thought terrified him, and he eased their bodies apart. "Time for a rinse, I think," he said. He turned Peta away from him, and smoothed the lather from her body, letting the water sluice away the soapy residue.

With a quick shake, he rid himself of any leftover foam, and reached for the towels as she turned off the water.

"How's the ankle?" He held out his hand and watched her as she stepped out of the tub cautiously.

"Good, thanks. I can't put my full weight on it yet, but it's holding up very nicely."

Max wished he could say the same. He rubbed her ferociously, reddening her body, and ignoring her protests.

"Max, you're going to take the skin off," she laughed.

"Not me. I have plans for that skin."

"Oh?" Her gray eyes gleamed at him. "What plans might those be, may I inquire?"

"No, you may not." He gritted his teeth. She was warm, dry, shining with her heat, and he wanted to take her right this minute. Lay her down on the damp towels and sink so deep into her he'd lose himself. Forever.

He got scared all over again.

* * * * *

Peta lay quietly on the bed and listened as Max finished up in the bathroom. He'd been almost curt with her, but the heat in his eyes had reassured her. And his hard cock had sent a message all its own. He was struggling for control.

She smiled to herself. She, Peta Matthews of the big hips and inadequate boobs, was making Max Wolfe struggle for control. Yes, Virginia, there was a Santa Claus. He'd brought Peta something she'd never believed she could have. Max.

She snuggled deeper into the covers, wondering what was taking him so long.

"Miss me?"

His light tones made her shiver as he appeared in the doorway, snapping the bathroom light off as he moved towards her.

Her breath caught in her throat. He was truly gorgeous.

His sandy hair had darkened beneath the shower, and a few damp strands clung to his face. His body was perfect, his chest a work of art that would have made Michelangelo weep and then reach for his chisel — and his eyes? Well, hell. There were no words.

Peta faced reality. She was helplessly, hopelessly in love with this man. Come what may, she'd gone and done it. Been really stupid and allowed him to touch her in more places than just her body. She'd let his warmth and

Sahara Kelly

his humor get inside her, to comfort her and enrich her life.

A life that would, in all probability, not include him.

But she'd have tonight. As Max had said, tonight was for them.

"Yes, I missed you," she answered. Her voice was throaty as her need bubbled up from her toes to her eyebrows.

Max prowled the room. He was looking for something it seemed, and then he reached for her cashmere scarf. "Aha."

"*Aha* what? I don't need a scarf. I'm quite warm enough now, thank you." And that was the understatement of the year. The soles of her feet were burning, and they were cool compared to the rest of her.

Max dropped the towel he'd been carrying into a pile on the floor next to the bed and sank down, making the mattress sag.

"Do you trust me, Peta?"

What a question. An immediate response sprang to her lips but she bit it back, trying to read the expression in his eyes. This wasn't just a simple sex thing, this was a real, honest-to-God, cross-your-heart-and-hope-to-die kind of question.

There could be no other answer. "I trust you, Max."

"Good." He leaned over, and with a quick move, tied the scarf around her eyes, blindfolding her.

"What the..." Her brain closed down along with her eyesight.

"I want you to be aware of your body, Peta. Only your body. By blindfolding you, taking away your sight, you'll have to use your other senses. It'll be good, honey. I promise you."

His words both soothed and aroused her, and she swallowed, finding her mouth suddenly dry. "Okay," she answered, trying to keep the nerves from her voice.

"Good girl."

She felt the bed lift as he stood up, and then — nothing. Nothing but the light brush of the covers as he pulled them away from her body, and the caress of the cool night air in the bedroom.

A moment or so later, she couldn't stand it any more. "Um, Max? What are you doing?"

"Looking at you." His voice was low, almost a whisper, and she felt her nipples harden in response to his words. She squirmed.

"Max, I...I don't know about this..." She felt vulnerable, exposed, and not being able to see the expression on his face robbed her of the ability to tell what he was feeling.

"I do. You're beautiful."

Peta snorted. "Am not. My hips are too big, I've got a belly, my — er — assets are less than impressive...want me to go on?"

There was no answer.

Then she felt warmth, heat, and the lightest touch of a tongue on her navel.

She gasped.

"Feel that?" he breathed.

"Oh yes, yes indeed," she croaked.

The touch came again, ringing her navel this time with moisture.

Her thighs widened as her arousal grew. But then, as soon as she was aching for the tongue to travel some more, it was gone.

She sighed.

There was silence for another moment or two, then something very cool pressed into her nipple, surprising a gasp out of her. It was gone before she could speak.

Max's sensual torture continued unabated, bringing sighs of pleasure to her lips when something soft brushed her clit, and sobs of surprise as other cool things caressed her breasts and her belly.

"Hell, Max," she moaned. "I'm going to die on you if you keep this up." Her head tossed on the pillow and her hands were fisted in the sheets. She knew her hips were squirming and she could feel her juices running everywhere.

"What a way to go," he chuckled. His deep voice was as arousing as anything he was touching her with, and she ached for him.

"Touch me with *you*, Max," she begged. "Please."

He didn't answer her, but she felt the bed sink as he clambered on and settled beside her.

She waited.

Something brushed her lips. It was hard, warm and smooth, and she felt a slight moisture. Hungrily she opened her mouth.

"Not yet, love," Max whispered, pulling away. "Not quite yet."

She licked her lips, tasting the drop of pre-come he'd left behind. "When?" she groaned.

"Soon, babe, soon..."

The touch came again, but this time to her breast, circling it in ever decreasing spirals until the heat of his cock was burning her nipple. Without thinking she reached for him, only to have him draw back.

"Hands at your sides, honey. No touching. Not allowed."

Peta choked. "You're impossible, Max Wolfe—" Her words were interrupted by another caress, this time to her other breast.

She clenched her fists and focused on the feeling as he rubbed her softness with his cock once more.

It was truly amazing. She was so sensitive to his touch that she swore she could feel the pounding of his pulse through the tip as it nuzzled against her nipple.

She strained her ears and caught his breathing, a little harsh now, as if he too were fighting against the urge that battered at her. The urge to spread her legs wide and get him inside her where she ached for him.

"Max, please, don't wait any longer, I can't stand it."

It was the unvarnished truth. It wasn't just her body that craved him, it was her soul. When he took her, filled her, she was complete.

Without him, she was desolate and empty, a needy mass of writhing nerve endings awaiting the touch that would send her spinning into a fiery void where bodies blended, spirits merged, and hearts beat as one.

Her head swam as she felt Max's thighs settle between hers. Super sensitive to the lightest touch now, the hairs on his legs brushed her and made her moan.

Then a soft sound intruded. A buzz.

And something touched her clit and nearly shot her up off the mattress. Bloody fucking *bollocks*. It was her vibrator.

Chapter 22

Max couldn't help the mighty grin that swept over his face as the woman beneath him practically levitated off the bed. He'd *really* surprised her this time.

"You bastard," she groaned.

He loved the way she cursed him, elongating the "a" and sounding like a furious Shakespearean heroine. He stifled his chuckle. *This* Juliet was seconds away from coming.

Of course, so was he.

He fidgeted around, moved her body slightly, and always kept the vibrator where it would do the most good.

He brushed her clit, then rubbed it, and then pulled back, letting her whimpers and cries tell him the best places and the best pressures.

Slowly, oh so slowly, he slid his sheathed cock into her cunt. Thank God he'd remembered protection a few minutes before, because he sure wouldn't have been able to stop for it now.

Not when her swollen flesh was pulling at him, widening for him and bathing him with her hot juices.

He slid deep, filling her cunt, catching the vibrator between them. It was wild, this thrumming against his body and hers. He could feel her responses as he moved it slightly, and he gritted his teeth.

She had to be there—at the very peak. The most enormously high, muscle—clenching, my-heart-is-gonna-stop peak, before he'd let her fall.

And then he'd catch her.

He pulled back out and then slid in again, pushing even harder this time. The vibrator buzzed, Peta sobbed and Max's cock swelled to its limits. He couldn't take much more.

He thrust into her, rapidly now, letting his control go, and his instincts take over. His balls had solidified between his legs, and his heart was pounding in his ears.

He sensed her gathering her strength...he even felt her cunt as the pressure of the vibrator hit exactly the right spot.

For them both.

Peta screamed. Her body went into wild and thrashing spasms as he held on, keeping the vibrator tight between them and hammering into her for all he was worth.

He couldn't last. And he didn't.

With a shout of his own, Max came. A crazy hot whirlwind rushed through him and spurted out into Peta, egged on by her cunt which grabbed him and massaged him and milked him, encouraging him to sink deeper and deeper as he let his come flood free and his balls empty their precious cargo into her.

He wrenched the vibrator from between their bodies and rammed himself home one last time, feeling her answering shudders beneath him as their flesh melded.

Another tremor shook Peta, and he relished it, letting her body tell him of its pleasure at his possession.

She sobbed, shaking around him, muscles weakening now, and rendering her limp.

Max himself was not entirely sure he was any better off. Lethargy flooded him, and he let his weight sink down onto the soft pillow of her breasts.

She sighed and rested a hand on his spine.

He carefully raised a hand and removed the blindfold, watching her eyes as she blinked at the light. They shone at him, as the haze of passion receded.

"Max," she whispered. "Max...*Max.*"

His heart thumped against hers, as he slid gently from her body to her side. His cock softened and slithered sadly from her cunt, relaxed now, and ready to rest.

Max's mind couldn't, however. He lay quiet, holding Peta, and wondering what the hell had just happened.

Then it hit him. For the first time in his life, he hadn't fucked a woman. He'd made love to her.

* * * * *

The dream began slowly, creeping into Max's sleeping mind with all the stealth of Mr. Peebles pursuing an elusive morsel of bacon.

He was standing by an open window looking out onto a strange and colorful landscape. Birds sang loudly, plants that he'd never seen before bloomed in profusion, and the air was soft and warm.

It certainly wasn't Mayfield in the winter.

He looked down. In his arms he was holding a soft bundle. Which moved. Surprisingly, his first instinct wasn't to drop it but to look more closely.

A pair of hazel eyes stared somberly back at him from beneath a soft cap of chestnut curls.

He wondered why on earth he was holding a baby.

He was quite surprised. Max had made no secret of the fact that he regarded children in the old fashioned way—they should be seen and not heard. And even then only seen from a distance. Preferably one that included at least two states. And possibly a river.

But few of those thoughts ran through his mind as he gazed at the tiny face studying his.

The little rosebud mouth opened in a large yawn, and revealed shiny pink gums. Obviously it found Max rather boring. Max wished he could say the same.

For some reason he was fascinated.

He gently settled the bundle more securely against his chest and brushed a finger over the satin cheek. The small head followed the move, responding automatically to the touch of another.

"Hello," said Max, unsure of what to say to someone this small. The little eyes blinked sleepily at him.

Then it struck him. They were *his* eyes. A junior version, but the hazel coloring was unmistakable. He gulped.

"Little sweetheart, isn't he?"

The voice behind him, although quiet, made Max jump and tighten his hold on the infant. A small whimper next to his heart recalled his attention and he quietly soothed the child, as he watched a man with very blue eyes stand next to him and smile down at the baby in Max's arms.

"Is he...is he *mine*?" Max stuttered the words.

"He could be." The answer was noncommittal and Max frowned.

"I don't understand."

"What's to understand? You're dreaming, right? None of this is real," said the man. He waved his hand towards the window. "You've never seen anything like this, have you? So how can any of it exist?"

Max closed his eyes for a moment as he wondered if too much tea induced hallucinations.

"Max, this child could be yours," said the man quietly. "If you set aside your instincts and learn to trust."

"To trust? Trust who?"

"Trust your heart, Max. You've never listened to it before. You've been too busy listening to another portion of your body."

Max felt himself blushing. Well, hell. Of course he had. His dick seldom failed him. His trust, however...well—that had let him down on more than one occasion. He had learned from his mistakes. He'd started trusting his parents, and right there had discovered a problem. They were little more than the biological creators of his person. They hadn't been there when he'd needed them. So who the hell else would be?

He glanced down at the child in his arms, who had quietly fallen asleep. Christ, if this *was* his kid, what kind of a father would he be? The kind who barely acknowledged his son's existence? The kind that sent a check and thought that was sufficient for birthdays, Christmases and whatever else came along?

He felt his lips tighten. *No.* This kid deserved more. He held the soft bundle more closely, wondering at the waves of warmth that seemed to be flowing from his body to surround his precious little cargo.

"That's it, Max. Let those feelings out. You're going to need them very soon."

"I am?" Max frowned. "Who are you? Where am I?"

"That doesn't matter. None of it matters. He..." The man nodded at the child. "He is what matters. He's going to be important to your world, Max. And you have to learn to trust in order for him to be born."

"Uhh...I do?"

"Yep."

Max struggled with this information. "I don't get it."

The man sighed. "You will. Just remember one thing, Max." His voice grew even quieter. "Trust your heart. Trust what it tells you. Trust *her*..."

Even as the last word was spoken, Max felt the world fade away.

He woke, his head snuggled into his pillow, and his arms cradling emptiness.

Max Wolfe began to sweat.

* * * * *

Peta's ears were ringing. She sighed and turned over, finding warmth next to her. A living warmth.

She smiled as she realized that Max was sleeping soundly, sprawled over a good three-quarters of the bed. God, great sex sure rang those bells.

An insistent sound pulled her into consciousness. It wasn't the sex, it was the phone.

Bollocks.

She picked it up and before she'd had chance to say anything, Phoebe's voice was yelling loudly from the receiver.

Well, probably not yelling, but it just sounded like it.

"Peta? Peta? I didn't wake you, dear, did I? I'm so glad you're up..."

Yes right. Up. *Up* implied a state of alertness. Perhaps even clothes. Neither of which applied to Peta at this particular moment.

"What's the matter, Phoebe? Everything all right?" Peta stifled a yawn, and noted that Max hadn't moved. God, he was sleeping like a log this morning. Of course, given their activities last night, she wasn't too surprised.

She grinned and pulled her attention back to the conversation Phoebe was busily having with no one in particular. "Sorry, Phoebe, say that again?"

"I *said*...I'm coming over. Struthers and I have just had breakfast, and he's offered to help me unload some of that junk from your place. Is that all right? Did you hear me?"

Peta struggled with this. Obviously it was now morning. And she was going to have to get up and get dressed. Probably shower too, since she was still all sticky. "Uh, well, certainly, Phoebe. Can you give me half an hour?"

A laugh echoed from the phone. "Half an hour. No more. Get Max to put coffee on, will you? And wake *up*, Peta. It's a lovely day. Time's wasting, you know." She hung up.

Peta sighed.

Carefully, so as not to disturb the sleeping man next to her, Peta eased from the bed, shivering a little as the cool air met her naked skin. She peeked out the window.

Phoebe had been right. The sun was shining so brightly, Peta had to squint to handle the brilliance as it reflected off the snow. She could hear the sound of snowplows, so the town must be pulling itself out from the depths of yet another spring snowstorm.

She shivered again. Definitely not the best day to hang around the house stark naked.

One quiet shower later, Peta emerged, only to find the bed empty, and the scent of coffee drifting up the stairs through the open bedroom door. Apparently Sleeping Beauty had arisen from his slumber.

Peta grinned and dressed quickly, slipping into jeans and a sweatshirt. Daringly, she left off her undies, surprised at herself, but accepting that there might be a chance she could lure Max back into bed after Phoebe left. And hell, if there was the slightest chance, she was damn well going to take it.

Make hay while the sun shines, her mother had always said. So this might not have been *exactly* what her mother had in mind when voicing that sentiment, but the heck with semantics. The sun was shining, and Peta was ready to make more hay.

Stepping in to the kitchen, Peta allowed herself a moment to appreciate the picture she found awaiting her.

Max was chatting with Mr. Peebles. Quite intently, apparently, since a small frown wrinkled that handsome forehead of his, and Mr. Peebles's tail was twitching.

She wondered if they were arguing. If they were, then Max was clearly unused to dealing with cats. One simply could not win an argument with a cat.

"Good morning, you two," she said.

Max glanced briefly at her and then turned back to the coffee pot. "Hi," he answered.

Peta blinked. "You look rather intense. Mr. Peebles giving you a hard time?"

Mr. Peebles lifted his nose in response, swept her with an indignant gaze, and then decided that he might as well investigate his food bowl to see if anything decent had appeared to replace his cat food.

Apparently it hadn't, since after several disdainful sniffs, he thought better of if and stalked off to his favorite patch of morning sunshine. He tucked his paws beneath him and settled down, presenting a large furry backside to the world.

It seemed Max was doing the human equivalent. "Coffee or tea?" he asked.

"Um, coffee, I think. Thanks. Phoebe and Struthers will be here in a minute. They're going to take all those boxes of junk out of here."

"That'll be good."

Peta frowned as a little chill of concern traipsed up her spine. "Max, is everything all right?"

Max turned and met her gaze. She nearly gasped at the expression in his eyes.. They were heated as they looked at her, but somewhere deep down in their hazel depths was a sort of anguish. Maybe even — pain.

"Max..." she began, taking a step forward.

The doorbell interrupted her.

Smothering a curse, she turned and left the kitchen to open the door to Phoebe and Struthers.

Neither seemed aware of any undercurrents as they settled themselves around the kitchen table, accepting coffee and chatting away as if it was just another morning.

Peta was almost glad of it. Taking part in the normalcy of conversation helped her keep her mind off the fact that Max hadn't touched her this morning. Hadn't kissed her. Hadn't...well, hadn't done anything. Had barely looked at her.

With an inner pang, Peta considered the possibility that this might be "it".. The end of the affair. The time when Max would pack and walk out of her life, leaving it dark and cold.

The time she'd expected would come, but not this soon. Her heart ached.

The discussion turned naturally to the horrible murder of Mike Dean, and Peta's brain swam with guilt. She found she couldn't bring herself to join in, since Mike Dean was beyond her help. It was a tragedy, of course, but it didn't touch her nearly as much as the thought of Max leaving.

"So anyway, we decided it would be a good idea," said Phoebe. "Don't you think so, Peta?"

"Umm...yes. Of course."

Phoebe chuckled. "You didn't hear a word I said, dear. Do try and concentrate."

"Sorry. I'm not quite awake yet, and with all the goings-on last night..."

Max's smile was horribly impersonal, polite, and superficial. Peta found herself waking up much too fast, and she didn't like what she was waking up *to*.

"Well, goodness me, it's past nine o'clock," laughed Phoebe. "So, as I was saying, Struthers is going to help me with these boxes of stuff. The books will go over to the library, and the rest to the dump. Or somewhere. I simply have to stop cluttering up your house with it all."

"No problem," said Peta. "You know I don't mind."

"Well, as Struthers pointed out, you do have a houseguest now." Phoebe grinned.

Silence fell.

Phoebe cleared her throat. "Anyway, if you don't mind, we'll throw it all into the car. Along with that other box full too."

Peta frowned. "Other box?"

"Yes, don't you remember? I dumped the last box in the dining room the other day. It should be under the table somewhere."

"Uh, no, I never noticed." Damn. One of these days she really was going to pull out the vacuum cleaner and do some housework. It was looking more and more as if she'd have plenty of time for it too.

Max still hadn't said a word.

Phoebe pushed back her chair and stood. "It should still be in there. Want to go check it out?"

Struthers grinned. "Can't stop Phoebe when junk is involved," he said.

Max smiled politely and Peta clenched her teeth. She just wished his arse was between them, because she'd like to take a chunk of him right about now. What the *hell* was going on with him?

They trooped into the dining room, and within moments Phoebe had dragged a crate from beneath the table, spreading the contents over the surface and digging amongst them with all the glee of a child on Christmas morning.

Peta noticed one large package at the bottom of the crate, and pulled it out. It was heavy and wrapped in what looked like vintage 1950's wallpaper. Smelly wallpaper.

She wrinkled her nose. "Ugh, Phoebe. What on earth did you buy this for?"

Phoebe glanced over. "Oh that. I have no idea. Except that I had a room with that stuff on the wall when I was younger. Sentimental reasons I suppose. I only paid fifty cents for it."

Peta gently peeled away the discolored roses.

She gasped. "*Phoebe...*"

Her voice trailed off as she uncovered the contents. Staring at her was the ancient leather cover of a very old book. A very old book indeed.

"Oh my *God*."

The others leaned in. "What the hell is it?" asked Max.

Right. *Now* he was talking to her. Now, when she could barely catch her breath, let alone her thoughts.

For lying amidst the remains of its wrapping was a Bible. The leather binding was dark with age, and the ornamentation almost obscured. But even so, Phoebe's hand trembled as she carefully reached out and opened it.

"Oh my word," breathed Struthers. "Is that what I think it is?"

"It could be," said Phoebe. "You'd know better than I. What do you think?" She moved aside and gave him room to sit down next to her.

Struthers's eyes were wide as he took her seat and reverently ran his fingers across the binding and the leaves.

The text was small, very ornate, and a few pages were browned with damp stains.

"My God. I think it *is*."

"It is *what*, Struthers? What the heck is it? A first edition? Tell me before I burst here," demanded Phoebe.

He raised his head. "Much more than a first edition, Phoebe. You've managed to get the buy of the century, I'd say."

Phoebe ground her teeth with frustration. "*WHAT IS IT?*"

"Well," said Struthers, carefully turning the pages with the tips of his fingers. "As near as I can tell, this is a 1611 King James Bible."

Max's eyes met Peta's, as they both recalled their research in the library. "You mean the one Edward was looking for?" asked Max.

Struthers's head shot up with a frown. "How did you know that?"

"Struthers, I'm sorry. When we were in the library, we happened to notice his book requests." Peta felt rather guilty, like she'd been caught prying.

Struthers's brow cleared. "Oh, yes. Of course. The computer." He bent over the book again. "Never mind. It's just that I never thought I'd see one, let alone touch it."

"So is it male or female?" asked Max.

"What the hell are you talking about, Max?" sputtered Phoebe. "It's a *book*, for heaven's sake."

Struthers chuckled. "These two have done their research, too, Phoebe. Max is right. Let me check here." He riffled the pages cautiously, reaching the Book of Ruth at last and staring intently at the page.

"My God. I can't believe it." He raised his eyes and stared at the three faces looking back at him. "It's a 'he' Bible."

Peta swallowed. "Is it real? A copy? Can you tell?"

Phoebe frowned. "I don't understand any of this," she moaned. "Will someone please tell me what's going on?"

Max took pity on her.

He needed something to distract him from Peta anyway. The look in her eyes had damn near knocked him off his feet this morning. So bright and full of love. And him terrified all the way to his toes, for the first time in his life.

With half his mind, he filled Phoebe in on the Bible and its significance, while the other half screamed at him to run. Run like hell, as fast and as far as he could.

The woman now leaning over the rare book was a threat to his very sanity. She represented everything he'd grown up avoiding. Security, warmth, love, a home, family — all the things that used to make Max's flesh creep. The sex between them was different, and that frightened him too.

When he'd woken up and found her place empty, his heart had damn near stopped until he heard the shower running.

Then the memories of his dream returned, and his terror began.

He had no idea what to do, except follow his usual course of action. Move on. Get as far away from Peta as possible and find his way back to his usual pursuits. Empty apartments and empty sex.

No longings, no urges to buy houses and minivans, and above all, *no babies.*

His heart lurched. And an odd pain started, spreading through him like a hangover. But this one wasn't in his head. It was in his soul.

He dragged his mind back to what he was saying. "So you see, Phoebe, this one, if it's genuine, is incredibly rare. And incredibly valuable."

Struthers nodded. "That it is, Phoebe. Very valuable indeed."

"God," said Phoebe, looking flabbergasted. "And it cost me fifty cents."

Peta chuckled. "A good buy, I'd say."

Struthers sighed and closed the volume. "It should be kept safe until we can get it appraised, you know. I could keep it in the library if you want?"

Peta thought for a moment. "Look," she said to everyone. "It's been here under my table for a while, and we're the only ones who know about it. Why don't we just leave it here? I'll...um..." Her gaze wandered around. "Here. In my bookshelf with my other hard covers."

She gently picked up the Bible and opened one glass door, laying it gingerly inside. "There. All safe. No one could tell at a glance that it's anything more than just another book. And you should call someone *today,* Phoebe," she said firmly.

Phoebe, for once, seemed at a loss for speech. She simply nodded.

Struthers stood up. "Well, well. This has been one surprising morning. Come on, Phoebe. We'll stop by the library and I'll pull up some phone numbers of a few antiquarians I know in Boston. I'll just guarantee they'll be out here in next to no time." He looked over at Peta. "You keep that safe now, young lady. That's quite a treasure there, you know."

Phoebe stood as Max pulled out her chair for her. "This is all a bit much to take in, isn't it?" she said.

Her face was pale, and Max took pity on her, giving her a quick hug. "Look at it this way, Phoebe. You could sell it and become a disgustingly rich woman. Or you could donate it, and become a disgustingly famous one." He grinned at her as he watched her eyes narrow.

"Hmm. Famous, huh? Well, there's a thought." She chuckled and let Struthers lead her out into the hall.

"Oh, by the way," said Max casually. "Is Cole's open this morning?"

Silence fell. Max knew everyone was familiar with the name. It was, after all, the only realtor in town. He swallowed. "Now that Peta is back on her feet, it's time I was thinking of finding someplace permanent to live."

Phoebe raised an eyebrow, and even Struthers looked oddly at him.

"Um, I should suppose so," muttered Phoebe. She flashed a look of concern at Max. "I really wouldn't know for sure, though."

Max just nodded. "Thanks. You be careful on the steps. Frank cleaned them up pretty good, but they may still be icy."

He closed the door behind them, leaving him alone with Peta. And his fears.

Chapter 23

The departure of Phoebe and Struthers left a silent void in the front hall.

Peta couldn't meet Max's eyes. She turned away from him and went back into the kitchen, finding comfort in the small chores she created for herself as she collected coffee cups.

"Peta, I..." Max stood in the doorway.

"No, Max, please. Don't say anything. I understand."

"You do?" His voice was odd, strained somehow. "I wish to hell I did."

"Look." She wiped her hands on her dishtowel. "It's quite simple. We've had fun, made a lot of noise, and enjoyed each other, right? Now, it's time to move on."

The words were calm, but Peta felt like she was bleeding them instead of speaking them.

Max blinked. "You want me to move on?"

"That's not what I said. But probably, yes. You will anyway, so why wait?"

Her question thudded between them. Better to at least retain a little pride. Screaming, carrying on, hanging onto his neck, no. That wasn't her style at all. Diana could get away with it, but not Peta.

"I suppose," he said, running his hand through his hair.

Bollocks. If only she didn't love him so much. Then perhaps this wouldn't kill her. But she did, and it probably would. Oh she'd survive physically, but she wasn't sure about her mental state.

She turned away again, to hide the sting of tears she could feel beginning behind her eyes.

"Well, all right then. I'll go and check in over at Cole's and see if they have anything." Max cleared his throat. "I'll be back in a while, okay?"

"Sure. Take your time."

Peta's voice was casual, miraculously so, since tears were pouring down her cheeks, and her throat was aching with the need to scream out her pain. Her hands trembled as she heard Max putting on his coat, and when the door slammed again she slumped, giving way to her grief.

She sobbed. Huge, hiccupping sobs that wracked her body and tore at her throat.

He was gone. Her house had never seemed so empty.

Peta dragged herself to the kitchen table and sobbed some more, ignoring Mr. Peebles who was expressing his concern by twining himself around her shins.

She sniffled, and grabbed for a tissue, blowing her nose hard, and trying to stop the flood that threatened to sweep her over the edge into despair.

He was gone. Max Wolfe had done what he did best. Loved her and left her. Why was she so surprised? Why was she acting like some twit, crying over a man she'd known from the beginning she could never hold?

Because you love him, you pea-brained moron.

Her thoughts allowed her no respite and the tears came again. Mr. Peebles jumped up on her lap, and she took some small comfort from stroking him.

"I love him so much, Mr. Peebles. It's going to be hell trying to live without him, you know," she confided with a sniffle.

Mr. Peebles looked thoughtful, then closed his eyes as her fingers scratched around his ear and under his chin.

Peta tried for a mental diversion. There was work to be done, edits and contracts to complete, and the office had to be checked up on, to see if she could actually get back to work. Get her life back to normal.

Normal. Hah. Nothing would ever be normal again. Her life was now PW and...and...PW. Pre-Wolfe and Post-Wolfe.

She blew her nose again, and stared at nothing in particular. In the last week or so, she'd crashed up her car, loved Max Wolfe, found out about her co-worker's murder, loved Max Wolfe, found a dead body, tried to solve a crime, and loved Max Wolfe.

Yes, there was definitely a trend. It was a damn shame that the Deans had been killed, but Peta was obsessed. Not by their murders, but by Max Wolfe.

She exhaled deeply, wondering if it was her heart leaving her body, and why it wasn't puddling on the table in front of her.

Mr. Peebles sat up on her lap, and did something quite un-cat like.

He licked her cheek.

A weak smile crossed her lips. "Aw, sweetie. Thanks for the comfort." She pulled in a shuddering breath. "I have to go on, don't I? I *have* to get past this."

Mr. Peebles obviously agreed. He jumped down onto the floor and Peta stood, looking vaguely around her.

"So where do I go from here?"

* * * * *

The cold air blasted Max's cheeks as he left Peta's house, and walked down the street. He had no idea where he was going, but some instinct took him towards the center of town.

He was two blocks away when he realized that he did, in fact, have a car.

It didn't seem to matter. Nothing seemed to matter. He was walking away from Peta and that was the only thing running through his mind.

His steps slowed, and for once he did something that was quite out of character. He started analyzing his feelings for Peta.

Until now, he'd never done stuff like this. Thinking about the women he'd slept with was so unlike him, he got a distinct shiver of concern as he began the process. What was the matter with him? Where was the love 'em and leave 'em philosophy that had served him so well in the past?

Where was the superstud Max Wolfe who merrily fucked his way through life, taking what was offered with a smile, a hard-on, and a cheery wave goodbye?

Peta Matthews had somehow eroded that carefully-constructed facade. She'd burrowed beneath his protective armor and reached a place inside him that was open to her, waiting for her, and she'd settled down there with all the enthusiasm of Mr. Peebles finding a comfortable lap and curling up on it.

Even Mr. Peebles liked her. And he'd been notoriously aloof with Max's other women. Not that any of them had stayed long enough to meet him, but still...

Max ignored the slippery sidewalk beneath his feet and the cold wind lashing the color into his cheeks as he strolled on, asking himself some unanswerable questions.

Why was it different with Peta? How was it different with Peta?

She was no better looking than many of his other women. She had hips, nicely rounded ones it was true, and she was no slender supermodel. There was a good amount of flesh there for his hands to sink into when he pulled her onto his cock.

His body flushed as he recalled the feel of her, the scent of her, the look of her as he buried himself in her.

He tried to remember that precise moment with any of the other women he'd fucked. He couldn't. They had all faded away, blown into obscurity by one eccentric chestnut-haired woman with a slightly British accent and a pair of gray eyes that spiked him to his soul.

Resolutely, Max turned his steps onto Main Street and headed for the realty office. He wanted his own apartment. He needed his own apartment. He was a loner by choice and by nature. He was after someplace that wouldn't collapse on him, had a reasonably comfortable bed to which he could bring his choice of women, and a rent that didn't require him to be a multi-millionaire.

He swallowed as he realized that no apartment would really offer what he wanted, because Peta wouldn't be in it.

Her ratty robe wouldn't be hanging behind the bathroom door. Her assorted shampoos wouldn't clutter up the shower. Her tea can, or as she called it, a caddy, wouldn't be brightening up the kitchen counter.

He chuckled as he realized how many Briticisms he'd come to accept. He'd always thought a caddy was someone loaded down with golf clubs. Now whenever he heard the word, he knew he'd see Peta, intent on her tea-making ritual, swirling water in the pot and then tucking it up under a hat-like lump of insulation.

He reached the door of Cole's Realty Office. He even put his hand on the doorknob.

But he stopped. The truth snuck up on him and landed him a blinding thump somewhere behind his left ear.

He wanted to go home. And "home" was anywhere Peta was.

It was too late for the old Max Wolfe. The man he used to be had ceased to exist the moment he'd buried himself inside Peta Matthews and taken them both to the edge of oblivion.

What was originally another in a series of conquests had become so much more. Something that overrode everything else in Max's mind and, he hated to admit it, his heart.

He wanted *her*.

He wanted her humor, her charm, her accent, and her deliciously rounded thighs. He wanted to see himself reflected in her eyes as she came in waves beneath him. He wanted to fall asleep with her curled up next to him and wake up wrapped around her. He wanted to drink tea until his bladder exploded, and even, possibly, eat beans on toast. He still wasn't sure if he could manage the poached egg thing, but for her, he'd try it.

And he knew why.

Because the conquering hero, Max Wolfe, had finally been conquered himself.

He'd gone and fallen in love with her.

As Peta herself was wont to say, oh *bollocks*.

Max turned away from the realty office and began the long walk home to claim his woman.

* * * * *

While Max was experiencing an enormous emotional epiphany, Peta was experiencing a wide variety of her own emotions.

Going upstairs to her room, the pain she'd been suffering gave way to anger. Her sheets were rumpled, the scent of Max and sweat and sex lingered, and Peta's temper boiled over.

"How *dare* he." She muttered to herself as she yanked the comforter off the bed and dumped it in a pile on the floor beside her. "That bloody bastard. How *dare* he just saunter out of here like that."

The flying linen unnerved Mr. Peebles, who attacked a pillowcase as it fluttered his way.

"He gives me the best sex I've ever had in my entire life and then acts like it's nothing." Holding a pillow to her chest, Peta sank down on the bed and stared at Mr. Peebles as he glared at the now-dead pillowcase. "Do you think it was nothing to him, Mr. Peebles?"

The cat wisely kept his silence.

Peta snorted. "Perhaps it's always like that for him. Perhaps it was disappointing, even. Perhaps...perhaps..." She thumped the pillow. "Oh how the bloody hell should I know?"

She stood and winced as her jeans chafed the bare skin beneath. Her temper rose again. "And to think I even left off my damned underwear. God, I am *such* a slut..."

She rummaged in her bureau, pulling out a bra and panties. Serviceable white cotton emerged, and Peta roughly shoved her lacier garments to the bottom of the drawer. It was unlikely she'd need *them* in the near future.

Scattering clothes right and left, Peta mumbled on. "Damn the man. How stupid could I have been? I knew what he was like right from the start, but did I listen to myself?"

Correctly deducing that this was a rhetorical question, Mr. Peebles hunkered down on his front paws and waited for Peta to offer her response.

"Noooo. Of course not. The stupid sex-mad Brit *idiot* couldn't wait to strip off her panties and...and fuck like a bloody rabbit." She glanced over at the cat. "Yes, I said rabbit. Aren't you supposed to look predatory or something?"

Mr. Peebles's nose twitched.

Peta sighed. "See? He's even got me talking to a cat. One good-looking man pays attention to me, takes me to bed, fucks my brains out, and here I am. A raving twit with no underwear, conversing with a creature who only gives me the time of day if I've got food in my hand."

Mr. Peebles took offense at that. He stood, stretched gracefully, and flicked his tail at her as he left the room.

Oh brilliant. She'd just been flipped the feline version of the middle finger.

With a muttered curse that had far more to do with the physical than the abstract, Peta stripped off her sweater and jeans and struggled into her panties.

They felt constrictive, too tight, and rubbed her in places that she hadn't realized were aching.

She closed her eyes and tried not to remember how they got that way. How Max had felt as his body had pressed her vibrator against her and how his cock had responded as she fell into a million pieces beneath him.

She sank down on the bed again, and fought the tears. Damn it, she was *NOT* going to cry again.

She bit down on her lip.

And cried.

Chapter 24

The timing was perfect.

Max Wolfe was gone, on foot too, which would take a lot of time, given the road conditions. He'd seen the shadows behind Peta Matthew's windows. She had gone upstairs.

He probably wouldn't get another chance like this. Maybe even try a little of that British cunt she seemed to guard so jealously while he was at it. God knew she'd been quick enough to share it with Wolfe.

Now it was his turn.

He chuckled to himself as he slowly eased the front door open.

At last. FINALLY. He'd be able to get his hands on what rightfully belonged to him. His heart pounded as he entered the small hallway.

He'd known it was here. Just as sure as he knew his own name. He could almost smell it. The trail had gone cold in Boston a few years ago, because people had a very distressing tendency to move around more than they should.

And to think of the hours he'd spent researching, digging, making endless and futile phone calls, only to have it turn up in that stupidly ignorant Phoebe's cache of junk. He'd been so close at the flea market. So fucking close.

If only he'd recognized the box for what it was. But it had taken more time to find the dealer than he had anticipated, and when he got there – it was gone.

Fortunately, the guy had at least remembered the bitch who'd bought it. And so the trail had led him here. To Phoebe, of all people.

He grinned. Sometimes the world was a truly funny place. To think that he could have actually skipped all that time-wasting stuff, and just waited for Phoebe to bring it back to Mayfield.

He closed the door behind him, and the damn thing clicked shut with a sharp sound.

A door opened upstairs.

He reached into his pocket and cradled the small caliber gun. The time was past for the niceties of doing it barehanded, or the innate satisfaction of a knife sliding home. This time, it was going to be obvious.

An obvious case of a lovers' quarrel, that is. And he'd have to make sure that the part about the 'lovers' was backed up by a whole lot of very convincing forensic evidence. He remembered the condom in his back pocket, and silently eased his hands into a pair of thin latex gloves. Peta would look used, all right. But the only physical remains would be those of Max Wolfe.

He smiled once more, and started for the stairs.

* * * * *

Peta's heart stopped as she heard the distinctive sound of the front door closing downstairs.

He was back. *Max had come back.*

Her ears rang and her vision blurred for a moment, as her heart started up again and roared into overdrive.

Would he come up and kiss her and sweep her off her feet? Or would he just casually mention that he'd found an apartment and was leaving shortly?

Well, screw that. Not if she had anything to say about it. She was dressed for sex, if wearing white cotton panties could be called sex-inducing attire, and if he thought he was going to get away without one last fuck, then he was wrong.

Peta rushed into the bathroom, splashed cold water on her face, ran a brush through her hair and then re-entered the bedroom.

The footsteps hesitated on the landing.

Aww. He was shy.

"In here, Max...I'm so glad you came back. There's something I need to talk to you about." Sitting on the edge of the bed, and trying to forget that she was almost naked, with her breasts on display, and her nipples putting on a rather obvious show of arousal, Peta waited.

The door opened.

"Max...I..." She gasped, and her heart stopped once again. But this time, it was with fear. Her eyes slid from the cold gaze of the man staring at her to the shiny little gun he was pointing at her.

"YOU!"

* * * * *

Max's pace quickened as he headed back to Peta's little house on Acorn Street. He felt as if a weight had been lifted off his shoulders, and his lips creased in a grin as he imagined her surprise when he walked into the kitchen.

Or the bedroom. Or her bathroom. He didn't care if she was sitting on the toilet at the time. Some things demanded immediate attention, and what he had to say was one of them.

"I love you." He tried out the words quietly to himself. "I love you, Peta." Yep. It sounded right. He wasn't sensing any urge to throw up, or run for the nearest train out of town.

He wasn't panicking. He was eager. For the first time in his life, Max Wolfe loved someone, and he couldn't wait to tell her. In detail.

And then show her. Also in detail. Most of which included them both naked, on the bed, the floor, the dining room table, and possibly next to the tea caddy. He wanted to lick her all over, and have her do the same.

A thought sobered him. Suppose she didn't love him back?

His steps slowed a little as he considered this possibility, and a chill slipped down his spine that had nothing to do with the weather.

He gritted his teeth. If she didn't love him back, then he'd damn well *make* her. He'd caress her, and touch her and drive her crazy, bringing that wonderful glaze of cloudy heat into those gray eyes of hers.

Then he'd sink deep into her and make her admit that she loved him too. She just had to. She could never have given herself to him, cuddled him, hell, made him tea like she did, if she hadn't felt *something*, could she?

Once again, Max found himself caught up in a maelstrom of questions to which he had no answers. It was an unusual feeling, and a sort of unpleasant one. He wasn't sure that he liked this whole "being in love" thing. Too many uncertainties, and too many unanswered questions.

There was only one way to find out. He had to go get answers, and he had to lay to rest his uncertainties. And then he was going to fuck Peta until they were exhausted, sticky, limp, and ready to plan their future.

And their family.

A small vision from his dream crept into his mind. He'd dreamed that he'd had a son. Where the hell had *that* come from? He knew, sure as shit, that Peta was the mother.

And he knew, just as certainly, that he wanted that child. Wanted to plant his seed in her and watch her grow as she nourished his son. And perhaps a daughter, too.

He chuckled as he quickened his steps. Maybe he'd send Emma Hansell a picture of the babies. She'd like that.

It seemed to take ages to get back to Peta's, but his long legs ate up the slushy sidewalk, and he found himself breathing quickly as he mounted the steps two at a time and opened the front door.

He frowned, as he realized that she really should keep it locked.

"Peta? Peta, it's Max..." he called.

The house seemed quiet. He glanced into the kitchen, but it was empty. There was a box of tissues on the table, but everything else was tidy.

Max frowned a little. Had she gone out? Dammit to fucking hell. She wouldn't. Not right *now*.

He peeped into the dining room to see if she was working, but her laptop was closed. All was silent.

Okay. She was upstairs. In her bedroom. Good. Saved them both some time.

"Peta, it's me..." he called, as he hurried up the stairs.

"In here, Max." The voice came from her bedroom.

Max opened the door.

And froze.

Peta was lying on the bed, wearing only her panties. Lying on top of her, sucking her breast — was *Struthers*.

He raised his head and grinned at Max. "Good to see you, Wolfe. Always glad to welcome a third to the party. Come on over and get some of this, why don't you?" He nodded at Peta's bared breasts.

Max couldn't breathe. Couldn't speak. Couldn't even formulate a thought.

"Max, it's not...what you think..." She gasped and thrust her breasts upwards.

"Oh, but it is, Peta dear. Max knows a slut when he sees one. Hell, Diana probably showed him how to handle a three-way. Max knows women well, you see. Isn't that so, dear boy?"

The "dear boy" was completely at a loss, stunned by the sight in front of him, and brain aching from trying to comprehend what he saw.

Peta looked like she was enjoying Struthers's mouth on her. Her back was arched towards him. But her eyes...

Max stared into her eyes.

"Trust me, Max," she sighed. "Please, *trust* me."

And there it was.

The evidence was right before his eyes, but she was asking him to trust her. Could he? Should he?

Did he love her enough to trust her?

Shit yes.

"I trust you," he answered.

"Pity," murmured Struthers. He cast a longing glance over Peta's nearly-naked body. "It would have been fun, I think."

He moved off her and revealed the hand that had been pressing into Peta's spine beneath her.

The hand that held a rather serviceable gun.

Max swallowed. "Oh fuck."

"Quite," answered the imperturbable Struthers.

* * * * *

Peta found herself pushed from the bed onto the floor as Struthers stood, gun firmly held in his hand.

She scrambled over to Max, and he automatically reached for her.

"Leave her be," came the sharp command. "Don't move. Either of you."

Hell, what chance did she have? She was damn near stark naked, and facing a madman with a gun. This was so *crazy.*

"Struthers, I don't understand," she said. Keep him talking, her mind told her. Distract him. Divert his attention so that Superman could fly in through the window and disarm him. Anything.

But the small barrel never wavered from Max's heart.

"What's not to understand?" asked Struthers. "The book is mine. That Bible has been mine all along. It was stolen from me years ago."

Peta sighed. So that was it. This was all about that dratted Bible. And the money.

"You probably think it's the money, don't you?" Struthers giggled, an unpleasant sound that warned Peta this was not someone intent on simple robbery. He was too near the edge.

Peta nodded. "Of course. That book is worth a lot."

Max moved slightly. "Just take the fucking thing, Struthers. Just take it. It's not worth...this..." He gestured at the gun, but froze as Struthers's hand moved upwards a quarter of an inch.

"Oh, but I can't do that, you see. Too many people know I've been inquiring about it."

"But," frowned Peta. "I thought it was Edward who wanted that information."

Struthers glanced down at her with a disdainful expression. "You were meant to. I had to cover my tracks here in Mayfield, didn't I? But they know me in Boston. They know that it has been my life's goal to get that book back into my family. Did you know—" His tone was almost chatty, and Peta tried to forget that he was pointing a gun at the two of them

"—That book was stolen from my family over a hundred years ago? I found out about it quite by accident, and then I knew."

"Knew what, Struthers?" asked Peta.

"Knew that it was ordained for me to return it to where it belonged. I was a librarian. I had the resources. Fate had put me in the perfect position to track it down. Of course, I didn't have the wherewithal to purchase it outright, not many people do." He paused thoughtfully.

"And so?" drawled Max.

Peta wanted to laugh hysterically. Max sounded almost—bored by the whole thing. And yet, from her position on the floor, she could see the slight tremble that shook him. Max Wolfe was not bored at all.

She prayed that he wouldn't do anything silly. They had to get out of this alive. She had things to tell him.

As if he heard her, his eyes dropped and met hers for a second or two. She sighed as she saw his raw emotions churning. He was as tense as she was.

"And so," continued Struthers. "And so here I am. I thought I could get it from Sandra, but she tried to play games with me. Stupid bitch."

"And so you killed her," said Max flatly.

"Yes, I did. And you know what?" Struthers licked his lips. "It was quite fun. You see I was fucking her at the time. She came and went, so to speak."

He giggled again at his own pun, and Peta swallowed down bile.

"Of course, it was annoying. But it really did reinforce my determination to get the Bible."

"What about Mike Dean?" asked Peta hoarsely.

"Ah yes. The late unlamented Mr. Dean. What an idiot he was. Do you know he actually thought he could blackmail me? I have to assume that Sandra's mouth was as big as her cunt. She'd blabbed to him everything she knew. So, of course, being the thickheaded lout he was, he tried to turn it to his advantage."

Struthers shook his head in disgust.

"So you disposed of him too?" Max's voice cut through the room.

"Yes indeed. Quite nice, that one was. Something so satisfying about the feeling of a sharp knife sliding between a couple of ribs. Which reminds me, I do have to apologize..." He glanced down at Peta.

"I had no intentions of having Dean die on your doorstep, my dear. Much too uncivilized. But it seems that his heart was a lot stronger than his brains. He managed to survive my knife, the trunk of my car, and the cold weather. Finally," Struthers snickered. "It was the snowplow that finished the job. Quite ironic, isn't it?"

He was mad. Clearly, undoubtedly, raving mad. Peta's blood churned as the full realization hit her.

Struthers was going to kill them both. There was no way he'd be telling them all this unless he knew they'd be permanently silenced.

"What about us?" she breathed.

Chapter 25

Max had no idea how he managed to stay still as he listened to the insane ravings of Struthers and watched the gun in his hand.

If Peta hadn't been on the floor between them, he'd have rushed the guy and taken his chances. But if he should fail...his blood chilled at the thought of her left alone to face this madman.

"Yes, what about us, Struthers? Oh and don't forget Phoebe. She knows too."

Struthers shook his head sadly. "Yes, poor Phoebe. I'm afraid I'm going to have to arrange for a slight accident there, my boy. Dear Phoebe. I couldn't bring myself to do her any harm personally. She's too sweet." He sighed. "This terrible weather. Cars go off the road all the time. Yours did, Peta. It'll be a dreadful coincidence when Phoebe's suffers the same fate. A simple fault in her brake lines...you know the sort of thing."

Max heard Peta's swallow as she digested this information. He stepped slightly to one side away from her.

The gun followed him. "I said don't move," Struthers rapped out.

"So what are you going to do with us? Remember, there's two of us. And don't think we won't do everything we can to stop you," warned Max.

"Bloody right, Max," echoed Peta firmly.

Max hoped he was the only one who heard that slight quaver in her brave words.

Struthers snickered. "Oh you two have made it all too easy. Why, I daresay the whole town is talking about the way you've moved in here, Max. And Peta hasn't kept very many things secret. Cary Stiles is still pissed that you told him you two were sleeping together."

"I did not," said Peta crossly. "He deduced that all by himself."

Struthers snorted. "No matter. It all adds to my story. Such a sad story too. You see, Max was about to leave you, my dear. You, being a reserved Englishwoman, stored up all your hurt and your pain. And when Max here returned from his trip to the realtor, you couldn't stand it any more."

"And she shoots me. What then? She turns the gun on herself?" Max's words dripped ice.

Struthers raised an eyebrow. "Very good, Max. I'm impressed. And here I thought you didn't actually read anything but the articles in Playboy."

Max's eyes narrowed. "It won't work, Struthers. People know us in Mayfield. They won't believe it for a minute."

Struthers let out that peculiarly horrible giggle and Peta shuddered on the floor. "Oh but it will work, Max. I'm very careful, you see. I like to take my time." He glanced down at Peta.

"And dear Peta's body is going to be quite ravished, don't you know. I'm afraid it will be quite obvious that you've been having rough sex before the end. There will be no doubt in anyone's mind what went on. In fact..."

He looked quickly around the room before snapping back into focus on Max. "You two have already set up quite enough evidence to persuade any investigator that sex took place in here."

Struthers paused and raised an eyebrow. "By the way, how was she? Any good?"

It was the last straw for Max.

The first woman he'd ever loved was practically naked at his feet and a madman was holding them immobile at the end of a gun.

He'd had quite enough. A red film of fury rose up behind his eyeballs, and his lips peeled back from his teeth as his anger grew.

"Like I'd tell you," he scoffed. "Although hearing it would probably turn you on, wouldn't it? I doubt that much else can. If you have to strangle a woman while you're fucking her, you're probably useless the rest of the time. Can't get it up, huh, Struthers? Got a needle-dick there? A *teeny* problem? Ever think of trying Viagra?"

Struthers' hand was shaking now. Definitely shaking.

"You filth," he spat at Max. "You fucking piece of ignorant shit. You nail every piece of cunt you can lay your hands on and you dare insult *me*?"

Max tensed. He had to get Struthers boiling. So angry that he'd lose focus. It was their only chance.

"Sure I dare. You're some limp-dicked piece of crap who gets off fucking dead women. There's a name for that, you know. Necrophilia. Ever heard of it? I can even spell it."

Unbelievably, he heard a quick chuckle from Peta. "You know, you're probably right, Max. I doubt if he's got anything in those pants besides that gun of his."

Oh Christ, no. Peta. Max tried to send mental messages to her. *Don't aggravate him. That's my job. I don't want him shooting you. I can't live without you.*

Struthers was sweating now, his hand wavering as his control slipped. "We'll just have to see about that, won't we?"

Max braced himself to move any which way he could once Struthers's finger tightened on the trigger. He met the man's eyes, watching for a sign that the moment was coming.

Like two gunfighters sizing each other up on some dusty western street, he faced Struthers and the gun, waiting, heart pounding, for the moment when he could release the adrenaline bottled up inside him.

Struthers laughed.

NOW.

* * * * *

The next minutes seemed to pass in slow motion before Peta's horrified eyes. Her brain stopped working, and her automatic reflexes took over.

As Struthers laughed, she could see his hand tense and knew that he fully intended to shoot Max, right there, in her bedroom.

It was something she couldn't allow. Every molecule in her body screamed out against it. She couldn't—*wouldn't*—lose him.

Gathering her strength, Peta leaped off the floor just as Struthers raised the gun and aimed at Max.

The sound of a shot rang in her ears, deafening her as it resounded through the bedroom.

Peta screamed. "Nooooooo..."

She fell against Max, knocking him off-balance, and tumbling them both to the floor.

Another voice cut through the confusion.

"*Stay down*," it commanded, and another shot followed.

Peta turned her head and watched, stunned, as a horrible red stain appeared on Struthers' chest.

He seemed surprised as he lowered his gaze to his jacket. "Good heavens," he muttered. They were his last words.

He slowly crumpled to the floor, the gun dropping from his limp fingers and clattering down beside him.

"Peta, Max...are you all right? *Peta*?"

Frank Summers stood in the doorway, his service revolver still gripped firmly in his hands.

Peta wanted to giggle. He looked like something out of every police drama she'd ever seen on TV.

"Oh sheeeiiiitt..." His voice was horrified and Peta followed his gaze downwards, looking at her own body.

She swallowed. Her white skin was no longer white. There was a neat hole just above her left breast, and her blood was flowing freely down and onto Max who was terribly still beneath her.

"Oh *bollocks*."

Peta Matthews' world went dark.

* * * * *

Somewhere, birds were singing. It was a soothing sound, and Max lay quiet, relishing the liquid notes that poured over him along with a gentle breeze.

Slowly, memories returned.

A gun. A shot. Struthers. Peta.

Peta.

Max jerked, opening his eyes wide in fear.

He was in a large room, with soft drapes moving slightly near the open windows. He was in bed, and as he turned, he saw Peta lying next to him. She was very still. He raised himself up on one elbow and stared at her.

She was pale, but her chest was moving beneath the sheet.

Max offered up a prayer of thanks. Tears sprang into his eyes. They were probably both dead, but at least they were together.

Gently he stroked her skin, loving the softness and the warmth beneath his fingers. There was so much he wanted to say to her, to tell her, but for now, he was quite content to lie next to her and watch her as she slept.

This had to be heaven. It was a miracle that they'd allowed him in, for sure, but an eternity next to Peta would be his own private heaven. Perhaps St. Peter had a soft spot for reformed superstuds.

Max felt his cock twitch in approval as his hands brushed Peta's flesh. Oh good. Sex was allowed in Heaven too. Things just got better and better.

He leaned over and dropped a gentle kiss on the pulse at the base of her neck, and she stirred, sighing a little and letting her lips curve into a small grin.

"Hi sweetheart," he murmured.

"Hi yourself," she mumbled back. "You all right?"

Max smiled. "Never better, babe. I'm next to you and we're in bed. I have no idea where, and right at this moment I don't care."

Peta slowly opened her eyes and looked at him. Max saw his world reflected in her gray depths and his heart thudded as she raised a hand to stroke his cheek.

He swallowed past the lump in his throat. "I love you, Peta Matthews. I was almost too late to say it. But I do. I love you." He dropped another kiss, this time on her lips.

"That's bloody brilliant, Max," she grinned. "Because I love you too." Her eyes changed. "But Max...Struthers...the gunshot..."

"I don't know, honey. I *think*—" He glanced around the strange room. "—I think we may be, er, dead?"

A light laugh sounded from the foot of the bed.

"No, Max, you're not dead."

A tall man stood there, with a woman beside him. His eyes were a very unusual color, and they were both dressed in flowing robes. No wings, however. And Max couldn't remember ever seeing pictures of angels that looked like these two.

The woman was incredibly beautiful, with raven black hair hanging past her waist, and the man's arm was holding her close. They looked...they looked *right* together.

Peta gripped the sheet firmly and struggled up onto the pillow, with a slight frown. "I remember you."

"Good," answered the man. "You should. We asked you to fulfill a special mission for us, and you have succeeded. The proof is lying beside you." He nodded at Max.

Max unstuck his tongue from the roof of his mouth. "Okay. I'm confused. You say we're not dead. But even a moron could tell that this isn't Mayfield. So where the hell are we?"

The man moved to the bed as the woman perched beside Peta. "It's a rather complicated story, Max, but to get to the root of the matter, you are in a place called Anyela. It's sort of—out of time—as you know it. It's where we keep an eye on the Universe. Make sure it's running smoothly. That sort of thing."

Max raised one eyebrow. "Right."

"No really, Max. It's true. I remember this place—these people. I was here before. Right after my car crashed." Peta turned to him. "Honestly. It's all coming back to me."

"You sure you don't have something in that tea caddy besides tea?"

Peta grinned. "I'm not joking, Max. This place is real. Well, perhaps not *real* in the sense that you and I would use the word. It's more...more...non-corporeal. Outside the normal space-time continuum, so to speak."

Max raised the other eyebrow. "Might I ask if Scotty is going to rush in and beam us up any minute? You been doing some Vulcan mind-meld thing with Spock here?" He tipped his head towards the man smiling at them.

Peta sighed and looked over at the woman. "Can *you* explain it to him?"

"Nope. You're on your own with this one. You're only here for a sort of debriefing, anyway."

Max moved his hips around. "We've been *de-briefed* already, by the feel of things."

Peta blushed.

The man sat down on the bed with a smothered chuckle. "Max, don't sweat it. You and Peta have played your roles perfectly. The problem that was about to interrupt the natural flow of time has been corrected. You are both still alive and matters will progress as ordained."

"Good to know." Max leaned back. He was definitely hallucinating. And it was rather nice. A lovely room, warm air, Peta naked beside him under the sheets...if these two visions would just evaporate or disintegrate or something, he could make it even better.

"We seldom interfere, Max," said the woman thoughtfully. "But there are times when intervention is the only way to avert a serious problem. We needed Peta to be in the right place at the right time. We needed her to save you, Max. You are important."

Peta looked at him. "He sure is."

The woman's lips twitched and she coughed a little. "Yes, well, be that as it may, everything has now been set to rights. In a little while, you'll go back to your own time. You will remember little, if anything, of this experience. Maybe a dream or two."

Max jerked a little. His eyes turned to the man. "My dream. Christ, it was you in my dream, wasn't it?"

The man grinned.

"What dream, Max?" Peta's question brought a blush to Max's cheeks.

"Never mind. I'll tell you later."

"Will you trust us? Believe us when we tell you that soon you'll be back where you belong?" The woman tipped her head at Max.

He shrugged. "What choice do I have?"

"None whatsoever," answered the man. "The reason you're not back right now is that your bodies have taken rather a beating, I'm afraid. You, Max, hit your head on Peta's bureau when she knocked you down, and are presently suffering a concussion. Peta..."

Max's heart thumped. "Oh God. She was shot, wasn't she? She took that damned bullet Struthers meant for me." He turned to Peta and let the anguish pour through him. "How could you?"

"Because I love you, silly thing," she soothed. "You'd have done the same for me. You were about to."

"Yes, but that's *different*," he began.

"Er, let's not squabble about it, shall we?" The interruption came firmly from the woman as she stood up from the bed and gave Peta's hand a little pat. "Peta was shot, but not fatally. Her body is resting and healing, and when you go back more healing will be necessary. Which is why..." She cleared her throat again. "Why my husband and I thought you might like some time here together, before you have to return. There's going to be a lot of resting and recuperating needed before you two can— um—" She blushed.

Max felt a slow smile creep around his lips. "Mighty thoughtful of you, Ma'am," he grinned.

"We like to think that our world runs along on wheels greased by love and passion, Max," said the man, with a knowing look in his eyes. "In another time, another place, you would have made a hell of a genie."

"A *genie*?" choked Max. "Oh I don't *think* so. Vests? Blue skin? A *bottle*?"

"Not quite." Two chuckles greeted Max's outrage. "Relax now. The next time you sleep you will return to your world, and your memories of Anyela will be gone."

They moved away from the bed, the man sliding his hand around the woman's waist. He spoke once more. "Thank you both. You have provided an invaluable service to the progression of time. Enjoy your reward."

They were gone.

Max was finally alone with Peta.

Chapter 26

Peta felt herself pulled close to a hard chest by a pair of strong arms, and she sighed with pleasure.

"Alone at last," murmured Max in her ear.

She giggled. "I thought they'd *never* leave." She daringly pressed her lips to the solid expanse of flesh in front of her. "Mmm. Max. You taste so good. I love you so awfully much, you know."

Max ran his fingers along her arm from her shoulder to her elbow and made her shiver. "I know. And I love you too. I'm just sorry it took me so damn long to realize it. If I hadn't left you that morning...this morning...hell, I'm lost. What day is it?"

"Who knows? Doesn't matter. And if you hadn't left, Struthers might have snuck in and shot both of us without a blink. At least with you gone he was offered the chance to set things up for himself, which bought us some valuable time. He was quite insane, I think."

"Did he hurt you? Before I got home?" Max frowned.

"No. He scared the shit out of me though. I thought it was you coming in, and that was why I had no—er—well, I didn't bother to dress too much."

He chuckled, making Peta's ear rumble. "So that's why you were in those enticing white panties."

"Yes. I think Struthers was rather shocked for a moment too. But it wasn't too long before he heard you come in the house, and the next thing I knew he was on top of me with that blasted gun shoved up under my back. He knew how to make it look like I was encouraging him, all right." She sniffed. "Stupid idiot. He should have known you better. As if you'd believe I could encourage *him*." She peeped up at Max. "You didn't believe I could, did you?"

"Absolutely not. I took one look in your eyes, and knew something was very wrong."

Peta snickered. "You're a very smart man, Max Wolfe."

Max snorted. "Of course. I have you. I'm smart enough to know that you're the only one for me. I could have been smarter and figured it out earlier, but hell. We made it. Now we can begin fulfilling our dreams." His hand crept to her breast, cupping it lovingly.

"Oh, that reminds me. What did you say earlier about a dream?"

Max sighed.

"Tell me? Please?"

"I have a better idea," he said. He rolled over onto Peta, nestling his cock between her thighs, which she obligingly opened for him. "Mmm. How about I show you."

"Oooh. It was *that* kind of dream, was it?" Peta couldn't help the little wiggle of her hips as she felt Max's hot cock slipping and sliding over her flesh. She adjusted her position to get him right where she wanted him. Up against her cunt. She raised and lowered her hips slightly, letting her juices moisten him.

He groaned. "Oh, babe. Any time you do *that* is a dream."

Peta slipped her hands down his back and filled them with his buttocks, pressing him against her. "God, Max. I was so *afraid*."

Max sighed with pleasure. "Yeah, I know. Me too. When I saw that damn gun—"

"No, not that. I was afraid you weren't coming back. When you walked out of my house, you took my heart, maybe my whole life, with you."

Max kissed her, thrusting his tongue deep, demanding she kiss him back. Which she did. With a great deal of enthusiasm. Kissing Max, decided Peta, was one of life's great pleasures.

He moved, rubbing his body against hers in a sensual slide. Okay, make that another of life's pleasures.

"Peta, I could never have left you. Every step I took away from you damn near killed me." He stared at her, his hazel eyes glowing.

"Thank heavens for that." She reached up and stroked his cheek lovingly once more, unable to get her fill of touching him. "I think you're stuck with me, Max."

"I think we're stuck together." His body moved a little, demonstrating the truth of his words. "And I have no complaints at all."

He reached behind him and found her hands, lifting them up and pinning them to the pillow behind her head. Her back arched, and Max lowered his head, suckling a nipple into his mouth.

Peta shivered. His touch, his tongue, his heat...they were stoking up her fires to inferno-like levels, and she felt that familiar emptiness in her cunt that told her something ought to be there. Something that only Max could provide.

"I want you inside me, Max," she breathed. "Right here, right now."

She spread her thighs wide, opening herself. Offering all that she was in a flagrant invitation.

He accepted.

Raising his hips, his cock found her wetness, her heat, the swollen tissues that wept tears of joy just for him.

Slowly, very slowly, as if he was relishing every single moment, Max's cock slid home.

* * * * *

It took milliseconds for Max to become aware that this was different. "Christ, Peta. You feel...you feel..." He moved experimentally. Yeah. She *felt*.

"Feel how, Max?"

His eyes closed as he gently slid out and then back into her again. "Hot. Slick. I don't know. Yes I do." He opened his eyes and stared at her. "This is a first for me."

He felt her body tremble as she giggled. "Oh come *on*." She didn't understand.

"Don't you get it? This is the first time I've ever, *ever*, made love without protection. With nothing between me and your cunt. Your wonderful—" He plunged again. "Boiling hot—" Another plunge. "—And snug little cunt."

Peta groaned as he thrust once more.

Max was beyond thought. His cock was wrapped in fiery silk, her muscles caressing and squeezing him into bliss.

"I never realized how different it could be," she breathed. "It's a first for me, too."

Max held himself deep within her as her eyes opened wide.

"I can feel you so much better. Every little part of you." She grinned. "Although I use the word 'little' in the metaphorical sense, of course."

Max grinned back.

With a swift move, he rolled them, ending up on his back with his cock still deep inside Peta. She settled herself astride him, folding her legs comfortably on either side of his hips.

"God, this is *fabulous*," she whispered.

Max let his hands roam. He found her spine and traced it lightly all the way down to the soft curve of her buttocks. He cupped her cheeks and tugged them slightly, stroking her cleft and bringing a moan to her throat.

"Ride me, babe," he encouraged.

Well, all right, she probably didn't need to be told what to do, since she was already leaning forward, taking her weight on her hands and lifting up a little. She was a natural at this. Just perfect.

And she'd managed to get those wonderful breasts right where he needed them.

He kept up his light touches around her buttocks as his mouth sought her nipple, swinging tantalizingly close to his mouth. There. He'd found it. He suckled her strongly, teasing the hard bud with his tongue and pressing it to the roof of his mouth, making her gasp.

He could feel her cunt clenching on him as he sucked. It was truly, absolutely amazing, and it blew Max away. Each strong pull of his mouth was answered by a ripple deep inside her around his cock.

There was a weird kind of symmetry to it that left him breathless.

His fingers found her puckered skin between her cheeks and pressed, making her sob with pleasure.

"Bloody hell, Max," she grunted.

He tried to grin, but she chose that moment to sink so far down on him that their bodies merged into one.

He realized that all those romance novels were right. There were times when two people lost themselves in each other. When they didn't know where one ended and the other began.

This was such a moment.

"Oh yeah," he breathed.

Peta's hands clawed at his shoulders as her body shuddered on top of his. She pushed herself onto him, sliding around him, cradling his cock inside her and loving it with every squeeze, every gasp, every little squirm she made.

The harder she pushed, the more he felt her clit against him, and he began to meet thrust with thrust, and downward slide with upward push.

It was an ancient rhythm, pounded out by hearts and bodies, and Max allowed his instincts to direct the moves of this dance. His instincts and his heart.

They were both panting now, slick with sweat and moisture, their flesh meeting and parting in a kiss all its own.

He pressed his finger past her anal muscles, penetrating her a little and adding a new touch to nerves he knew were screaming.

She cried out and pushed him so deep inside her he could feel her womb pressing on the tip of his cock.

It was truly a moment out of time. Max's soul crumpled, stunned by the feel of her, both inside and out. His balls contracted, he gasped for air around her breast, and with a sharp cry he felt himself erupt.

She was right there with him.

Peta ground herself against him, and the increased pressure seemed to send her off the edge of heaven. No sooner had he begun to come than she was shivering and shaking around him and over him.

His spurts began, intense and strong, filling her with his come. Her cunt contracted tight around him, sucking the life out of him, pulling it all deep within her.

Max knew this was more than just an incredible fuck. This was a life-altering, mind-bending, heart-shattering orgasm for both of them.

He let go, let it happen and lost himself in the wonder of it all.

Peta didn't know anything at all.

She was completely and absolutely immersed in the experience of loving Max with every single bit of her.

Her orgasm threatened to explode through her ears, and she screamed out his name as the convulsive shudders spread from her clit to the top of her head. Her thighs gripped his hips so hard that his bones dug in, adding a weird dash of pain to her pleasure.

His finger was pressing into her arse, taking her even higher as new sensations wracked her and stole the breath from her lungs.

She choked in a great lungful of air as she fought to prolong the moment.

His cock was pulsing inside her, each twitch sending her higher and higher. Oh *Christ*. It was happening *again*.

Peta sobbed as more tremors racked her body, and Max's cock spurted its warmth into her deepest places.

Surely she could not survive this. How could anyone live through such pleasure, time and time again?

Eyes closed, Peta let the waves take her, her world narrowed down to one man, one cock, and yet another trembling surge of ripples washing through her.

It was heaven. It was beyond belief. And it was exhausting.

Finally, it ended.

Peta collapsed with a thud onto Max's chest, bringing a grunt to his throat.

His heart was beating furiously beneath her head, matching her own pounding pulse.

She was helpless. She couldn't move a muscle. Perhaps she *was* dead. She sincerely hoped not, since once she got her breath back, she thought she'd rather like to do it again.

But a gentle caress up her back told her that she wasn't a corpse. Far from it. Max's loving strokes were helping her down from that wild peak she'd just scaled, and her lungs filled with a huge sigh of contentment.

"Bloody hell," she sighed.

"Fucking *A*," he agreed.

"I love you."

"I love you too."

Peta nestled herself into Max, feeling his softened cock slip from her body. She smiled sleepily. "I like this, Max. I *really* like this a lot."

Max yawned. "No more than me, I'll bet. Give me a few minutes and we'll go again, okay?"

Peta chuckled. "Give me an hour. I'm not up to your speed yet."

"You will be, sweetheart. I plan on a lifetime of teaching you."

She raised her head a little and glanced up at his chin. "You do?"

"Oh yeah." He bent his head down and dropped a kiss on the top of her head. "We've got something very special to do. I have it on the *highest* authority."

She groaned. "Not another sleuthing job, I hope. We did a lousy job first time around."

"Nope. Not this time."

"Ah." She waited. Max was silent. "So, are you going to share this *special thing* we've got to do?"

"Nope."

"Rat." Peta nipped his chest.

"Ouch." His mock-pain wriggle made her smile.

"I can think of a thousand ways to torture it out of you, you know. My ancestors invented hanging, drawing and quartering." She giggled.

"My ancestors were probably hung."

Peta traced a hand down to his groin and let it rest on his cock. "I'll just bet they were."

Max laughed. "You, woman, are insatiable."

"And I don't hear any complaints."

He sighed and pulled her even closer against his body. "And you never will, darlin'. Just keep loving me, and we'll fulfill all those dreams. You and me."

His voice trailed off, and Peta found her eyelids growing heavy at the rhythmic sound of his heart beating beneath her ear.

She sighed deeply, contented all the way to her soul. For once, her wishes had been granted and her life had become the stuff of fantasies.

For a shy, well-rounded British girl, it wasn't bad going. Not bad going at all.

She closed her eyes and followed her lover into sleep.

Chapter 27

Something terribly sharp was digging into Peta's chest. And something else really heavy was sitting on it.

She struggled to catch a breath and gasped as a savage pain shimmered over her. "*Bollocks. I hurt.*"

"Easy, Peta, easy," said a calm voice. "Just breathe naturally. Don't struggle, dear."

Peta fought to open her eyes. As soon as she did, something very bright shone into them and she snapped her lids shut again immediately.

"Just checking, hon. Have to make sure you're okay."

Well damn it. Searing her retinas wasn't the way to go about it. She frowned as the unmistakable feel of a blood pressure cuff clamped down on her arm and the whuffling sound of pumped air tightened it snugly.

"Good, sweetheart. You're doing fine."

Velcro ripped and her arm was freed. "Where am I?" She opened her eyes again.

Okay. Stupid question. She should have opened her eyes first. It was very obvious where she was. Clinical white drapes surrounded her bed, generic sheets covered her, and some equipment was beeping quietly behind her.

The pain came again and she winced.

"Don't struggle, Peta. Just rest. Your body needs time to heal." Peta turned her head and met the sympathetic eyes of a nurse. "Is the pain bad, honey?"

Peta considered the question. "Only when I do something stupid. Like breathe, for instance."

The nurse grinned. "You're doing great. It will pass. We gave you a little pain medication but not too much. You had to wake up first." The woman nodded to the IV drip that was attached to Peta's hand. Funny thing, that. She didn't feel it at all.

Memories came flooding back to Peta as she looked down to see her chest swathed in bandages.

"Oh my God. I was *shot*—" She looked at the nurse. "Max? Max Wolfe? Is he—"

The question trembled on her lips, and her heart rate made the monitor beep frantically.

"Whoa. Calm down, sweetheart. He's fine. Although I must confess—" She leaned closer to Peta. "Once I got a good look at him, my heart rate went up by twenty points, too."

Peta managed a painful grin. "He's mine. Sorry."

The nurse sighed. "Yeah, he made that very clear. We had to sedate him to get him away from you. But he should be here any minute...aha. Speak of the devil—"

The curtains were swept back, and Peta's eyes feasted on the sight of Max smiling at her. The bandage around his head gave him a rather piratical look, and although he was in a wheelchair and an ugly hospital gown, he still looked good enough to eat.

The heart monitor shrieked again.

"You're out of here if you upset her," warned the nurse. Max smiled at her, and she melted. "Well, okay. Just for a little while. You both need rest."

"Thanks honey. I need this woman a lot more than I need rest. And she needs me. You can just leave us if you want." Max rolled his chair up to the side of the bed and took Peta's free hand in his. "We'll be fine now."

Oh yes indeed. Peta felt the warmth of his hand and saw it matched the heat in his eyes. *They would indeed be fine now.*

She smiled. "Hello Max."

"Hi yourself, babe." He stroked her hand and played with her fingers. "You scared the life out of me."

"Funny. I seem to remember a dream..." She blinked and the images were gone. "The head...what happened?"

Max grimaced. "I fell down and hit it on the bureau. Pretty embarrassing, huh? Trying to be a hero, and you're the one who took the bullet. I was fucking *unconscious* while you were getting shot." He gritted his teeth.

"But what about Struthers? He was shot too...oh wait, Frank was there." Some of the mists cleared from Peta's memory.

"Yep. The cavalry arrived in time, thank God." Max's grip tightened. "I won't let myself think about what might have happened if Frank hadn't come in when he did."

"How did he—Max, I'm confused." Peta wrinkled her brow.

"Perhaps I can help out." Frank Summers peered around the curtains. "Okay if I disturb you two for a moment? I've got Doc's permission." He looked a little uncomfortable at the sight of Peta and Max holding hands and staring into each other's eyes.

He cleared his throat.

Peta tried to ease her hand from Max's, but he refused to let go. His fingers tightened as he nodded at Frank. "Come on in. We have a lot of questions." He glanced over at a chair. "Cop a squat, Frank."

Peta groaned.

"Sorry. No pun intended," chuckled Max.

Frank ignored the by-play, sitting down and resting his forearms on his knees. Peta thought he looked tired.

"Frank, tell us. How did you come to be there? What happened?"

He sighed and ran his hand through his hair. "What a damn mess. Not the sort of thing I'm used to, Peta, that's for sure." His hand shook a little. "Never killed anyone before. Hell." He tried for an awkward grin and almost made it. "I've never even discharged my weapon in the line of duty before. Except for the time that Mrs. Grunson's dog went crazy, and even then I didn't—"

"Frank?" Max gently interrupted Frank's reminiscences.

Frank recalled himself. "Sorry. Yeah. About that morning. You can thank Phoebe."

"*Phoebe?*" The word came from Max and Peta simultaneously.

Frank dredged up a smile. "Yeah, Phoebe. One sharp lady. Apparently, she felt that Struthers was acting kind of odd that morning. He dropped her at the library and couldn't wait to leave her there. It was, according to her, out of character. And the other thing was, he was sweating."

"*Sweating?* And that was enough to bring you to my house?" Peta frowned.

"Well, given that it was a damned cold morning, and Phoebe told me you had a book or something worth damn near half a million dollars sitting in your dining room, yeah. It was quite enough."

"Oh shit, that book," said Max. "Damned near forgot about it."

"Well Struthers hadn't," answered Frank. "We did some backtracking, and it turns out he'd been obsessed with it for years. Thought it was rightfully his, or some such thing. He'd worked himself into some kind of madness over it. Never realized that a damned book could drive someone to murder, though."

"You heard him? You heard him say he killed Sandra and Mike Dean?"

"Not all of it." Frank winced. "But enough to know that he meant business. If I could have gotten off a shot earlier, Peta, I could have saved you this...I'm so sorry."

"Frank," said Max calmly. "If it hadn't been for you, neither of us would be sitting here right now, and you'd be investigating what was supposed to be a murder-suicide. A crime of passion."

"Max is right, Frank. We owe you our lives," added Peta.

Frank blushed. "Just trying to do my job. But Christ, when I heard that first shot..." He dipped his head.

"He is dead, then?" Peta couldn't help asking the question. She had to know the threat no longer existed.

"Yeah. I may not shoot too often, but I don't mess around when I do," sighed Frank.

"Good thing too." Max's voice was firm. "He was mad as a hatter, Frank. He'd have killed us without a blink. He'd probably have enjoyed it. The world is better off without him."

Frank sighed. "I know. But damn, the paperwork's a bitch and a half."

Peta and Max chuckled.

"I'll bet," she added. "What about the book?"

"Oh yeah. Phoebe had some guy from a Boston museum in yesterday. It's been taken over there and put into a safe. I guess it has to be authenticated or something."

She smiled. "And to think we were lining up all kinds of suspects. I figured Edward was a good candidate. He needed money."

"I was betting on Cary Stiles. He's in debt to some rather nasty folks. He sure had the motive," mused Max.

Frank's tired face softened into a grin. "Doing my job for me, were you?"

Peta looked shamefaced. "Well, not exactly. But it was sort of natural to wonder. After all, Mayfield is a quiet town. This isn't a big city where things like that happen every day."

"And thank God for it."

Another voice chimed in and Phoebe peeked around the curtains. "How are you, darlings? Oh my goodness, you both look like war victims."

Frank stood and offered Phoebe his seat. "Hello Phoebe." He glanced over at Max and Peta. "It's okay. I have to go. I'll have some questions for you both later, but the Doc has given me strict instructions not to bother you with them right now. They can wait."

He left with a nod, as Phoebe took his seat and leaned forward eagerly. "So dears, tell me everything."

Peta gawped. "Good grief, Phoebe, it's you who has to tell us everything. How did you know about Struthers?"

She hated to ask the question, since Phoebe had made her personal interests plain in that direction. But she didn't look shattered. On the contrary, she seemed quite bubbly this morning.

"Oh, simple really." She waved her hand airily. "He was just acting all *wrong*. Not like himself at all. I have no illusions about my charms, Peta," she chuckled. "But this was the first time Struthers had ever acted like he couldn't wait to get rid of me."

Max opened his mouth.

"No, Max, let me finish, dear." She frowned him down, and he subsided. "I knew Struthers well enough—or I suppose I should say I *thought* I did—funny thing, isn't it? You think you know someone and they turn out to be quite the opposite from what you imagined?"

"*Phoebe.*" Peta couldn't help the exclamation. The nurse would be back dragging Max away from her before Phoebe had finished her story if she didn't get a move on.

"Yes, sorry." Phoebe sighed. "Well, it was just all wrong, you know? He kept trying to leave, to make *me* dig up all those names of people in Boston, and usually he didn't let me anywhere near his computer. He was always so territorial with the darned thing. And then, when I kept asking him what was wrong, he started with this story about a touch of the flu. And I saw him sweating."

She paused dramatically. "In all the time I've known Struthers, I've *never* seen him sweat."

Max was staring at Phoebe. "That wasn't much to go on, Phoebe. Calling Frank must have been a difficult decision."

"Not when a book worth a cool half-million or so is lying around loose," she answered caustically. "I know they say there's no fool like an old fool, Max, but even I'm not *that* much of a fool." Her lips pursed. "There's something about a lure like that that exercises a kind of horrid spell on people. Greed, avarice, call it what you want." Phoebe frowned. "Whatever it is, Struthers got that look about him as soon as he touched the blasted thing. I'm surprised you two didn't notice."

Peta remembered her state of mind as she'd watched Struthers and the Bible. It hadn't had anything to do with books. It had all to do with Max.

She sighed. "Well, whatever it was, Phoebe, you do know that your quick action saved both our lives, don't you?"

Max pulled his hand from hers, wheeled his chair awkwardly over to Phoebe and held out his arms. "Come here, you," he said roughly.

With a giggle, Phoebe leaned over and allowed herself to be thoroughly kissed. "Oh my, Max. Don't do that again. It's not good for my heart at my age."

Peta chuckled and watched as Max returned to her side, picking up her hand and twining their fingers together.

Phoebe sighed. "Well, all's well that ends well, as the Bard so aptly put it. Now." She stared at the two of them. "Am I to lose a couple of editors? Have you two finally sorted things out between you? Can I be step-grandmother to the kids?"

Peta choked back a gasp as Max laughed. "We're working on it, Phoebe," he grinned.

Peta flashed him a look and got one back that nearly blew out the monitors. She breathed deeply and told her errant hormones to back off. This was not the time or the place. Dammit.

Clearing her throat, she glanced down at herself. "I think you may be in for a bit of a wait on the grandchildren thing, Phoebe."

Max frowned, as did Phoebe. "Well, darn it," she said. "I forgot. You two just look so—so—glowing there, it's hard to remember you're both hurt. How bad is it anyway?"

"Good question," answered Peta thoughtfully. "I don't know yet. I'm sore, but I seem to be okay other than that."

"You're doing very well, Peta." The quintessential medical face appeared around the curtains, sporting a stethoscope instead of a tie, and a white coat. He was also grinning, a fact which gave Peta a considerable amount of reassurance.

"I am?"

"Yep." The doctor pulled her chart from the bed and ignored Phoebe's snort of impatience.

"The bullet entered your chest, but whether it was the fact that you were moving at the time, or just sheer providence, it missed everything vital and lodged in a rib. Never seen anything quite like it, actually. Neither had anyone else. Had a lot of company in OR when we retrieved the bullet, I can tell you."

Peta blushed at the thought of numerous faceless physicians watching as her chest was thoroughly investigated.

Next to her, Max bristled. "Well, that's good to know, *Doctor*." He emphasized the last word as he held Peta's hand even more tightly. "When can I take her home?"

The power in his words took Peta's breath away far better than some silly old bullet. He was claiming her. Talking about taking her home. And oh my, she liked it. She liked it a lot.

Unfazed, the doctor grinned at Max. "In a couple of days if she continues to improve and you show no signs of concussion. But rest is the order of the day for both of you for at least forty-eight hours."

Phoebe stood. "Wonderful news, dears. You just rest and get well again. Nothing that won't wait until then. Oh, before I go...I hope you don't mind, but I did drop in to see about that cat of yours, Max."

Max looked relieved. "Phoebe, you are an angel, I swear. He's okay?"

"Yep. Did you know he's got a fetish for bacon, though? I gave him cat food, and he just looked at it. Wouldn't touch it. I was afraid he was pining for you, so I thought I'd try and get him to eat *something*. Well, I mean, those eyes, you know? Anyway, he seemed to be okay with a couple of rashers. So he'll be waiting for you when you get out."

Max shook his head and grinned. "I'll be in touch, Phoebe," he called as she gathered her things. "I owe you."

"We both do, Phoebe," added Peta.

Phoebe smiled as she made her way from the room. "Just be happy, dears."

The doctor hung the chart back up on the bed. "Five more minutes, you two. Then it's nap time for both of you." He looked pointedly at their hands, still clasped together. "That'll be nap time in separate beds, Mr. Wolfe."

Peta blushed, and Max snarled at him. "Thanks. I think."

The curtains swayed behind him, and Max leaned over Peta. "Jesus. I didn't think we'd ever be alone."

His hazel eyes bored right into her, so full of emotions it made her shake. "I love you, Peta Matthews. I seem to remember saying that before, but I want to make sure you get the point. I love you. Totally. You've taken my world and completely obliterated it. You've given me a new world. And I want that world because you're in it. Forever."

Peta's eyes filled with tears. "God, I love you too, Max. So much I just want to burst with it."

"How about bursting with my babies instead?"

Peta's eyes widened and her jaw dropped. "*Babies*?"

"Yeah. Babies. You know, little things that make a lot of noise and smell godawful on occasion. Small yous. And perhaps a small me. Grandkids for Phoebe."

Peta's brain tripped and skinned its knees, leaving her thoughts blinking on her mental sidewalk. "You want babies?"

Max gritted his teeth. "Yes. In my undoubtedly clumsy way, I'm asking you to marry me. To live with me, *and* Mr. Peebles, for better or for whatever, til death does its thing. To bear my children and let me love you until we're both pushing up daisies."

As a proposal it probably lacked a certain style, but to Peta's ears it was greater than the most passionate love poem she'd ever read. It was about the future, their future. One that would take them on their most thrilling adventure yet.

She raised her hand carefully to Max's cheek, ignoring the trailing tubes across the white sheets and focusing completely on his handsome face.

"Yes."

And she kissed him.

The nurse who answered the summons of the rapidly-beeping heart monitor took one look around the curtains and quietly turned the machine off. There was nothing wrong with Peta Matthew's heart. Nothing at all.

Except for the fact that she'd given it to Max Wolfe.

Forever.

Epilogue

"Well, that went well."

The raven-haired beauty sighed as she leaned back against her husband's hard chest.

"Indeed it did," he murmured. "Although I am forced to point out that even though Peta was our first female genie, she didn't really do the whole 'genie' thing."

Neala laughed. "She didn't need to. Women have different ways of going about things. A good fuck isn't always the answer, you know."

"Oh really?" The voice was low and deep, and a pair of strong hands slid around her waist and upwards to cup her heavy breasts. "Do you want to re-think that statement, my love?"

Neala sighed. "Cullen, my sweet, for us a good fuck was certainly one of the answers. But there were a lot more. Don't you remember?"

Cullen's turquoise blue eyes danced. "I remember the good fucking parts best," he breathed.

Neala sucked in her breath as his fingers found her nipples. He knew so well how to love her to the edge of madness. He always had.

"And look at us now." Her eyes closed as she rested her head in the exact spot on his shoulder that had always seemed made just for her.

"Yeah, just look at us."

She could feel his hardness against her buttocks through the thin silk that covered her, and wondered once again at the strange quirks of fate that had brought them together. "Are you happy, my love?"

Her question made Cullen pause in his investigation of her breasts. "More than I could have imagined possible, sweetheart. I have you and Lalla, our life here on Anyela — what more could I ask?"

She smiled. "Well..." She took his hand and lowered it slightly until it covered her belly. "Perhaps the addition of a small Celtic warrior might complete our joy?"

Cullen froze, not misunderstanding her at all. "Good God. Really?"

Neala chuckled. "Really. And you shouldn't be surprised, given what we get up to. And how often we get up to it."

He turned her in his arms, and she sighed with pleasure at the love she saw in his eyes. "I didn't think life could be any better," he said. His hand slipped to her cheek and caressed it with such love she felt her heart turn over as it had so often since she'd met this man. "I was wrong."

With strong arms he swept her up, and as she tangled her hands in his long fair hair, she banished all thoughts of distant moors and savage people to the recesses of her mind.

Perhaps one day, they'd tell their son of Cullen Teague and his exploits. But probably not too many of the details. Certainly not how he'd won the heart and the body of a fiery Celtic woman. Neala blushed and hid her grin against her husband's neck as he carried her off to their bed.

That was a tale that was *not* for the ears of their children.

Enjoy this excerpt from
BEATING LEVEL NINE
© Copyright Sahara Kelly 2004

"God fucking *DAMN* it."

The expletive shot from the lips of the man sitting in a ring of light radiating from a computer monitor. Not just any monitor, of course, this was a state-of-the-art, micro-thin, twenty-three inch plasma job, which would have made even the most hardened of techno-geeks drool with envy.

It was surrounded by a deluxe home theater surround sound system, and in front of it was an ergonomically-designed leather chair that other folks would have considered to be the height of extraordinary decadence.

Not the man sitting in it. All he could do was grasp the remote mouse, and curse luridly.

Once again, he'd failed to beat Level Nine.

His nemesis. The ultimate level in the ultimate game. Nihilism On Line — or NOL as it was known to its fans. And he probably qualified as *the* prime fan, since he played the game incessantly from dusk to dawn, night after night, and had done ever since its release a few months before.

After all, what else was there for a fully-fledged vampire to do in this day and age? He couldn't go terrorize the peasants any more — most of them now drove sedans and scared *him* a lot more than he scared them. He'd learned the true meaning of "liberal conservatism" the first time he'd seen a Volvo with a gun rack.

Sucking the blood of virgins during their deflowering might be all very stimulating, but virgins weren't exactly thick on the ground these days. He had no taste for kids anyway.

Goth clubs were plentiful, but were peopled with weirdos that made his three-hundred-year-old hair stand on end, and he'd gotten close to one woman's neck only to get a lungful of cheap perfume and a bad case of the sneezes.

No, things just weren't the same for the old ones anymore. Some of them held to the traditional ways, lurking in the dark forests of middle Europe. At least the bits of the forests that hadn't been turned into suburban developments. And even *they* had to be careful of mad Mercedes drivers taking hairpin bends on moonlit nights at speeds that flaunted the laws of gravity.

He'd chosen the life that suited him best. Businessman, entrepreneur, quiet—almost reclusive—in his habits, he managed a small financial empire from the solitude of his historic home and was perfectly content.

His body's need for blood was satisfied by the synthetically produced plasma-substitute he ordered by the case from an online supplier. He was able to cater to his rather appalling addiction to ham and pineapple pizzas and not have to explain to anybody that of *course* vampires could eat real food. He had a nice pair of dark glasses for sunny days, and snickered whenever he read the apocryphal stories about his kind bursting into flames in the light of day.

It was all nonsense created by overdramatic novelists with overheated imaginations. It was, in fact, a rather nice lifestyle, with a great many benefits that he'd enjoyed for several hundred years and he was happy living it.

Until he'd run into NOL and Level Nine.

And the German Whore.

About the author:

Sahara Kelly was transplanted from old England to New England where she now lives with her husband and teenage son. Making the transition from her historical regency novels to Romantica™ has been surprisingly easy, and now Sahara can't imagine writing anything else. She is dedicated to the premise that everybody should have fantasies.

Sahara welcomes mail from readers. You can write to her c/o Ellora's Cave Publishing at 1337 Commerce Drive, Suite 13, Stow OH 44224.

Why an electronic book?

We live in the Information Age—an exciting time in the history of human civilization in which technology rules supreme and continues to progress in leaps and bounds every minute of every hour of every day. For a multitude of reasons, more and more avid literary fans are opting to purchase e-books instead of paperbacks. The question to those not yet initiated to the world of electronic reading is simply: *why?*

1. *Price.* An electronic title at Ellora's Cave Publishing runs anywhere from 40-75% less than the cover price of the <u>exact same title</u> in paperback format. Why? Cold mathematics. It is less expensive to publish an e-book than it is to publish a paperback, so the savings are passed along to the consumer.

2. *Space.* Running out of room to house your paperback books? That is one worry you will never have with electronic novels. For a low one-time cost, you can purchase a handheld computer designed specifically for e-reading purposes. Many e-readers are larger than the average handheld, giving you plenty of screen room. Better yet, hundreds of titles can be stored within your new library—a single microchip. (Please note that Ellora's Cave does not endorse any specific brands. You can check our website at www.ellorascave.com for customer recommendations we make available to new consumers.)

3. *Mobility.* Because your new library now consists of only a microchip, your entire cache of books can be taken with you wherever you go.

4. *Personal preferences are accounted for.* Are the words you are currently reading too small? Too large? Too...**ANNOYING**? Paperback books cannot be modified according to personal preferences, but e-books can.

5. *Innovation.* The way you read a book is not the only advancement the Information Age has gifted the literary community with. There is also the factor of what you can read. Ellora's Cave Publishing will be introducing a new line of interactive titles that are available in e-book format only.

6. *Instant gratification.* Is it the middle of the night and all the bookstores are closed? Are you tired of waiting days—sometimes weeks—for online and offline bookstores to ship the novels you bought? Ellora's Cave Publishing sells instantaneous downloads 24 hours a day, 7 days a week, 365 days a year. Our e-book delivery system is 100% automated, meaning your order is filled as soon as you pay for it.

Those are a few of the top reasons why electronic novels are displacing paperbacks for many an avid reader. As always, Ellora's Cave Publishing welcomes your questions and comments. We invite you to email us at service@ellorascave.com or write to us directly at: 1337 Commerce Drive, Suite 13, Stow OH 44224.

Discover for yourself why readers can't get enough of the multiple award-winning publisher Ellora's Cave. Whether you prefer e-books or paperbacks, be sure to visit EC on the web at www.ellorascave.com for an erotic reading experience that will leave you breathless.

WWW.ELLORASCAVE.COM